Shadows Found

Zora Stone

Print ISBN: 978-1-971405-02-5

Publisher: Smut by Design

www.zorastone.com

There's beauty in knowing the story isn't over yet.

(Don't tell Finn.)

Content Warnings

This book contains mature themes, emotional intensity, and explicit content. Please read with care.

Violence & Combat

- Large-scale fantasy battle sequences
- On-page deaths of antagonists
- Graphic descriptions of blood and injury
- Magical corruption and its physical effects
- Confrontation with a god-level entity

Mental Health & Trauma

- Panic attacks and anxiety episodes
- Emotional breakdowns and psychological distress
- Themes of guilt, self-doubt, and unworthiness

- Characters processing past betrayal and violation

- Trauma responses during intimacy

Sexual Content

- Explicit sexual scenes between consenting adults

- Multiple romantic/sexual relationships (reverse harem)

- MMF content (male/male/female intimacy)

- Group intimacy dynamics

- Detailed intimate encounters with emotional intensity

Magical Coercion & Consent Issues

- Aftermath of forced magical bonds

- Characters reckoning with violations of agency

- Bond corruption and its emotional toll

- Healing and reclaiming autonomy

Emotional Manipulation & Betrayal

- Trusted characters revealed as compromised

- Psychological manipulation by antagonists

- Characters used as unwitting pawns

- Confronting those who caused harm

Family Trauma

- Major family revelations (hidden bloodlines)

- Deceased parents and their legacy

- Generational secrets exposed by enemies

- Characters redefining family on their own terms

Loss & Grief

- On-page mourning and emotional processing

- Confronting the death of loved ones

- Themes of sacrifice and survival

- Mass death referenced (historical and present)

Cosmic/Existential Themes

- Direct encounter with a deity

- Souls awaiting passage (visible, numerous)

- Questions of fate, choice, and purpose

- Reality-bending magical events

Note: While *Shadows Found* explores mature and intense themes, all romantic relationships occur between consenting adults. The story centers agency, healing, and choosing love in the aftermath of manipulation.

Note 2: The next page contains spoilers from Books One and Two—a quick recap to get you caught up.

A Quick Recap from Your Friendly Neighborhood Author

Because it's been a minute. And honestly? A lot happened. Even Bob needed a spreadsheet.

So! When we last left our disaster found family, things had escalated from "complicated" to "actively on fire" (sometimes literally, thanks Torric).

Let's catch up:

Kaia's still the last Valkyrie, still bonded to way too many gorgeous men, and still carrying the Heart of Eternity like the world's most stressful necklace. Her shadows—Bob, Patricia, Finnick, Mouse, and the chaos crew—are still judging everyone. Walter's still doing... whatever Walter does. (Honestly, even I'm not sure. He just vibes.)

The bonds? Yeah, about that.

Kieran—ancient dragon shifter, centuries-old guardian, and walking disaster of good intentions—forced the mate bonds without consent. All of them. At once. Because he thought it was the only way to save Kaia's life and he's been waiting literal centuries for her.

Spoiler: she did not take it well.

Neither did anyone else.

The group fled to Kieran's sanctuary in Absentia, the corrupted shadow realm where everything is wrong and the vibes are immaculate (if you like existential dread). They're hunting Seren and Lira, who were taken by forces connected to Alekir.

Speaking of Alekir—the Soulbinder, the Valkyrie-murderer, the ancient evil bleeding through the cracks between worlds—he's still out there. Still planning. Still using Lady Virath as his puppet on the inside.

Darian? Still complicated. Still bonded to Kaia in ways neither of them asked for. Still carrying corruption that feels wrong at the edges but right at the core. The jury came back, and the verdict is: *it's messy*.

Callum came with them on this little journey through Absentia. Kieran trusted him completely. Then Callum betrayed them all.

(File that under "things that might be a problem later.")

As for the rest of them:

Finn's still using humor as a shield, still desperately in love with Kaia, still pretending he's fine. (He's not fine.)

Malrik's still holding everything together while quietly falling apart.

The twins are still protective, still traumatized, still ready to burn the world for her.

And Kaia? She's leading them into the unknown, carrying guilt she won't let go of, and refusing to forgive Kieran even though the bond keeps reminding her it exists.

Book Two ended with Kaia finally letting herself rest.

And then a voice in the darkness:

"Hello again, Little Shadow."

Ready for Book Three?

Because the shadows have been waiting.

And they're not the only ones.

CONTENTS

Chapter 1
KAIA

"Hello again, Little Shadow."

The voice curls through the space between sleep and waking—soft, familiar, wrong.

Cold ground beneath me. Firelight somewhere close, embers crackling low. My pulse slams against my ribs.

Pressure blooms sharp against my chest.

The bond.

But it feels wrong. Tainted at the edges. Right at the core but twisted somehow.

Fuck.

My eyes snap open.

A figure stands over my bedroll, backlit by moonlight filtering through trees. Tall. Still. Close enough I should've heard him, felt him, *something*.

Recognition hits like a fist to the sternum.

Darian.

My breath catches. Every instinct screams *move*—but the bond presses harder, pinning me in place like a hand over my heart. Reminding me it's still there. Still tethered. Still *his*.

I hate it.

Bob surges between us, edges sharp as broken glass. Mouse materializes at my side, ears flat, violet eyes burning. His growl rolls low and lethal through the dark.

I force myself to look at Darian properly.

He's a wreck. Unshaven, dirt streaked across his jaw. Hair falling loose from its usual perfect style. His uniform—if you can even call it that—is torn at the shoulder, stained dark near the hem. He looks like he's been walking for days.

But his posture doesn't waver. Hands hang loose at his sides. Empty.

His eyes—storm gray, shadowed—hold mine without flinching.

A memory flashes. The arena. His smile turning cruel. *You weren't teaching me. You were studying us.*

Every training session replays in sickening clarity. The way he pushed me to show him every defensive pattern. Every instinct. Every vulnerable truth about my shadows.

So he could use them against me.

Bob shifts closer, bristling. Mouse's growl deepens.

Darian's gaze flickers to the shadows, then back to me.

He doesn't speak.

The silence stretches. Suffocating.

"What are you doing here?" My voice comes out rough—sleep and adrenaline shredding it.

He exhales slow, like he's been holding his breath.

Then he drops to his knees.

Not a stumble. Not a collapse.

Deliberate. Controlled. Like he's choosing it.

Patricia flickers into view, notebook blazing—then glitches, a blot of ink spreading where no ink should be. Carl appears near my ankle, vibrating too fast, like he's picking up signals no one else feels.

Mouse's ears flatten further. His growl wavers.

"Kaia." Darian's voice is quiet. Steady. Nothing like the cold precision I remember. "I came because I needed you to hear this. From me."

A flicker crosses his expression—pain? Confusion? Like something inside him pulls the wrong direction.

I should tell him to leave. Wake the others. Let my shadows tear him apart for daring to kneel like that means something.

But I don't.

The bond hums low in my chest. Quiet. Constant. Wrong but real. Inescapable.

"I know what I did in the arena." He doesn't look away. Doesn't soften it. "Every choice. I told myself I was protecting academy, the balance—whatever let me sleep at night." His jaw tightens. "But I wasn't protecting anything. I was protecting myself. From you. From what you made me feel."

The words land wrong. Too honest. Too raw.

I want to interrupt—to tell him I don't care—but something in his voice roots me.

"You deserved someone who stood beside you," he continues. His hands rest open on his thighs like an offering. "Not someone who studied your shadows like they were a problem to solve instead of—" He stops. Swallows. "Instead of seeing them. Extensions of you. Proof you're stronger than any of us gave you credit for."

My throat tightens. I press my palm flat against the ground. Dirt and grass, rough under my fingers.

Bob's edges soften slightly. Carl drifts closer to Darian—curious now, not defensive.

Walter drifts into view, bobbing lazily. He hovers closer to Darian, pulsing once—bright—like he's tasting something in the air. Then he drifts to my chest, pulses again. Back to Darian.

"I'm not asking for forgiveness." Darian's voice drops lower. Almost too quiet. "I needed to tell the truth. And to kneel here—" A ghost of bitter humor crosses his face. "Without running from it."

"Get up."

The words slip out sharp. Defensive.

He doesn't move.

"Get up, Darian."

"If I stand too soon," he says quietly, "it looks like I came here to win. Like this is strategy." His gaze holds mine. Unflinching. "I didn't. I came to own it. Every lie. Every betrayal. Every moment I made you doubt yourself." He pauses. "So I'll stay here until you tell me what comes next."

My chest aches. The bond pulses once—faint, echoing his honesty but wrong at the edges—and I fight the pull.

Steve materializes suddenly, thrusting a scroll at Patricia. She takes it without looking away from Darian.

I open my mouth to respond—

Steel flashes in moonlight.

A blade appears at Darian's throat. Cold. Precise.

Aspen steps from the shadows behind him, silent as death. Ice-blue eyes blazing with controlled fury. The blade doesn't waver. Neither does his voice.

"Move, and I'll open your throat before you take your next breath."

Panic hits—not for him. For what killing him would do to us. To the bonds already stretched thin.

Bob positions himself beside Aspen, backing the threat.

Darian doesn't flinch. Doesn't look at the blade. His eyes stay locked on mine. Calm. Resigned.

Like he expected this.

"Aspen—" My voice cracks.

"Don't." Aspen's tone is ice. Absolute. "Don't defend him, Kaia."

Mouse flicks his tail once—Aspen's grip on the blade tightens, but he doesn't move.

"I'm not—" I scramble to my feet. Carl darts anxiously around my ankles. "I'm not defending him. I just—"

Noise erupts beyond the firelight. Footsteps. Voices. The camp waking in shouted questions and chaos.

Torric arrives first, shirtless and radiating heat. Golden eyes locked on Darian with murderous intent. Finn's right behind him, chaos magic sparking at his fingertips. His usual grin replaced by something sharp. Deadly.

Malrik steps from the tree line. Silver eyes cold. Shadows coiling at his feet like waiting serpents.

And Kieran.

He moves through them with quiet authority. Never needs to raise his voice. His golden eyes sweep the scene—Darian kneeling, Aspen's blade at his throat, me frozen between them.

His expression hardens into something unreadable.

Finnick somersaults through the air, landing with dramatic flair before mimicking Darian's kneeling position. Bob appears behind him, yanking him upright by the scruff.

"Report." Kieran's single word carries weight.

Aspen doesn't look away from Darian. "Found him kneeling over Kaia."

Torric snarls. Fire licks up his forearms. "I'll burn him where he—"

"Don't kill him."

The words tumble out before I can stop them. Loud. Desperate.

Everyone stares.

Finnick stops mid-mockery. Goes still.

Finn recovers first, voice tight with disbelief. "You're joking."

"I'm not." My hands shake. I clench them into fists. "Just—don't."

Kieran's gaze shifts to me. Searching. "Kaia—"

"I know what he did." My voice trembles but I don't take it back. "I know. But killing him won't—" I stop. Swallow hard. "It won't change anything."

The silence feels suffocating.

Malrik steps closer, voice low and dangerous. "He betrayed you. Studied your shadows so he could destroy you."

"I know." The bond flares hot against my ribs—wrong, tainted, but still there. I press my hand over my heart like I can smother it. "I know."

Linda appears at my shoulder, already trying to organize the chaos. Patricia's notebook glows brighter—*this is going in the report.*

Darian's eyes haven't left mine. No pleading. No desperation.

Just quiet acceptance and something that looks dangerously close to regret.

Kieran exhales slowly. The sound carries centuries of weariness. "Bind him. North edge of camp. We'll deal with this at first light."

His tone leaves no room for argument.

Not execution.

Interrogation.

Torric moves forward, grabbing Darian by the arm with barely restrained violence. Darian doesn't resist. Doesn't fight. He lets Torric haul him to his feet, Aspen's blade still pressed to his throat until the last possible second.

As they drag him away, Darian's voice cuts through the tension. Quiet but clear.

"I'll wait as long as it takes."

Finn mutters, standing close—"Either brave or staggeringly stupid."

"Both," Malrik says from my other side.

We watch Torric and Aspen drag Darian away, and I'm not sure how I feel watching him go without a fight.

No one speaks.

Bob positions himself at my feet, shaking what might be a finger at me. Possibly just vibrating with disapproval.

I want to explain. To justify. To make them understand something I don't even understand myself.

But the words won't come.

Malrik looks at both of us—something knowing in his expression—then steps away into the shadows.

"Get some rest," Kieran says quietly. Voice gentler now. "We'll talk in the morning."

They leave one by one, until it's just me and Finn and the dying embers.

Mouse materializes beside me. Solid. Warm.

Finn lingers near the bedroll, hands shoved in his pockets. Doesn't push. Doesn't ask questions I can't answer.

"Stay?" I ask quietly, looking at him.

His expression softens. "Yeah, Trouble. I'll stay."

"I didn't forgive him," I say quietly. "I just didn't let them kill him."

He's quiet for a moment. "What's the difference?"

I don't have an answer.

He nods. Like he expected that.

"There's room," I whisper.

He hesitates—just for a breath—then lies down beside me.

"Thank you. For staying."

"Always, Trouble."

I reach back, finding his hand. Pulling his arm around my waist. He goes rigid, then slowly relaxes. His warmth settles against my back.

The bond I never chose sits deep in my chest. A bond I wish I didn't feel. A connection that should have been beautiful but was stolen from me.

Darian Luthar just knelt at my feet and confessed his sins.

And I stopped them from killing him.

I press my palm over my heart and try to name what I feel.

I can't.

Chapter 2
ASPEN

The frost spreads without permission.

I watch it creep across the ground beneath my boots—delicate crystalline patterns that shouldn't exist in pre-dawn warmth. My water rune pulses cold against my upper arm, responding to emotions I don't want to think about.

Fury. Guilt. A protective instinct so sharp it borders on violence.

I haven't slept.

Every time I close my eyes, I see Darian kneeling in our firelight. See my blade pressed to his throat—close enough to feel his pulse against the steel. Close enough to end him.

Close enough that Kaia stopped me.

That's what I can't process. She looked at the man who never saw her at all—only what she could do, never who she was—who dissected her wonder and called it research, who decided what she was worth and handed it to Thorne—and said *don't kill him*.

Ice veins outward from where I stand, climbing the tree trunk beside me. I don't bother stopping it.

"You're going to freeze the whole camp if you keep that up."

I don't turn. Torric's heat signature washes over me before he settles against the opposite tree, radiating warmth that makes steam curl between us.

"Let me," I say quietly.

"Can't." His voice carries an edge I recognize—the same barely restrained violence I'm fighting. "Apparently we're not allowed to solve problems by burning them anymore."

"Or freezing them."

"Shame."

I feel his fury mirroring mine. The fire rune on his chest pulses hot enough I can sense it from here. We're both wound tight, magic leaking in ways we haven't lost control of since we were children.

Since Father branded us and told us it was for our own good.

"Kieran's calling a meeting," Torric says. "Dawn. Everyone."

"To decide what?"

"What to do with him." His jaw tightens. "Like there's anything to decide."

I breathe out slowly, trying to rein in the cold. Failing.

"If she asks us to let him live—" Torric starts.

"Then we let him live."

"Even if—"

"Even if." I finally look at him, meeting molten gold eyes that mirror my own conflict. "Her choice. Her bond. Her decision."

"I hate it."

"So do I."

Bob materializes between us, his shadowy form rigid with disapproval. He shifts between Torric and me like he's trying to decide which of us needs the lecture more.

"Yeah, yeah," Torric mutters. "We're terrible. We know."

Bob turns toward me specifically. His edges sharpen.

"I wasn't going to kill him," I say.

The shadow's posture suggests he doesn't believe me.

"Fine. I wanted to. But I stopped."

Bob's form flickers—satisfaction, maybe. Patricia appears next, notebook blazing as she underlines something emphatically, then adds a dramatic asterisk that somehow feels judgmental.

"Camp's waking up," Torric says, pushing off the tree. "We should—"

"Give me a minute."

He studies me with the kind of scrutiny only a twin can manage. "You're thinking too much."

"Someone has to."

"That's what Malrik's for." But he doesn't leave. Just stands there, heat signature steady and familiar. "She didn't forgive him, you know. She just didn't let us become murderers."

The distinction matters. I'm not sure why, but it does.

"Come on," Torric says finally. "Let's go hear Kieran explain why we shouldn't kill the traitor."

The clearing sits at camp's northern edge. Dawn light filters through leaves overhead, casting everything in gray and gold.

Everyone's here. Malrik leans against a boulder, silver eyes unreadable. Finn's propped against a tree, arms crossed, his usual mischief replaced by something colder. Kaia stands slightly apart, Mouse pressed against her leg, her shadows forming defensive patterns around her boots.

She looks exhausted. Dark circles beneath violet eyes. Jaw set with determination that makes my chest ache.

Kieran stands in the center, golden eyes landing on all of us with ancient weariness. The sanctuary magic clings to him, making the air shimmer.

Darian kneels at the clearing's edge. Bound. Ashen. Still somehow managing to look composed.

His storm-gray eyes find Kaia immediately.

Cold bites through my veins before I can stop it.

"Tell me," Kieran says.

No one speaks.

"I found him kneeling at her feet," I say finally.

Kieran's gaze doesn't waver. "Did he threaten anyone?"

"No," Kaia says. Her voice is steady but strained. "He confessed. Everything. Then waited for judgment."

"Very noble," Torric's sarcasm could cut steel. "Doesn't change what he did."

"No," Darian says quietly. "It doesn't."

Torric moves before anyone can stop him. Fire coils around his forearms as he crosses the clearing, stopping inches from Darian. Heat radiates in visible waves.

"Then give me one reason," Torric growls, "why I shouldn't burn you where you kneel."

Darian doesn't flinch. "I can't."

"Torric." Kaia's voice cracks like a whip.

He doesn't move. Just stares at Darian with murder written across every line of his body.

"Don't," Kaia says.

That's what makes him step back. Not Kieran's authority. Not logic. Just that single word from her.

Bob shifts position, moving to stand between Kaia and Darian. Patricia's notebook flares brighter. Even the newer shadows cluster closer to Kaia like they're trying to protect her.

Kieran exhales slowly. "We need to decide—"

"No." Kaia's voice rings out, clear and certain. "You don't get to decide this. None of you do—because he's *mine* to deal with."

The words land like stones in still water.

Kieran goes very, very still.

"Explain," he says carefully.

"He's mine." Kaia's hands curl into fists. "The bond isn't just the five of you. It's him too."

The silence that follows could shatter mountains.

Kieran's face drains of color as realization dawns. His eyes widen before he schools his expression.

"How?"

"When you forced the bonds, it wasn't just you, Malrik, Finn, Torric, and me." She glances at Darian, then back to Kieran. "It was him too."

Understanding crashes through the clearing. The way Darian found us. The way he knew exactly where to look.

Kieran turns to face us—all of us. His expression shifts through shock, betrayal, fury, before settling on something that looks dangerously close to hurt.

"You all knew."

It's not a question.

Torric's jaw tightens. Finn looks away. Malrik's shadows deepen. And I meet his gaze steadily. "Yes."

"How long?"

"Since she told us," I say quietly. "After Callum cornered her at the lake."

"And no one thought to tell me?" Power bleeds around the edges of his control. The ancient kind that reminds everyone why he's called the Dragon of the Void.

"Would you have believed us?" Malrik's voice cuts through the tension. "Or would you have assumed we were protecting our own interests?"

"I deserved to know."

"So did she." Finn steps forward, chaos magic sparking. "So did all of us. Before you forced bonds that weren't ready to form." He laughs without humor. "You trapped us all—not just her. Made decisions for people who should have had a choice. And now you're angry because we kept one truth from you? That's rich."

Kieran's hands flex. "I was protecting—"

"Yourself," I interrupt quietly. "You were protecting yourself from knowing something that would force you to question whether you made the right call."

His eyes snap to mine. For a moment, I think he might unleash the full weight of his power. Instead, he just looks tired.

"You should have told me," he says again, softer.

"And you should have asked," Torric shoots back. "Asked if we wanted these bonds. Asked if she was ready. Asked literally anything before you trapped us all in connections we can't undo."

Carl tumbles out of a nearby tree with a scroll clutched in his shadowy grip, landing in an undignified heap. He scrambles up, salutes Bob with obvious pride, and presents his "intel" with earnest determination. Bob takes one look at the blank parchment and his form visibly deflates with disappointment.

The absurdity of it cuts through some of the tension.

Kaia steps forward. Her shadows move with her—Bob at her right, Mouse at her left, Patricia hovering near her shoulder. The newer recruits form a protective semicircle behind her, their movements slightly off-sync but earnest.

"This isn't about you, Kieran." She looks around at all of us. "Or any of you. This is about him." She gestures toward Darian without looking at him. "And what happens next is my decision. Not yours. Not theirs. Mine."

"Kaia—"

"I'm not asking permission." Her violet eyes blaze. "I'm telling you how this is going to work. He's my bond. My problem. My choice."

Kieran studies her for a long moment. Something shifts in his expression—resignation, maybe. Or respect.

"If that's what you want."

"It is."

The finality in her voice ends the discussion.

Kieran nods once. Sharp. Then turns and walks away, ancient power trailing him like a cloak.

His absence leaves the air thin, like the world is waiting to exhale.

"Well," Finn says into the silence. "That went great."

I turn my attention to Darian. He's been silent through the entire exchange, watching with carefully neutral expression except for the faint tremor in his bound hands.

"He followed the bond," I say. "Straight to us."

Kaia goes still.

"We can use that," I add.

Cold spreads across the ground.

She meets my gaze. Understanding passes between us—gratitude, maybe. Or just acknowledgment that sometimes mercy needs an excuse.

"Fine," Torric says finally. "But I'm burning him if he so much as looks at her wrong."

"Get in line," Finn adds.

Malrik's shadows still. Then, quietly: "We'll hold him."

We fall in behind her. Nothing else matters.

Linda appears beside Bob, placing what looks like a shadowy hand on his shoulder—reminding him to stand down now that the crisis has passed. Several of the newer shadows mirror the gesture with each other, as if they're learning from her example. Walter drifts upside down for a moment, inspecting Darian like a puzzle before bobbing away to investigate a nearby rock.

Kaia turns to face Darian fully for the first time. Her shadows shift with her, forming patterns I don't fully understand. Bob positions himself protectively. Patricia's notebook blazes brighter. Even Mouse's violet eyes narrow with warning.

"You'll stay bound," she says quietly. "You'll answer every question. And if you lie—" She doesn't finish the threat. Doesn't need to.

Darian's voice is rough. "Whatever you need."

"Good." She takes a breath, steadying herself. "Because if you do, I'll let them kill you. And I won't stop them twice."

The words settle like frost on stone.

Finn moves to her side immediately. Torric follows, heat signature blazing with protective fury. Malrik drifts closer, shadows intertwining with hers.

And I stay where I am. Watching. Letting the cold spread beneath my boots in patterns that mirror the ice in my veins.

Her choice. Always.

But if Darian so much as breathes wrong, I won't ask permission again.

The blade will find his throat. This time, nothing will stop it.

Chapter 3
MALRIK

The clearing empties in patterns I've learned to read.

Torric leaves first, heat signature blazing, fire barely leashed. Aspen follows—quieter, colder, frost trailing his boots like a threat he hasn't finished making. Kieran moves last, ancient power wrapped around him like storm clouds, his silence heavier than words.

And Finn.

Finn pretends to linger near the fire, adjusting his pack with movements too careful to be casual. His chaos magic sparks and settles—restless energy pretending to be calm.

He's watching Kaia without watching her.

I see it because I see everything. It's what I do. The others burn or freeze or command. I observe. I calculate. I notice the fractures before they break wide enough for anyone else to see.

My shadows coil at my feet, calm but alert. They sense what I sense—tension stretched thin, bonds pulling in directions that don't align, something building that none of us are ready for.

Kaia hasn't moved since Kieran left. Mouse stays close, violet eyes tracking every shift in the group. Her shadows form tighter patterns than usual—defensive, but also exhausted. She's running on fumes and pretending otherwise.

And Finn.

Finn starts walking toward her before he realizes he's doing it.

I watch the exact moment he catches himself—shoulders tensing, steps faltering, chaos magic flickering brighter like static charge. He adjusts course, angles toward the supply packs instead.

Distance as punishment, not her request.

He doesn't fool me. His trajectory still curves in her direction. Gravity never asks permission.

Kaia sits by the fire, finally letting exhaustion catch her. She sinks onto a log, spine straight despite everything, hands curling into fists on her thighs.

Finn approaches casually. Too casually. The kind of ease that takes effort.

"Mind if I—" He gestures at the space beside her.

She glances up. Something flickers across her expression—relief, maybe. Or just the comfort of familiar chaos.

"Sure," she says quietly.

He does. Not close enough to touch, but near enough that his chaos magic sparks softer around her. I notice the shift immediately. The way his power gentles in her proximity, like fire banking itself without conscious thought.

My shadows shift, recognizing the pattern.

"You okay?" Finn asks.

"Fine."

"Liar."

The corner of her mouth twitches. Not quite a smile, but close. "You're one to talk."

"I'm an excellent liar." His grin appears—bright, sharp, armor made of mischief. "Years of practice."

"I know."

The smile falters. Just for a breath. Then it's back, locked in place like muscle memory.

Bob shifts position slightly, edges softening. Even he sees it—the way Finn stabilizes her without meaning to. The way she lets him closer than she lets most of us.

Of all of us, he's the one she lets see the cracks.

I remember when our bond locked. The way Kaia looked at me in the water, choosing me in her moment of need. The rightness of it settling into place. And underneath all of it—faint but unmistakable—Finn's presence flickering through. Feeling what we felt. Breaking quietly somewhere across camp where we couldn't see him shatter.

He hasn't recovered. He just learned to joke around it.

Torric appears at my shoulder, heat signature washing over me before he speaks. "You going to do something?"

"Not this time."

His golden eyes narrow. "What does that mean?"

"It means if Finn breaks, she breaks. If she breaks, everything breaks." I keep my voice low, measured. "Let them breathe."

"You're playing strategist with people's lives."

"I'm always playing strategist." I meet his gaze steadily. "Someone has to."

He studies me for a long moment, jaw tight with frustration he can't quite articulate. Then he exhales, shaking his head. "I hate when you do this."

"I know."

He leaves. Fire trailing him like discontent made visible.

I don't worry about romance. That's not what this is—not yet, maybe not ever. What worries me is the chaos magic.

Finn feels too much. It's his strength. The reason his power responds to emotion, adapts, flows. But it's also his flaw. When he gets too tied to something—someone—his magic destabilizes. Becomes unpredictable. Dangerous.

My shadows deepen, reflecting the unease I won't speak aloud.

Carl tumbles out of a tree nearby, landing in a heap with what looks like a stick clutched triumphantly in his shadowy grip. He scrambles up, salutes Bob with obvious pride, and presents his "discovery."

Bob's form deflates with visible disappointment.

Linda appears, gently redirecting Carl toward actual patrol duties. Patricia's notebook flares brighter, documenting the chaos with what I suspect is extreme judgment.

The absurdity cuts through some of my tension.

Kieran stops Finn as he stands to leave, golden eyes serious. "I need you on first watch tonight."

"Sure thing, boss." Finn's voice is casual. His shoulders are rigid.

"With Torric."

"Perfect. Love spending quality time with fire and fury."

Kieran's expression doesn't shift. "Finn—"

"I'm fine." The smile sharpens. "Really. Totally fine. Never better."

Kieran looks like he wants to push. Instead, he just nods once and walks away.

Finn glances toward Kaia without meaning to.

I catch the slip. The way his gaze finds her automatically, like checking a compass. The way he forces himself to look away half a second later.

My shadows tighten.

Kaia stands and steps forward before anyone can settle into the plan. "As long as it's while we're moving."

Kieran turns back, surprise flickering across his face. "Kaia—"

"Seren is still out there." Her voice is steady, absolute. "We need to find her. And that means we keep moving."

"We need rest," Kieran says carefully. "The group needs—"

"No." She cuts him off. "We're moving. Pack up."

The clearing goes quiet.

Kieran's jaw tightens. He looks like he's about to argue—ancient authority bristling against being overruled.

But Kaia doesn't back down. Doesn't soften. Just holds his gaze until something in his expression shifts.

"Fine," he says finally. "We move at first light."

"Now, it's still morning," Kaia corrects. "We've wasted enough time."

Finn mutters under his breath—"Trouble"—but there's something almost relieved in the way he says it. Like her pushing forward gives him permission to stop pretending he's fine.

Kieran exhales slowly. Then nods once. Sharp. Final.

"Pack up," he calls to the group.

Kaia eventually moves toward her bedroll, exhaustion catching up now that the decision's been made. Finn moves toward her again, chaos magic sparking brighter as if responding to her proximity.

She sways. Just a little.

Finn's hand snaps out before she falls, catching her elbow with precision that speaks to instinct, not thought.

She steadies. His hand withdraws instantly, like he touched fire.

"Thanks," she says quietly.

"Yeah. Sure. No problem." He shoves his hands in his pockets. "You should rest. Before we go."

"I will."

"Good. That's... good."

The awkwardness hangs between them. Unnamed. Obvious.

Kaia walks away. Mouse follows, tail flicking once in what might be approval.

Finn watches her go, chaos magic dimming as distance grows between them.

My shadows shift, recognition settling cold and certain in my chest.

Chaos always chooses its anchor.

And she has no idea she's holding the rope.

Chapter 4
FINN

I'm fucking this up.

My pack won't close. The bedroll won't roll. Everything I touch either tangles or falls or decides gravity is a suggestion I should've ignored.

Chaos magic pops at my fingertips like static charge looking for somewhere to ground. I shove it down. It sparks anyway.

I drop my canteen for the third time and swear under my breath.

"Real smooth, Veylan," I mutter. "Very competent. Very together."

Across the clearing, Kaia seems to move effortlessly, packing her gear like she's done this a thousand times. Mouse supervises from her shoulder. Bob hovers nearby, edges sharp with disapproval that probably has nothing to do with packing technique.

I try not to look at her.

I fail.

Again.

My chest does that thing—the tight, wrong, aching thing that's been happening since the lake. Since Malrik's bond locked into place and I felt every second of it like I was drowning in someone else's happiness.

I shouldn't be here. Shouldn't be this close. Shouldn't want things I have no right to want.

Distance is kindness, and it's fucking smart.

So why does it feel like punishment?

Because I am not a smart man. Okay, I am, just not when it comes to her.

I grab my pack straps and yank too hard. Something tears. Of course it does.

"You're packing that like you're trying to lose it."

I don't jump. Barely. Malrik's voice comes from directly behind me—calm, measured, the kind of steady that makes my chaos magic flicker nervously.

"I'm fine," I say without turning around.

"Try again."

I exhale through my teeth. "I said I'm fine."

"Your magic's loud again."

"Yeah, well." I gesture vaguely at the air around me where sparks dance like angry fireflies. "It does that."

Malrik moves into my peripheral vision, silver eyes tracking my hands as I fumble with a buckle that suddenly has too many moving parts.

"Finn."

Just my name. That's all. But the way he says it—quiet, certain, like he sees straight through the armor I've been wearing since I learned to talk—does something to me.

I drop the buckle. Stare at my hands. They're shaking.

"I don't know what I'm supposed to do," I say quietly. "I don't know what I'm allowed to feel."

The words slip out before I can stop them. Raw and honest. Dangerous.

Malrik steps closer. Silent. Solid. Like he's drawn to me as much as I am him.

Then his hand settles on my wrist, warm and steady.

My chaos magic flickers once, then quiets.

"You're allowed to feel whatever you feel," Malrik says. "That's not negotiable."

I laugh. It comes out broken. "Pretty sure it is."

"It's not."

I finally look up at him. He's close enough I can see the way shadows cling to his edges, the silver of his eyes reflecting firelight. Close enough to notice he's not looking at me like I'm a problem to solve.

He's looking at me like I matter.

My breath stumbles.

"Mal—"

"Whatever you need, Finn." His voice is low, certain. "I'm here too."

The words hit harder than they should.

I don't decide to lean in. My body just does it—gravity pulling me forward like I've been fighting this current for too long and finally stopped resisting.

Malrik meets me halfway.

The kiss is soft at first. Tentative. Like he's giving me room to pull back if I need to.

I don't pull back.

His hand comes up to cup my jaw—warm, steady, grounding—and I feel my chaos magic flicker once before settling into something I haven't felt in days. Weeks, maybe.

Quiet.

Not gone. Just... calm.

He tastes like smoke and certainty, and when he tilts his head slightly, deepening the kiss, I make a sound I don't mean to make—something between relief and desperation.

His other hand finds my hip, anchoring me like he knows I'm about to float away if he doesn't hold on.

And I let him.

I let myself sink into this—into the warmth of his mouth, the steadiness of his hands, the way his shadows curl around us like they're giving us privacy even though we're in the middle of camp.

My hands find his chest. His heartbeat is steady beneath my palm, and I focus on that—the rhythm of it, the proof that he's here, that this is real, that I'm not imagining the way he's holding me like I matter.

When he pulls back—just an inch, just enough to breathe—his thumb brushes along my cheekbone, and I realize I'm trembling.

Not from fear.

From relief.

"Finn," he murmurs. The way he says it—low, careful, like it matters—makes my chest crack open.

I'm staring at him like I've forgotten how words work. Like my brain's been rewired and all I know is the warmth of his hand on my face and the way my magic finally stopped screaming.

"I shouldn't—" I start.

"You didn't do anything wrong."

"But Kaia—"

"Isn't carrying you alone." His hand is still on my jaw, thumb still tracing small circles that make my thoughts scatter. "Neither am I."

I shake my head. "She doesn't—"

"She does." Malrik's voice is certain. Absolute. "Remember the first time? In my room? When you kissed me and she watched?"

Heat floods my face. My chaos magic sparks once.

"I saw her, Finn. Her pupils blown wide. The way her breath caught. She wasn't tolerating it." His thumb brushes my cheekbone again. "She wanted it. Wants it. Wants *us*."

The words settle somewhere deep. Somewhere I've been too afraid to let myself believe.

"You're sure?" My voice comes out rough.

"I'm sure."

I exhale slowly. The tension in my chest doesn't disappear, but it... shifts. Becomes something I can breathe around.

"Okay," I whisper.

"Okay?"

"Yeah. Okay."

His mouth curves—just barely. Almost a smile. "Good."

"Come on," he says quietly. "We move."

He bends down, picks up the canteen I dropped earlier, and hands it to me.

I take it. Our fingers brush. My magic doesn't spiral.

"Everyone ready?" Kaia's voice cuts through the clearing.

I look toward her automatically. She's standing near the fire, shadows clustering at her feet, determination etched into every line of her body.

My chest aches. But differently now. Less like drowning. More like longing I can actually name.

Malrik stands beside me, close enough our shoulders almost touch.

"Ready," he calls back.

I nod. Force my voice to work. "Yeah. Ready."

We walk out together.

My chaos magic stays quiet.

For the first time in days, I feel like I can breathe.

Chapter 5
KAIA

We move.

Because I said so. Because Seren is out there. Because sitting still feels like waiting to die.

Kieran disagreed. I watched his golden eyes hold mine—ancient authority versus someone who's done listening. He backed down.

Damn right he did.

Now everyone's following in silence, exhausted and pissed off, and I'm pretending my hands don't shake every time I adjust my pack.

Mouse perches on my shoulder, tail twitching against my neck. Bob's at my right, bristling. Patricia walks beside me, notebook blazing—scribbling what, I don't know, but it looks aggressive.

The newer shadows keep glancing at the trees like something's going to step out.

My legs ache. My chest feels tight. The bonds pull in directions that don't make sense.

Keep moving. Just keep moving.

I look back. Finn's near the front, quieter than usual. His chaos magic sparks but doesn't spiral. Malrik stays close to him, shadows softer around them both.

Torric and Aspen seem restless, their magic flaring as steam rises between them.

Kieran keeps his distance, watching me like I'm about to break.

I won't.

Something's off.

They're judging me. Have to be. For Darian. For claiming him when I don't even know what that means.

Finn won't look at me.

Malrik's hiding something.

Kieran's angry.

I'm being paranoid. Right?

But the bonds feel wrong—strained, pulling, like wounds that won't close.

And my shadows are acting weird.

Walter drifts toward the trees, pulses once, then floats back. He does this three times in five minutes.

Carl vibrates too fast, like a compass that can't find north.

Linda keeps tugging shadows backward, forcing them into formation.

Bob stops walking entirely and just stares into the woods, edges flaring.

Mouse growls low. A warning.

It's exhaustion. Or the weirdness in the bonds. Or hell, maybe it's nerves because Darian's somewhere behind us, bound and guarded, and I swear I can feel the resignation in his soul.

It's not that.

The pulse hits without warning.

Sharp. Static. My heartbeat glitches.

I stumble.

Mouse hisses, claws digging into my shoulder.

Bob flares so hard his edges warp.

"Not now," I whisper. "Please not now."

It pulls again. Stronger. Insistent.

I clutch my chest, pressing my palm over my ribs like I can smother it.

They're around me before I can wave them off. Too close. Heat and cold and magic pressing in from all sides.

It feels like drowning.

"I'm fine," I mutter.

Kieran's voice cuts through. "Kaia—"

"I said I'm fine."

Silence.

"We stop here," Kieran says.

I push forward between Malrik and Finn. "No. We keep moving."

"We assess before crossing." He gestures toward the river cutting through the forest ahead—wide, fast-moving, the current dark.

"No. We move. Now."

His jaw tightens. "Kaia—"

"We're not stopping."

The silence stretches between us.

Kieran exhales slowly, then nods once. "Five minutes. Then we cross."

I turn away before he can see my hands shaking.

I walk to the river's edge, needing air and space and the fucking bonds to stop screaming.

Mouse leaps down, settling near my feet. Bob positions himself at my side. Patricia hovers close, notebook dim but watchful.

I try to focus. Breathe. Calm the shadows clustering too tight.

Ignore the pull I feel to Darian that's now impossible to ignore.

Then everything stops at once.

Bob freezes as Mouse bristles, ears flat.

Patricia's notebook goes dark.

Walter appears again, pulsing frantically.

Carl launches himself sideways like he's dodging something I can't see.

I scan the trees.

It's just a forest, but it feels wrong. There's no birds chirping, not even rustling leaves. Even the wind stops.

"Something's not right," I whisper.

I hear footsteps behind me. Kieran.

His hand touches my shoulder—

And then everything detonates.

The creature explodes from the treeline.

Massive, with mangy fur matted with something dark. Bone spikes jut from its spine at wrong angles. Its limbs bend in ways that shouldn't work. Eyes too intelligent. Too aware.

An evolved version of the beasts that attacked us the first time we entered Absentia.

Twisted. Corrupted. Wrong.

It charges straight at me.

Before I can blink, Kieran throws himself in front of me.

The creature slams into him with the force of a battering ram. I hear the impact—bone against muscle, air punching from his lungs—and then he's airborne, crashing into a tree with a sickening crack.

He crumples to the ground.

"Kieran!" I scream.

Finn's chaos magic explodes outward—wild, arcing through the air like lightning with nowhere to ground. Torric's flames erupt beside him, heat washing over the clearing in visible waves.

Mouse launches toward the creature, a streak of violet fury.

Bob doubles in size, edges sharp as broken glass.

Patricia's notebook blazes so bright it hurts to look at.

And Darian—somewhere behind us, bound and guarded—flinches. I feel it through the bond. Like he took the blow himself.

My shadows go feral.

The ground shudders beneath my feet. My wings burst free as darkness pours from my hands, wild and uncontrolled, rage and fear igniting magic I can't contain.

Blood streaks down Kieran's temple. He's breathing—harsh, shallow—but his eyes won't focus.

He's down. Not dead. But not fighting.

The creature turns back toward me.

It charges again.

I don't have time to breathe.

Chapter 6
TORRIC

Move.

Move.

Fuck, move.

Get to her. Get to her *now*.

Flames break free—wild and pissed off. Fire cracks across the ground as I force my body faster than physics should allow. The underbrush ignites. I don't care. I don't slow down.

Kieran's down.

Kaia's exposed.

The creature's turning toward her.

Her shadows are losing control—wild, feral, trying to protect her but she's not commanding them. She's just standing there, wings flared, darkness pouring from her hands like she doesn't know how to stop it.

If she dies, the world fucking ends.

The creature charges.

I'm not close enough.

Not fast enough.

Fuck.

It lashes out as I close the distance—bone spike swinging toward my ribs.

I duck. Fire bursts from my palm, deflecting the blow just enough that it grazes instead of impales.

Pain lances across my side.

I don't stop.

"Get the fuck out of my way," I snarl.

It doesn't listen.

And the world detonates.

The scream hits like a physical blow.

Ear-splitting. Ancient. *Furious.*

I stumble, hands flying to my ears as the sound tears through my skull. Heat rolls across the clearing—hotter than my fire, hotter than anything I've ever felt.

I look up.

Revna.

Phoenix form. Massive wings spread wide, feathers made of flame blazing so bright I have to squint. Talons big enough to crush bone.

She dive-bombs from above.

The creature doesn't have time to react.

She *slams* into it with the force of a collapsing mountain. Talons dig into its back, piercing through matted fur and corrupted flesh. It screams—high, wrong, inhuman.

Revna drags it backward, wings beating once, twice, lifting it off the ground.

Then she *throws* it.

The creature's body arcs through the air and crashes into the river with a spray of dark water.

But its momentum catches Kaia on the way.

The impact jerks her sideways. She doesn't have time to brace. Her wings fold as she's knocked off balance, stumbling—

And then she's in the water.

"*No.*"

The word rips from my throat.

No no no *NO.*

I dive.

Zero hesitation.

The river slams into me like a wall. Cold punches the air from my lungs. My fire extinguishes instantly—every spark, every ember, gone.

I force myself forward. Muscles screaming. Current dragging at me like it wants to pull me under.

I see her ahead—hair streaming dark in the water, arms flailing, trying to surface but the current's too strong.

She's going under.

No.

I kick harder. Force my way through water that feels like molten lead, heavy and brutal and *wrong.*

The current shifts.

Slows around her.

Frost forms on the surface—delicate patterns spreading outward like someone's redirecting the flow.

I don't look. Don't need to—Aspen's right on the bank. I can feel the cold tug of his magic.

Twin bond or instinct or both—I know he's with me.

I reach her. Grab her arm. Pull her against my chest.

Her head breaks the surface. She gasps—chokes—coughs water.

"I've got you," I rasp. "I've got you."

The current surges again, trying to rip her from my grip.

I hold tighter.

We're being dragged downstream. Fast. Too fast.

I can't stop us.

A tree groans ahead—chaos magic sparking wild along its bark.

Finn.

It tilts. Cracks. Then crashes across the river, slamming into the water with enough force to send spray into the air.

A barrier.

A place to stop.

"Finally," I snarl, using it for leverage.

I angle us toward it, kicking with everything I have left.

We hit the log so hard I know my ribs are bruised. Pain explodes across my chest but I don't let go.

Kaia's weight sags against me. Her breathing is shallow. Rattling.

"Torric—"

Malrik's voice cuts through the roar of water.

He's already in the river, wading toward us. Shadows lash through the current, stabilizing the surface around us like he's forcing the water to obey.

He grabs Kaia's arms. "I've got her—Torric, let go—"

"Like *fuck* I'm letting go."

His silver eyes flash. "Then push while I pull."

I adjust anyway. Not because I want to—but because Malrik's right.

We move together.

Malrik pulling from the front. Me pushing from behind, one arm locked around her waist, the other gripping the log for leverage.

Aspen's frost spreads further, slowing the current.

Finn's chaos magic holds the tree steady, trembling but solid.

Revna circles overhead, phoenix wings blazing, ready to strike again if the creature resurfaces.

Teamwork.

We drag her onto the bank.

Malrik helps me lay her down gently. Her chest rising with shallow breaths. She's unconscious.

Because I didn't get to her fast enough.

Aspen flicks a glance behind us. "Kieran's breathing," he says. "Unconscious, not gone."

Mouse is shrieking somewhere behind us—high, furious, terrified.

Bob hulks beside her, shaking with rage, edges so sharp they cut the air.

I fall to my knees beside her, hands hovering over her face because I don't know where to touch, where it's safe, where I won't hurt her.

Then shadows curl around her—dark, wrong, not hers.

They move differently. Heavier. Tainted at the edges.

Darian's.

The air even smells wrong—metallic and cold.

They press close to her skin like they're trying to warm her. Comfort her.

Bob surges forward, doubling in size, snarling as he blocks them.

But the shadows don't fight back. Don't lash out.

They just... reach for her. Like they're begging.

I look back.

Darian's still bound, kneeling in the mud fifty feet away. His hands are tied behind his back. But his face—

Raw. Desperate. Terrified.

His shadows tremble between us, caught between her and him, not knowing where to go.

"Get them *off* her," I snarl.

Malrik's hand lands on my shoulder. "Torric—"

"I said get them—"

"They're not hurting her." Malrik's voice is quiet. Certain. "Look."

The shadows settle against her ribs in a way that doesn't seem natural. Warmth bleeds through where they touch.

A faint pulse thumps through them—like a heartbeat that isn't hers.

Her breathing steadies. Deepens.

Color returns to her face.

I hate that he's helping.

I hate that she needs it.

I hate that I'm grateful for it anyway.

My lungs finally unlock.

I slump forward, pressing my forehead to her shoulder.

"Never—*fucking*—do that again."

My hands are shaking.

Fire flickers back to life along my knuckles—weak, guttering, but there.

Finn's hand lands on my shoulder. Squeezes once.

Malrik's shadows curl protectively around all of us.

Aspen doesn't move. Just keeps watch.

And Kaia breathes.

Chapter 7
KAIA

Golden light behind my eyelids.

Warm. Gentle. Pulling me toward consciousness.

I blink, and the world comes into focus slowly.

Clean sheets beneath me. Soft blankets tucked around my legs. The distant sound of voices—real voices, not shadows or magic or danger—drifting through an open window.

A cart wheel creaking. A dog barking. Someone laughing.

Normal sounds.

Safe sounds.

The room smells like soap and sunlight.

I'm not used to waking up without fear.

My body doesn't know what to do with safety.

I try to orient myself. The room is small but well-kept. Simple wooden furniture. My pack sits folded in the corner, gear laid out like someone took care of it.

Took care of me.

Mouse is curled on my hip, warm and solid, purring softly in his sleep. When I shift, he lifts his head and nudges my cheek gently. He noses under my jaw like he's checking for injuries.

Bob stands at the foot of the bed like a bouncer who takes his job way too seriously.

The newer shadows cluster around the edges of the room—watchful, protective, refusing to leave.

I try to sit up.

Pain lances through my chest. Sharp. Immediate.

I gasp, and the shadows rush in like I'm about to fall apart.

"Whoa—slow down."

Torric's voice cuts through the chaos, low and rough.

I turn my head.

He's sitting in a chair pulled close to the bed, slouched forward with his arms crossed, exhaustion written across every line of his face. His hair's a mess. His shirt is half-burned at the edges, streaked with soot and river water.

He looks like he hasn't slept in days.

He's been watching over me.

"You almost drowned," he says quietly. "River nearly took both of us."

I push myself upright anyway. Slowly. Stubbornly.

"I'm fine."

Torric gives me The Look™—dry, disbelieving, fond in a way that makes my chest ache for reasons that have nothing to do with bruises.

"Sure," he says. "And I'm a delicate snowflake."

"You?" I manage. "You'd melt the entire mountain."

His mouth twitches. Almost a smile.

"Dammit, Sunshine." His voice softens. "It's good to see your eyes."

He pauses, jaw tight, like he's choosing his next words carefully.

"But if you're trying to die on me? Stop. It's bad for my nerves."

Something in my throat tightens.

Relief. Embarrassment. Guilt.

I scared him. Really scared him.

"I wasn't trying to—"

"I know." He leans back in the chair, exhaling slowly. "Doesn't make it easier."

I try to sort through what I remember.

Pieces. Fragments.

The creature charging.

Cold water. So much cold.

Strong arms grabbing me. Warmth cutting through the river's grip.

Torric. That was Torric.

And something else. Something warm. Something that felt like home that shouldn't have been there.

I can't place it.

"Where are we?" I ask.

"Small town. Allied village." Torric gestures vaguely toward the window. "Part of Kieran's network. These people owe him favors—respect him. They took us in without question."

I glance around the room again. The care in how everything's arranged. The clean linens. The sunlight. It feels like the sanctuary did, but warmer.

"They gave me this?"

"Gave us a whole safehouse, actually. Separate rooms. Food. Water. Privacy." He shrugs. "Kieran's built loyalty over the years. It shows."

A soft knock interrupts before I can respond.

The door cracks open and Aspen walks in, holding a tray with broth, bread, and tea.

"Hey, Torric. Thought you could use—" He stops mid-sentence, eyes locking on me. "Holy shit. You're awake."

His voice doesn't change—still controlled—but his face shows his surprise, and settles on relief.

"Nevermind, Torric. It's for her."

Torric sits up straighter, eyes widening in mock betrayal. "Excuse me?"

Aspen ignores him entirely and sets the tray on the table beside me.

"Betrayal," Torric mutters, crossing his arms dramatically. "In my hour of need."

I almost laugh. This time I manage not to wince.

Aspen's mouth twitches—barely, but it's there—as he straightens and meets my gaze.

"How are you feeling?"

"Sore. Weak. Alive."

"That's better than the alternative."

His ice-blue eyes flick toward Torric—assessing him, not speaking.

"The others?" I ask.

"Malrik and Finn are talking to the village leaders," Aspen says. "Making sure we're clear to stay as long as we need."

"Revna?"

"Returned to the sanctuary after she escorted us here. She'll check in again soon."

I nod slowly, processing. Then: "Darian?"

Torric's jaw tightens. "Still bound. Quiet."

There's something in the way he says it. Something I'm missing.

But before I can ask, my memory flickers.

"The creature?"

"Dead," Torric confirms. "Revna made sure of it."

Relief washes through me, followed immediately by exhaustion.

Aspen watches me carefully. "You should eat. Rest."

"I will."

He doesn't look convinced, but he doesn't push. Just nods once and steps toward the door.

"Aspen?"

He pauses, glancing back.

"Thank you."

His expression softens—just a fraction. "Always," he says, like it's not a promise but a fact.

Then he's gone, and it's just me and Torric again.

I reach for the broth, hands shaking slightly. Torric doesn't comment, just shifts closer like he's ready to catch the bowl if I drop it.

I don't drop it.

The warmth settles in my stomach, grounding me.

"What about—"

I stop.

A memory slams into me without warning.

The creature charging.

Kieran stepping in front of me.

The impact—bone against muscle, air punching from his lungs.

The sound of his body hitting the tree.

The crack.

The crack from the tree keeps echoing in my head.

My breath shudders.

"Kieran," I whisper.

Torric's face shifts. Subtle. But I see it.

"He's alive," he says carefully. "He's... not great. He won't admit how bad the hit was."

My stomach drops.

"Where is he?"

"Kaia—"

"Where?"

Torric hesitates. "Next room. Resting. Or supposed to be." He exhales. "He's conscious. Just... don't let him pretend he's fine."

I put the broth down and push the blankets off, ignoring the way my ribs protest.

"Kaia, wait—"

"I need to see him."

Torric stands, blocking my path without actually blocking it. "You can barely stand."

"I don't care."

Bob shifts position, edges softening like he's debating whether to help me or stop me.

Mouse lifts his head, tail flicking once.

Torric studies my face for a long moment. Then he sighs.

"You're going whether I help or not, aren't you?"

"Yes."

"Stubborn."

"You knew that already."

He mutters something under his breath—probably a curse—then offers his arm.

I take it.

My legs shake. My ribs ache. My chest feels tight with something that has nothing to do with bruises.

But I move anyway.

Because Kieran saved me.

And I need to see him.

Chapter 8
KIERAN

Pain lances through my ribs when I reach for my shirt.

I don't let it show.

I've endured worse. Survived worse. This is nothing—a bruise, swelling, the price of moving too slow.

The price of failing her.

I force my arms through the sleeves, fabric catching on bandages Malrik wrapped earlier despite my protests. He'd been methodical, silent, disapproving. Finn had offered to stabilize the bruising with chaos magic. I refused. Aspen suggested ice. I declined.

I don't need help.

I never have.

I never deserved softness anyway.

I step toward the small mirror propped against the wall, assessing the damage. Bruising spreads across my ribs in dark, mottled patterns. Swelling beneath the bandages. Nothing broken, Malrik said. Just fractured pride and strained muscle.

I button the shirt slowly, each movement calculated to hide the way my breath catches. Control is discipline. Discipline is survival. Weakness invites chaos—and my chaos, not Finn's, means danger.

Danger to her.

I will not be the reason she's hurt again.

The memory replays whether I want it to or not.

The creature charging.

Her standing exposed, wings flared, shadows wild around her.

The sound when it hit me—bone against muscle, air punching from my lungs.

Then nothing.

I woke here. Bandaged. Bruised. Alive.

They told me what happened after I went down. How Revna intervened. How Kaia was thrown into the river. How she almost—

I stop the thought before it finishes.

She nearly drowned because I wasn't fast enough.

It could have been worse.

It should have been worse.

She didn't need me stepping in front of her like some martyr playing hero.

But a life without her isn't a life at all. I should know. I've lived centuries like that.

The thought settles cold in my chest.

I shut it down immediately. Push it away. Lock it behind the walls I've spent lifetimes building.

I'm not allowed to need anything from her. Even if it betrays everything I am.

I will not make that mistake again.

A knock at the door.

I straighten, ignoring the way pain spikes through my side.

"I'm fine," I call out, voice steady. "Tell them I'll be ready in a moment."

The air changes before the door opens—warmth where there shouldn't be any.

Then I hear her breath.

Soft. Uneven. Real.

My entire body stills.

Her shadows slip into the room first—Linda drifting close, protective and calm. Carl darts forward, inspecting the bandages like he's assessing the damage. Bob yanks him back with a sharp tug, edges bristling.

Mouse pads through the doorway behind them, tail low, eyes locked on me.

Then Kaia steps through.

Pale. Bruised. Unsteady on her feet.

She shouldn't be walking. She shouldn't be upright.

And she's here.

For me.

Everything I rehearsed vanishes.

"You're hurt," she says quietly.

Just that. Two words.

They hit harder than the creature did.

I try to deflect. "It's nothing."

Her eyes land on the bandages visible beneath my half-buttoned shirt. On the way I'm holding my ribs. On the shallow breaths I can't quite hide.

"Kieran—"

"You shouldn't be up." My voice is too sharp. Too defensive. "You should be resting."

She doesn't move. Doesn't look away.

"You saved me," she says.

The words crack something inside my chest.

I didn't do it to earn gratitude. I did it because I would take a thousand hits before letting something touch her.

"I should have been faster," I say quietly. "Should have shielded you better."

"You stepped in front of me."

"I failed you."

"You protected me."

I can't look at her. Can't hold the weight of what she's saying.

Because she's wrong.

She has to be wrong.

She steps closer.

Too close.

Her shadows follow—gentle, careful, curling around my legs like they're checking on me too.

She reaches out, fingers hovering near the bandages.

I tense. Instinct. Centuries of silence. Centuries of putting armor over everything that hurt.

Then, slowly, my shoulders drop.

I let her touch me.

Her hand settles against the edge of the bandage, warm and steady.

"Does it hurt?" she asks.

"No."

Her eyes flick up to mine. She knows I'm lying.

"Kieran."

I exhale slowly. "Yes."

She doesn't pull away. Doesn't flinch. Just stays close, her hand still resting against my ribs like she knows I need it.

"You didn't fail me," she says quietly. "You were there. That's what matters."

Something inside me shatters.

Like a wall I've built over centuries finally crumbling under the weight of someone who sees me and stays anyway.

She came for me.

Hurting. Unsteady. Stubborn as ever.

Because she needed to see me.

I don't know what to do with that.

"If I had to take that hit again," I say, voice low, "I would."

Her breath catches.

"Every time," I continue. "Without hesitation."

"Kieran—"

"I will not fail you again."

She shakes her head. "I don't need you to be perfect. I just need you to be here."

The words settle somewhere deep. Somewhere I didn't know was still capable of feeling.

I reach up slowly, carefully, and brush a strand of hair back from her face.

"I will be what you need," I vow.

She leans into my hand, just slightly, and I feel the shift in everything.

She chose to come here. Chose to see me. Chose to stay.

And I will spend every day earning that choice.

"Stay," she whispers.

I don't hesitate.

"I'm not leaving."

Her forehead presses against my shoulder—gentle, careful, trusting.

I won't give her a reason to pull away again.

Not now.

Not ever.

Chapter 9
KAIA

My eyes open to sunlight.

Softer this time. Warmer.

My ribs ache. Not the stabbing kind—just a deep, annoying throb. I'm weak. But I'm not dying.

Good enough.

Mouse is glued to my side, purring hard enough I feel it in my bones. Bob's guarding the foot of the bed like he's expecting someone to burst through the door. The newer shadows have parked themselves against the walls—tense, but not freaking out.

So... that's something.

I sit up carefully.

Pain. Manageable.

I can do this.

A knock at the door.

"Kaia?" Finn's voice. Bright. Cautious. "You decent?"

"Define decent."

The door cracks open and Finn pokes his head in, grinning when he sees me sitting upright. His chaos magic flickers around his hands—calmer than usual. More focused than frantic.

"Look at you," he says. "Vertical and everything."

He steps inside, smirking. "Kaia, I know you don't *need* my help, but—"

"I can walk by myself."

"Sure you can, Trouble. But have you *seen* Torric and Aspen? Big. Scary. Very stabby when people they love get hurt. So just... let me help before they invent new ways to kill me, yeah?"

My ribs disagree loudly.

He offers his hand like he already knows I'll cave.

Fuck it.

I take his hand.

Carl darts forward, wrapping around Finn's ankle. Bob yanks him back with a sharp tug, snarling.

Mouse huffs.

Finn glances down. "Your shadows have opinions today."

"They always have opinions. I don't ask for them."

"Fair."

We slowly make our way out of the room, while I try, and fail to keep my breathing even.

The stairs suck.

Every step pulls at my ribs. Finn sticks close—not hovering, just... around. Annoying. Helpful. Both.

"Survival Tip #368," he mutters as we pass a creaky step. "Don't come between a Berserker and their Valkyrie."

"Is that what I am now?"

He glances at me. Grin softening. "You've always been theirs, Trouble. They're just gonna be less subtle about it now that you almost died... again."

We pass people in the hallway. We're greeted with warm nods. Respectful glances. Kieran's people. They know him. Trust him.

"You doing okay?" Finn asks.

"Yeah."

"Liar."

I glance at him. "I'm functional."

"That's what I thought." He grins. "Progress."

The smell of warm bread and something herbal drifts up. My stomach growls.

Finn nudges my shoulder. "See? Your body agrees with me. Breakfast fixes everything."

"Does it fix almost dying?"

"I mean... it helps."

The main room is bigger than I expected. Wooden beams. Sunlight through wide windows. A long table set with plates and cups.

And everyone's there.

Torric and Aspen sit opposite each other, bracketing the table like bookends. Malrik's got a clear view of the door—shoulders relaxed but his eyes land on me as soon as we walk in. Kieran sits near the head of the table, posture perfect even though I know he's hiding bandages under that shirt.

And Darian.

He's sitting opposite where I'm clearly meant to go. Between Torric and Aspen. Watched. But included.

He's eating quietly. Head down. Not speaking unless spoken to.

The tension isn't hostile anymore. Just... wary.

They're being careful, I get it.

Finn guides me to the seat between him and Kieran.

Kieran's posture shifts when I sit. Just barely. The smallest easing in his shoulders.

I move to sit—and suddenly my shadows converge at once.

Bob positioning himself like a bodyguard. Carl darting between my feet. Patricia's notebook blazing. Linda hovering protectively. Mouse pressed against my ankles, purring hard.

The others follow from the corners of the room, clustering close like they're all trying to help me sit.

It's… a lot.

The table notices.

Torric's mouth twitches—almost a smile.

Aspen's ice-blue eyes soften.

Malrik watches with quiet fascination.

Finn grins. "Entourage."

Kieran's gaze flickers to the shadows, then back to me. Something unreadable in his expression.

Even Darian glances up briefly before dropping his eyes again.

I finally manage to sit and Torric slides a plate toward me like nothing happened. "Eat."

"Bossy," I mutter, stabbing a piece of bread.

"You're still pale," Aspen says. "You need food."

Finn elbows me. Carl tries to elbow him back and hits the table instead.

"See? Told you. The twins will have my head."

Malrik smirks. "Your breakfast plate is a disaster, Finn."

Finn glances down at the chaotic pile of bread, eggs, and something that might be jam. "It's *organized* chaos."

"That's not a thing," Torric says.

"It is now."

My shoulders loosen.

Just a little.

For the first time since we left the sanctuary, the group feels... almost normal.

The banter keeps going. Light. Easy.

God, I missed this.

Torric teasing Aspen about giving me his soup last night.

Finn cracking a joke about Malrik's "resting disapproval face."

Malrik pointing out that Finn's shirt is on backwards.

Kieran watches silently. But there's something softer in his eyes. Relief, maybe.

And Darian—

He eats slowly. Politely. Doesn't speak unless spoken to.

But he's here.

And no one's shutting him out.

I set my fork down.

The sound is louder than I meant it to be and the table goes quiet.

Everyone looks at me.

My chest tightens. But I need to say this.

"Thank you," I say quietly. "All of you. For what you did."

No one speaks.

"I should have listened. I pushed too hard. I was..." I swallow. "I was wrong."

Silence settles—thick, real.

Malrik leans forward, voice low. "We know how badly you want to find Seren."

The words hit somewhere deep. I shift in my seat. "You're right. Just… not for what it cost us."

Kieran's hand lands on the table near mine—close enough I feel the heat coming off him. "We didn't lose anything that matters, Kaia. We're all still here. Still standing."

I shake my head. "That's not the point."

Finn studies me—really looks at me. "That's exactly the point," he says quietly.

My breath catches.

Darian clears his throat. "I've never seen a group work so effortlessly together. Not without years of training."

"Speak for yourself," Torric mutters.

"He's right," Aspen says quietly. "You and I might have trained our entire lives. But not together. Not like this."

Something in my shoulders loosens. I didn't even notice I'd been holding that tight.

Kieran speaks again, steady and sure. "We'll find her, Kaia. For you."

I meet each of their eyes. Conviction. Unity. No hesitation.

Tears well before I can stop them.

"Is this a group bromance I'm not aware of?" I try—and fail—to joke.

No one laughs.

Finn's hand lands on my knee. Warm. Grounding. Mouse nudges my ankle gently.

They're with me. All of them.

Chapter 10
MALRIK

Her voice cracks on the joke.

No one laughs.

Kaia's hand presses briefly to her ribs—quick, instinctive—before she swallows once, twice, and pushes her chair back slowly.

"I need some air," she says quietly.

No one stops her.

Her shadows peel off immediately—Bob bristling protectively, Mouse trotting after her, others dissolving into her wake like a quiet escort.

Kieran shifts forward slightly, like he's about to stand, then stops himself.

The door closes behind her.

The room shifts.

Lighter without her tension.

Heavier with worry.

No one moves at first.

No one wants to be the first to speak.

Finn pushes his hair back—anxious tic I've seen a hundred times. Aspen's jaw flexes. Torric looks like he's physically restraining himself from going after her.

Kieran's posture is rigid, watching the door like he's still deciding whether to follow.

And Darian—

Darian freezes in place, hands curled around a cup he isn't drinking, shoulders tight, body angled away from the table like he's trying to disappear.

Torric breaks first.

"She shouldn't be walking that much," he snaps—too sharp, too fast.

Fear, dressed up as anger, of course it is.

Aspen doesn't look away from the door. "Her ribs aren't stable," he says quietly. "She needs rest, not guilt."

Always calculating the risk.

Finn drags both hands through his hair, chaos magic flickering around his knuckles. "She's upright. I'll take the win." He pauses. "But yeah... she's not okay."

His magic always gives him away before his voice does.

And Darian—

He folds in on himself. Shoulders curled. Eyes down. Hands white-knuckled around the cup he's still not drinking.

The look of a man who expects to be cast out again.

Finn notices too. His gaze flicks to Darian, lingers for a moment, softens.

Aspen studies him with that quiet, analytical intensity he uses when he's working through something.

Darian whispers, almost too quiet to hear.

"I shouldn't be here."

The table reacts instantly.

Torric's growl is sharp. "NO."

Finn's head snaps up. "Oh for—no, dude."

Aspen straightens, ice-blue eyes sharp.

Kieran freezes for half a second, then his expression closes. But he doesn't disagree.

I lean back in my chair, shadows curling lazily around my feet.

"You're hers too," I say simply.

Silence.

Then chaos.

Torric slams his hand on the table. Heat rolls off him.

Finn's eyebrows shoot up. "Well... he's not wrong."

Aspen tilts his head, studying Darian thoughtfully.

Kieran's jaw tightens, but he doesn't object.

Darian looks like I just shattered his entire worldview.

"No." He shakes his head. "She shouldn't— I don't deserve—"

He can't finish the sentence.

I keep my voice calm. Logical. "Deserving has nothing to do with it."

"Your bond with her, whatever it is..." I pause. "It's real. You *both* feel it. You're as much a part of her as she is of you. That means something—whether you think it should or not."

Walter bobs through the doorway—unbothered, curious, pulsing softly with faint purple light. He drifts toward Darian, hovers near his shoulder for a moment, then floats away like he's satisfied.

Finn repositions in his chair, chaos magic settling slightly. "Sorry, man. It's a package deal. Welcome to the madness."

Torric mutters, "I am not babysitting his guilt spiral—"

Aspen smacks him lightly on the arm. "You're being dramatic."

Torric whirls on him. "I AM DRAMATIC."

Finn cracks up.

I don't bother hiding my amusement. He is—painfully so.

Kieran's voice cuts through the noise. Quiet. Steady. Absolute.

"He stays."

The room goes still.

Darian stares at Kieran like he doesn't understand what just happened.

Kieran doesn't elaborate. Just holds Darian's gaze until Darian looks away first.

Torric mutters something under his breath but doesn't argue further.

Aspen nods once—small, certain.

Finn grins. "See? Democracy."

Idiotic. But apparently it works for them.

Darian's hands loosen around the cup. Slowly. Like he's afraid to believe it.

"...Thank you." Barely a sound. Like he's afraid saying it out loud will undo it.

He means it. That's the part Torric hates the most.

The table softens.

It's not forgiveness, but acceptance. For now.

I watch them all carefully.

This isn't coincidence.

This is alignment.

Darian is no longer an outsider.

Torric is reluctantly accepting.

Kieran is steady—old power held tight under control.

Finn is the emotional glue holding us together.

Aspen is quiet support, calculating every move.

And Kaia—everything in this room pivots around her now, whether any of us want to admit it or not.

We're in this together. Because of her.

Whether it saves us... or takes us apart piece by piece.

Chapter 11
KAIA

Two days.

Two days of rest, careful movements, and shadows hovering like overprotective nursemaids.

I'm almost healed now. The sharp pain in my ribs has faded to a dull twinge—barely there unless I move wrong. My body feels lighter. Stronger.

But I need out of this house.

I'm already dressed. Boots laced. Nowhere to go.

I've been staring at the same four walls, the same concerned faces with too many questions for too long.

I need air.

The shadows hover near the walls—watching, waiting, but not crowding me like they did before.

Calmer today.

A knock at the door.

"I know you're pacing in there," Revna calls through the wood. "Come walk with me before you wear a hole in the floor."

The door opens before I can answer.

Revna leans against the frame, eyebrow raised, looking entirely too smug.

I move to step forward—and Mouse flops dramatically across my boot, pinning me in place.

"Mouse."

He doesn't budge.

"Mouse, I need my boot."

He flops dramatically to the side, purring louder.

I roll my eyes and step over him. "You're ridiculous."

Bob salutes as I follow her out.

We pass Torric and Aspen in the hallway—Torric mid-argument with Finn about something, Aspen shaking his head. Torric clocks me, eyes narrowing like he's assessing damage. I wave him off before he can say anything.

The village is small. Lived-in. Warm.

Smoke curls from chimneys. Kids run between houses, laughing. The smell of bread and something herbal drifts through the air.

And people notice me immediately.

Fantastic.

Respectful nods. Wide eyes. Some awe.

But not fear.

Because these are Kieran's people. They trust his instincts.

A baker—older woman with flour on her apron—hands me a sweet bun with a shy smile. "For you, miss."

I take it, surprised. "Thank you."

She nods and disappears inside.

A mother pulls her child closer as we pass, but the kid whispers loudly, "She's the wing lady, Mama."

I freeze.

Revna smirks. "You're already a legend."

"I didn't—"

"Doesn't matter. You are."

We're halfway through the square when a little boy—maybe six or seven—walks straight up to me.

He's got messy dark hair, dirt on his knees, and the kind of fearless curiosity only kids have.

"Is it true you have wings?" he asks.

I stare at him.

Revna raises an eyebrow, amused.

"I—" I glance at Revna.

She nods. "Go on."

I swallow. Look back at the kid.

He's waiting. Eyes wide. Hopeful.

Fuck it.

My shoulder blades warm as I let my wings flare—just a little. Light and shadow rippling softly behind me.

The kid's face lights up like I just gave him the best gift in the world.

His mother gasps. A dozen people stop what they're doing and stare.

And I let them sprawl out behind me.

It's awkward as hell. But the look on the little boys face is what I focus on.

Because it feels a lot like belonging.

It hits me hard. I've never felt that before.

Mouse flops proudly at my feet. Bob stands like a sentinel. Linda's notebook flickers—probably documenting "appropriate wing display protocol."

The boy grins. "They're so cool."

I can't help it. I smile back.

We wave goodbye and keep walking. I catch sight of movement across the square.

Darian.

Malrik's explaining something to him—hands gesturing, voice low. Darian's listening hard, posture smaller than usual.

Our eyes meet for half a second.

No guilt. Just acknowledgment.

Darian looks away quickly.

Malrik glances between us. Says nothing. He noticed. Of course he did.

Revna lifts one brow. "Interesting."

"Don't."

"I didn't say anything."

"You were thinking it."

She smirks. "Guilty."

We end up at a bench near the edge of the village, overlooking small fields that seem impossible in this corrupted place.

Revna sits with the kind of ease that comes from centuries of existing. I sit carefully, ribs protesting slightly.

"You're carrying too much for one person," Revna says.

I deflect immediately. "I'm fine."

"You're not."

I don't answer.

She doesn't push. Just waits.

Finally, I exhale. "I don't know how to do this."

"Do what?"

"Be what they need. Be what I'm supposed to be."

Revna tilts her head. "Who says you're supposed to be anything?"

"Everyone."

"Everyone is an idiot."

Despite everything, I almost laugh.

Revna's expression softens—just slightly. "Kieran wasn't always like this, you know."

I glance at her. "Like what?"

"Quiet. Controlled. Brooding." She waves a hand. "He used to laugh. Loudly. Dangerously."

I try to picture it. Can't.

"What happened?"

"He learned that caring too much burns the world down." She pauses. "So he stopped letting himself care. Until you came back from the dead. When he felt you again."

My chest tightens.

"He's a complete disaster around you," Revna continues. "Won't admit it. Everyone sees it. Malrik's keeping score."

"Revna—"

"I'm just saying." She grins. "It's entertaining."

I try not to react. Fail miserably.

Revna pauses, her eyes narrowing thoughtfully.

"Oh—reminds me. That little glowing menace—Walter, I think? He brought me to something yesterday. Wouldn't leave me alone until I found it."

She reaches into her pocket and pulls out—

The Heart of Eternity.

My breath stutters. I go still.

The shadows press closer—gentle, relieved.

Mouse purrs softly like he's content.

Revna holds it out gently. "He seemed very sure you need this now."

I take it carefully. The pendant is warm in my palm. Something in my ribs loosens.

"How did he—"

"He was... persistent," Revna says. "To say the least."

I close my fingers around it. The warmth settles something I didn't realize was still fractured.

"Thank you," I say quietly.

I hold the pendant for a moment, feeling its weight, then secure it around my neck.

The warmth settles against my chest.

Movement catches my eye—three shadows I don't recognize drifting toward me from the edges of the square. Hesitant. Curious.

They settle near my feet alongside the others.

Revna watches with quiet amusement. "Cute. Your little shadow family is growing."

I glance down. Bob's already organizing them into formation. Linda's hovering protectively. Mouse looks smug.

"I didn't—"

"You did," Revna says. "Whether you meant to or not."

The village hums around me. Kids still watch from corners.

I'm not invisible here.

I'm not a weapon.

I'm not a mistake.

Mouse headbutts my ankle gently.

Like he's saying, *It's time.*

Chapter 12
DARIAN

I've been staying close.

Not too close. Just... near enough.

Helpful when asked. Silent when not. Careful not to intrude.

It's a careful dance I've been performing, and I'm exhausted.

Malrik notices.

Fuck.

We're walking through the village when he stops and turns to face me.

"You've been circling her like you're afraid to get too close," he says. "We need to talk about that."

I tense immediately. "I'm not—"

"You are." His tone is matter-of-fact. "And it's not helping either of you."

I don't have a response to that.

He gestures for me to follow. We walk slowly through the square.

"I need to know nobody followed you when you came here," Malrik says without preamble.

My shoulders stiffen. "Nobody followed me."

"You're certain?"

"Yes."

He studies me for a long moment. "Good. Because I had you watched from the moment you left that arena."

My breath catches. "You—what?"

"You attacked Kaia," Malrik says calmly. "You were imprisoned. Alenya Virath visited you in that cell—I know what she offered you. I know you escaped. I know you went back to them."

The words hit like stones.

"And yet you're here," Malrik continues. "So I need to know why."

I open my mouth to speak, but then I see *her*.

Kaia.

Walking with Revna on the far side of the square. Her shadows move with her like a quiet escort. People notice her immediately—and why wouldn't they? Even still healing, she's breathtaking.

My chest tightens.

I force myself to look away. Focus on Malrik.

It doesn't work.

She glances over.

Our eyes meet for half a second.

There's something in her gaze—soft, unguarded. Almost like...

No.

I look away quickly, heart hammering.

I'm imagining it. I have to be.

Malrik glances between us. Says nothing. But I know he noticed.

A little boy approaches her. I can't hear what he says, but I see her hesitate. Glance at Revna.

And then her wings flare.

Light and shadow ripple softly behind her—just the edges at first, tentative.

I saw them once before. In the arena. When I attacked her.

But I didn't see them. Not really. Not like this.

The village stops. Stares.

And then she lets them sprawl out fully.

Massive. Breathtaking. Hers.

And I—

I can't breathe.

Something in my chest pulls—sharp, involuntary, undeniable.

My shadows writhe as light magic flickers beneath my skin in response.

Kaia's wings fold back. She waves to the boy, smiling, and she and Revna start walking again—toward the far edge of the village.

"As I was saying," Malrik continues, voice steady. "I need to know if I can trust you. Callum betrayed us. Led us into a trap. Kaia thinks Seren's been captured—that's why she can't sit still and heal."

I nod, trying to focus on his words.

We keep walking.

Malrik's still talking—something about trust, about the group's dynamics, about what happened after the academy—but the words blur.

My feet keep moving.

And then Malrik stops.

I take two more steps before I realize he's not beside me anymore.

I turn back. He's watching me with that sharp, assessing focus.

"You're leading us," he says quietly.

I blink. "What?"

"You've been following her for the last three minutes. I don't think you've noticed."

My breath stutters. I glance around—and realize we've drifted in the exact direction Kaia and Revna walked.

Away from the square. Toward the edge of the village.

"I didn't—"

"You did." Malrik's tone isn't angry. Just observational. "Your feet made the choice before your brain caught up."

He pauses. "Now answer the question. Why are you here?"

I swallow. Force myself to meet his eyes.

"I felt her," I say quietly.

Malrik waits.

"When Kieran forced the bond, maybe even before, if I'm being honest with myself," I continue, the words dragging out of me like broken glass. "I felt everything. Every emotion. Every..." I stop. Can't finish.

"Every intimate moment," Malrik says.

I flinch. "Yes."

"And you stayed with Alekir anyway."

"I thought—" My voice cracks. "I thought she'd chosen. That she'd never choose me. That I was better off..."

"Better off with the man who manipulated you?" Malrik's voice is sharp now. "Who used you as a weapon against the one person your power was meant to protect?"

The words hit too close.

"I didn't know what else to do," I whisper. "I had nowhere else to go."

Malrik gestures toward a quieter spot—still within sight of where Kaia and Revna are walking. We move there, and I force myself to keep my eyes off her.

Malrik leans against a post, arms crossed, studying me.

"And now?" he asks.

"Now I'm here." I force myself to hold his gaze. "Because I felt her again. Because all I can do is *feel* her. When she…" I stop. Breathe. "When she needed me."

"And if she doesn't need you?" Malrik asks. "If she chooses someone else? If she never forgives you for what you did?"

The question settles like a weight in my chest.

"I'm still here," I say quietly. "Not because I think I deserve her. Not because I think she owes me anything. But because leaving her again would kill me."

Malrik studies me for a long moment.

"She doesn't trust easily. You already know that. She's been abandoned, controlled, and manipulated by people who were supposed to protect her."

He pauses. Holds my gaze.

"You were one of them."

I flinch.

He doesn't soften it. "But she let you back in. That means something. Don't waste it by drowning in guilt."

I try to breathe. It comes out unsteady.

"I don't know how to be around her without—" I stop. Can't finish.

"Without what?" Malrik asks.

"Without feeling like I'm… taking something I don't deserve."

Malrik's voice is calm. Precise. "You're not taking anything. She's offering it. Learn the difference."

I want to argue. Want to tell him he's wrong.

But the words won't come.

"How do I make this right?" I ask quietly.

Malrik doesn't answer immediately. Lets the question sit between us.

"You can't undo what happened. That's not what she needs."

My chest tightens. "Then what does she need?"

He considers me carefully. "Consistency. Presence. Proof that you're choosing to stay—not because you owe her, but because you want to."

I nod knowing he's right.

Malrik straightens. His tone shifts—tactical, strategic.

"She needs you to be steady. Not perfect. Steady."

I force myself to meet his eyes.

"She needs you to show up without apology or self-flagellation," he continues. "She needs you to stop treating yourself like the enemy—because if you do, she will too."

His eyes narrow.

"And for fuck's sake, stop looking at her like you're waiting for permission to exist near her."

The words settle like stones in my chest.

I look back toward where she was.

In the distance, I can just barely see her—sitting on a bench with Revna. Talking. Her shadows gathered around her.

Movement catches my eye—new shadows drifting toward her from the edges of the square. Hesitant. Curious.

They settle near her feet.

Something in my chest tightens.

She glances over.

Our eyes meet again.

I don't look away this time.

Something in me steadies.

Something in me breaks.

The bond hums between us—quiet, inevitable, and absolutely undeniable.

Malrik watches the entire exchange. When I finally manage to tear my gaze away, he's watching me with that same sharp focus.

"That's what she needs," he says quietly. "Exactly that."

I don't respond.

Can't respond.

The pull is too strong. Too real.

Malrik turns to leave, pauses. "You're staying, Darian. Stop fighting it."

He walks away, leaving me standing there—caught between guilt and inevitability, between what I think I deserve and what I can't stop wanting.

I look back toward Kaia.

She's still watching.

And this time, I don't look away.

Chapter 13
KAIA

I can't bring myself to look away. He's still watching me—standing there like he's waiting for something. Or maybe just waiting.

Move, Kaia. Stop staring.

Something tightens low in my chest.

I stand and start walking toward him before I can talk myself out of it. Movement catches my eye halfway there—Malrik, walking away from Darian. Just as I look, he turns back. Eyes on me.

He smirks.

The bastard.

He's definitely up to something. Probably been plotting this whole thing.

I turn back to Darian.

I'd like to say that every time I look at him it doesn't do things to me I don't want to think about. I'd be lying. He's cleaned up since his late-night entrance—complete with groveling. The shadows around him move almost mechanically, there's tension in his shoulders. But he's still as breathtaking as he was the first time I saw him at the academy.

Fantastic.

My shadows drift forward before I consciously decide to move. Bob positioning himself at the front, his silhouette arching taller. Linda hovering near my shoulder. Carl uncertain, flicking between me and Darian like he's confused.

Finnick appears at my feet—sharp edges, no playfulness. Unusual for him.

Mouse's tail is low, ears back, watchful.

They remember.

Of course they remember.

I walk slowly. My ribs protest a little with each step.

Darian goes completely still. Shoulders tight. Hands curling into fists like he's bracing for something. His shadows twitch—reacting to mine.

I hesitate.

What am I doing?

But I keep walking.

Darian opens his mouth—probably to apologize again. I raise my hand. "Don't."

He stops. Swallows. Nods.

Good.

I force myself to look at him. Really look at him.

"I still hate what you did," I say. He flinches.

"The arena. What you did to me there." My chest tightens. "I can't pretend it didn't happen."

"Kaia—"

"I don't know if I'll ever forget it." The words taste bitter. "But..." *Fuck.* "Forgiving you isn't impossible."

Darian looks like I just broke him and put him back together wrong.

"I don't deserve—"

"No. You don't." My voice is sharper than I mean it to be. "But I'm not doing this for you."

He nods. Doesn't argue.

Smart.

Silence stretches between us.

Then Darian speaks, voice rough. "There's something I need to tell you."

Oh gods. What now?

"What?"

"I felt the bond snap into place," he says quietly. "I don't know how it happened. But suddenly you were just... there. In my head. I couldn't stop thinking about you."

I swallow. *Okay. That's—*

"And then..." He stops. Like he's forcing himself to continue. "And then it happened."

My stomach drops. "What happened?"

"I felt you." His voice cracks. "Not like the bond. More than that. *Through* the bond. I didn't know what was happening. Feelings... sensations..." He looks away. Mumbles, "A climax."

Oh gods—he felt that. I want to crawl into a corner and die.

Heat floods my face.

"Darian, I didn't—I wasn't thinking—I didn't *know*—"

"Don't apologize for wanting," he says quietly.

I stare at him.

"I wasn't meant to feel it," he continues. "But I did."

Great. That's just perfect.

"I—" The words catch in my throat. My shadows shift, uneasy.

"That was the moment everything shifted," he says.

Darian takes a step closer.

Why is he closer?

"I couldn't stay away after that," he admits. "Every instinct. Every piece of magic in me pulled toward you."

I should step back. I don't.

Why aren't I moving?

Our shadows drift toward each other. Bob's edges soften. Patricia's notebook stops flickering. Mouse's ears flick forward.

Finnick does one cautious flip.

Testing things, I guess.

And then Walter bobs through—unbothered as always, pulsing faintly. He circles us once—slow, deliberate. Observing. Then drifts away.

What the hell does that mean?

"I didn't know I needed you, Kaia," Darian says. Raw. Honest. "But I do. And I wouldn't want this any other way."

My breath catches.

Don't cry. Do not cry.

"No matter how long it takes," he continues. "I'm here."

My shadows tighten around me—not possessive. Something softer. Bob's posture shifts. Linda stops hovering so close.

They're letting him closer.

I reach up. Slowly.

Bob shifts—but doesn't move to stop me.

Darian freezes. Eyes wide, holding his breath.

I press a soft kiss to his cheek.

It leaves me a little unsteady.

His entire body shatters.

When I pull away, he's staring at me like I just handed him the sun.

Don't look at me like that.

Bob's posture softens completely. My shadows seem to breathe outward, calm now.

I force myself to hold his gaze.

"I'll keep that in mind, Darian."

Then the warning. Because I need him to *hear* this.

"But if you ever cross me again—bond or not—I'll kill you myself."

Darian doesn't flinch. "I know."

Good.

My shadows settle. Calm now.

His shadows move toward mine—subtle, instinctive, unconscious.

Mine don't pull away. Mouse stops guarding. Linda drifts back. Bob stands down.

Okay. We're okay.

I turn first, walking back to through the village.

Darian watches me go. I can feel it.

And something in my chest shifts.

Not forgiveness.

Just the start of something that might survive it.

Chapter 14
TORRIC

I've been pacing this hallway for the last ten minutes like an idiot.

Pretending to check the wards. Adjusting my weapons belt. Anything to look like I have a reason to be here instead of the truth:

I'm waiting for her.

I felt her leave earlier. Felt the pull of the bond shift when she walked away from the house with Revna. I followed her, then finally walking away when I saw her with Darian. I just can't. And I've been on edge ever since.

Get it together.

I drag a hand through my hair and force myself to breathe.

Then I hear footsteps.

I turn.

Kaia.

Walking toward the house alone, shadows drifting beside her. Calm. Alert. But softer than before.

She looks... gods, she looks healed. Stronger. Changed.

Mouse is at her heels. New shadows follow her—tentative, careful. And there's something around her edges that wasn't there this morning.

Softness.

I can't look away.

Movement catches my eye. Malrik steps out from another hallway, clearly coming from wherever Darian went.

He sees me watching Kaia.

He smirks.

He knows exactly what he's doing. Probably orchestrated this whole thing.

Kaia comes up the stairs, notices me. Changes direction. Walks toward me.

My chest tightens.

Say something. Anything.

"Hey," she says.

"Hey." My voice comes out rougher than I mean it to.

Silence.

I try to look casual. Fail spectacularly.

Heat rolls off me in waves. My fire rune burns against my chest—a sign I'm not controlling my emotions worth a damn.

My jaw locks. I force it to relax.

Just say it.

"I saw you," I manage. "Ya know. Talking to him."

She tenses immediately. "Torric, look—"

"You don't have to explain." The words come out sharper than I intended. I force myself to soften. "He's yours... as much as I am."

I take a breath. Keep going before I lose my nerve.

"You deserve whoever makes you happy. Even if I don't like it." My jaw clenches. "Even if it fucking tears at me. I'll deal with that."

Because wanting you is mine to deal with, not yours.

She steps closer instead of away.

I freeze.

What—

My breath catches. My hands clench at my sides. Heat flares beneath my skin—my magic responding before I can stop it.

The berserker strength stirs just under the surface. It's not anger. It's something deeper, more primal.

Because this woman has gotten under my skin.

Every instinct screams at me to reach for her, pull her close, keep her safe.

But I don't move.

Can't move.

"I don't want you to deal with it alone," she says softly.

Something in my chest hurts.

No. Don't do this. Don't say things like that unless—

"Kaia..." My voice drops. Rough. Desperate. "Please don't say things like that unless you mean them."

I can't take pity. Can't take her trying to make me feel better if she doesn't actually want—

"I meant every word."

She steps even closer.

Close enough that I can feel the warmth of her skin. Close enough that her shadows brush against the heat radiating off me.

Oh gods.

She wants—

She's choosing—

My restraint cracks.

I raise my hand. Slow. Careful. Touch her cheek with one finger.

She's soft. Warm. Real.

"I don't know how gentle I can be," I whisper.

It's the truth. I'm terrified. Terrified of being too much. Too rough. Too intense.

Terrified of hurting her when she's still healing.

Terrified my strength—berserker and fire combined—will break her if I lose control.

She meets my eyes. "I don't want gentle."

I break.

I kiss her like I'm starving.

Like I've been holding back for months and finally—*finally*—I don't have to anymore.

My mouth crashes against hers. Hungry. Desperate. But I brace my hand on the wall above her head because if I don't anchor myself somewhere I'll crush her.

She pulls me closer instead. Fingers tangling in my hair. Body pressed against mine.

I groan into her mouth and the sound is wrecked.

Heat floods through me. Not just desire. My magic flaring in response to her.

The bond hums.

Her shadows wrap around me like they're steadying me. My fire pulses in answer—controlled, but barely.

She's choosing me.

We stumble backward. Still kissing. Breathless.

I reach past her, shove her door open, and we fall through together.

My hands are everywhere—her waist, her back, tangling in her hair—but I'm careful. So fucking careful.

She's still healing. Her ribs are still bruised. I can't—

She tugs at my shirt.

I pull back just long enough to yank it over my head. Her eyes go wide for half a second—taking in my chest, the fire rune glowing faintly over my heart, pulsing with my heartbeat—before I'm kissing her again.

Her shirt follows. My hands slide up her ribs—gentle, checking—and she gasps when my thumb brushes the edge of the bruise.

I freeze. "Did I hurt you?"

"No." She grabs my face. Pulls me back. "Don't stop."

Gods help me.

We fall onto the bed together.

I hover over her, chest heaving, trying to hold onto the last threads of my control.

The rune pulses brighter. My jaw locks again—fighting the urge to just take what I want.

Then I stop.

Cup her jaw.

"Tell me you want this," I say quietly. Seriously. "Tell me it's you choosing me. Not the bond. Not the day. You."

I need to hear it. Need to know this is real.

She reaches up. Touches my face.

"I want you, Torric."

My breath shudders out of me.

"Then gods help me... I'm yours."

I move slowly at first.

Deliberately.

My mouth trails down her neck, pausing to scrape my teeth along her pulse. She arches into me with a broken sound and I nearly lose it right there.

Control. Keep control.

I keep going. Down her collarbone. Over the swell of her breast.

When my mouth closes over her nipple, she cries out.

I cover her mouth with my hand—not silencing, just muffling—and look up at her through my lashes.

"Quiet, sunshine," I murmur. "Unless you want the whole house to hear."

She bites her lip.

Good girl.

I reward her by sucking harder, teeth grazing sensitive skin, and she arches off the bed with a whimper that goes straight to my cock.

Fuck.

My free hand slides down her stomach. Hooks into her waistband.

"Can I?"

"Yes. Gods, yes."

I strip her pants off in one motion, taking her underwear with them.

I go still.

Just... stare.

She's perfect. Every inch of her laid bare for me to see. Curves and soft skin and strength.

Heat flares beneath my skin—my magic responding to the sight of her, the scent of her.

"You're so beautiful," I murmur. "You have no idea."

She flushes. "Torric—"

"I mean it." My hand skims up her thigh. Stops just short of where I can smell how wet she is. "I've wanted this. Wanted you. For so long."

She reaches for me. Pulls me down. "Then take me."

I kiss her again—deep, consuming—while my hand finally moves higher.

When my fingers brush between her thighs, she gasps into my mouth.

"Fuck, Kaia," I breathe. "You're soaked."

She can't respond. Can't do anything but whimper as I move—slow, deliberate circles that make her hips jerk.

"Is this okay?"

"More," she manages. "Please, Torric—"

I slide one finger inside.

She moans—loud, broken—and I cover her mouth again.

"That's it, sunshine," I murmur against her ear. "Let me feel you."

I add a second finger. Curl them just right. My thumb finds her clit and she clenches around me so tight I nearly lose my mind.

"Gods, you're perfect," I growl. "Give me more."

She's close. I can feel it. The way her body tightens. The way her breath comes faster.

But not yet.

Not until I'm inside her.

"Torric—" Her nails dig into my shoulders. "I need—"

"I know." I kiss her. Pull my hand away and she whimpers at the loss. "I know what you need, sunshine. Let me give it to you."

I strip off the rest of my clothes.

Kaia's eyes go wide when she sees me fully bare.

Her gaze drops. Lingers.

I smirk despite myself. "Eyes up here."

She drags her gaze back to my face.

Flushed. Breathless. Wanting.

Gods, she's perfect.

I settle between her thighs.

The smirk fades.

This is real. This is happening.

"Tell me if it's too much," I say quietly. "Tell me if I hurt you."

She nods.

I line myself up. Push inside slowly.

So slowly I want to scream.

The heat. The tightness. The way she gasps and clenches around me.

Control. Don't lose control.

I'm too strong. Even without fully triggering the berserker, my strength is too much. If I slip—if I lose focus for even a second—

When I'm finally seated fully, we both freeze.

Breathing hard. Trembling.

"Kaia?"

"Don't stop," she breathes. "Please don't stop."

I exhale shakily and start to move.

Slow at first.

Controlled.

Every thrust deliberate. Deep. Careful.

But it's killing me.

Every instinct I have is screaming at me to move faster. Harder. To claim her completely.

The berserker strength surges just beneath my skin—not anger, but raw, primal need.

But I can't. She's still healing. I'm too strong. If I lose control—

She shifts her hips. Pulls me deeper.

I groan—low and broken. "Fuck, Kaia—"

"More," she whispers. "I can take it. I promise."

Her hand comes up. Touches my jaw. Soft. Trusting.

"I know you're holding back," she whispers. "You don't have to. Not with me."

"Kaia—" Her name breaks on my lips. Wrecked.

She's going to kill me.

My control fractures.

I shift my grip. Hands on her hips—firm but careful.

My rhythm changes.

Still controlled. Still watching her face for every reaction.

But intense now.

Deep. Consuming. Every thrust hitting exactly where she needs me.

She arches into me. Nails raking down my forearms enough to sting.

The pain grounds me. Keeps me from losing myself completely.

"You feel so good," I lean down to murmur against her ear. "So perfect. Like you were made for me."

She pulls me closer. Wraps her legs around my waist.

Gods.

The angle shifts and I hit deeper. My hands grip her hips—guiding, adjusting—lifting her slightly so I can drive in exactly where she needs me.

She cries out and I swallow the sound with a kiss, still moving, keeping the rhythm steady even though every muscle in my body is screaming at me to let go.

Heat builds between us—literal heat, my fire magic responding to hers, to the bond, to everything we are together.

Her shadows pulse around us—soft, rippling, alive. My magic flares in answer—controlled, but barely.

The rune burns bright against my chest.

The bond hums between us—louder now, insistent, alive.

"Torric—" Her breath catches. "I'm close—"

"I know," I growl against her throat. "I want to feel it, Kaia. Let me feel you come around me."

I shift slightly. My hand slides between us, thumb finding her clit.

I press down. Circle. Match the rhythm of my thrusts.

"Kaia—" I groan her name against her throat, voice breaking. "Gods, Kaia—"

She shatters.

Her entire body shakes. She cries out my name and I kiss her through it, still moving, dragging it out until she's trembling and gasping beneath me.

Her shadows flare—a soft, brilliant pulse that ripples through the room.

I follow a heartbeat later.

Buried deep. Her name on my lips like a prayer.

Heat floods through me—my magic, the bond, everything—and for one perfect moment we're completely aligned.

I collapse on top of her, trembling, forehead pressed to hers.

Careful not to crush her even now.

She chose me.

For a long moment, we just breathe.

Then I shift carefully, pulling out. Roll onto my side and bring her with me.

I wrap my arms around her. Not trapping. Just... holding.

Safe.

My fire magic settles. Her shadows curl close but calm.

I press my forehead to hers.

"You can have all of us," I say softly. "But this... this part of you? The part that chooses me? I won't take it for granted."

She reaches up. Touches my face.

"You didn't take anything," she whispers. "I gave it."

Something in me shatters.

I glance up—and freeze.

Lined up along the headboard—perfectly spaced, eyes (If you can call them that) wide—are Bob, Patricia, Finnick, Carl, Linda, and Steve.

Just... watching.

"Um... Kaia?"

She stirs slightly, follows my gaze, and goes completely still.

Bob's posture is stiff, like he's pretending he didn't just witness the whole thing. Patricia's notebook flickers in her smoky little hands. Finnick does a slow, approving nod. Carl looks confused. Linda's expression is somewhere between maternal approval and mild exasperation. Steve is upside-down.

For a long moment, neither of us moves.

Then Kaia starts laughing.

Not a polite laugh. A full, breathless, uncontrollable laugh that shakes her entire body.

I can't help it. I start laughing too.

"Oh my gods," she gasps, covering her face with her hands. "You all are *terrible!*"

Bob salutes.

Finnick bows.

Patricia's notebook flares brighter—probably adding an appendix.

Kaia groans and buries her face in my chest, still laughing. "I can't believe them."

I grin, pressing a kiss to the top of her head. "They've been here the whole time, haven't they?"

"Probably," she mutters.

The shadows finally drift down from the headboard, settling around us.

They around us like a blanket. My heat wraps around her like a shield.

Chosen.

She falls asleep against me.

I stay awake for a long time—holding her like she might disappear if I let go.

Just before sleep takes me, I whisper:

"I'm not going anywhere."

I mean it with every part of me.

Chapter 15
MALRIK

The bond shifts in the night—warm, final, chosen.

Torric.

Good.

She needed that. He needed that.

From across the hall, I hear Finn turn over in his bed.

He doesn't make a sound.

That's worse.

Chapter 16
FINN

I feel it the second it happens.

The bond snaps into place—solid, warm, certain—and it's not mine.

Torric.

Of course it's Torric.

I stare at the ceiling and try to remember how to breathe around the weight crushing my chest.

Good for him. Really. I'm happy for them both.

I turn over and bury my face in the pillow so no one hears me laugh.

Or maybe it's crying.

I can't tell anymore.

Chapter 17
KAIA

Something's different.

I know it before I'm fully awake. The air feels warmer. Heavier. There's weight against my back and—

Oh.

Torric.

His arm is draped over my waist. His chest pressed against my back. The fire rune pulses faintly against my spine, syncing with his breathing.

He's out cold. Completely dead to the world.

My shadows are curled around us both like they've given up on being dignified.

I let myself have this. Just for a second. Just this one quiet moment before everything starts moving again.

Then I see movement in the doorway.

Aspen.

Grinning like an absolute bastard.

"Morning," he says.

Oh gods.

"...how long have you been standing there?"

"Long enough."

Heat floods my face. "Aspen—"

"Relax." He leans against the doorframe, arms crossed. "I'm just glad you both finally stopped running."

I carefully untangle myself from Torric. He doesn't wake—just shifts, reaches for where I was, then settles back into sleep like nothing happened.

My shadows scatter.

I grab my clothes off the floor and start getting dressed.

Aspen doesn't look away.

His gaze isn't leering—it never is—but it's not neutral either. There's heat there.

He wants me.

I know he does.

I'm okay with that.

But he just watches quietly, like he always does. Besides, he'd never do anything without asking me first.

"I knew you two would work it out eventually," he says softly.

I pull my shirt over my head. Meet his eyes.

"Aspen. I need to talk to Kieran."

The grin disappears.

"You want to move out."

Not a question.

I nod.

"We have to find Seren." I take a breath. "We're rested. Kieran's rested. There's no point waiting."

Aspen studies me. Then nods slowly.

"I'm glad you gave yourself time to heal first."

My chest tightens.

Because he's right.

I smile. Grateful.

"Thank you."

He pushes off the doorframe. "Come on. He's out back."

We walk in silence.

The air is cool. Soft. Dew clings to everything, catching the early light.

It's almost easy to forget we're standing in the middle of corrupted Absentia. That just beyond the wards, the realm is still twisted. Broken. Here, inside Kieran's sanctuary, everything feels normal.

Like a mirage in a wasteland.

Aspen slows as we approach the garden.

Kieran is there. Adjusting a ward or... something, that I definitely don't understand. He's moving carefully, deliberately.

He looks peaceful.

I haven't seen that in a long time. Maybe ever.

Aspen gives him a quiet nod—some kind of unspoken guy thing—and walks away.

Kieran sets down whatever he was holding. Turns to face me.

Gods.

I forget sometimes. How beautiful he is. How the light catches the sharp lines of his jaw. How his eyes hold centuries but still manage to look at me like I'm the only thing that matters.

It's annoying, honestly.

I steady myself, clasping the Heart of Eternity feeling the weight of it in my hand, and start with the truth.

"I haven't gotten a chance to thank you yet."

His expression shifts. Guarded. Like he's bracing for a hit.

"For what?"

I step closer. Let my fingers brush his bicep.

He goes still. Completely still.

"For saving me." My voice comes out softer than I intended. "For protecting me. For everything you've done since we got here."

I take a breath.

"Well. You know. Besides the whole forcing the bonds thing." I hold his gaze. "And at some point we're going to talk about that. But not right now."

Kieran flinches. Just barely.

Good. He should.

"I don't know how I'll ever repay you," I continue. "For the rest of it."

His jaw tightens.

Not guilt. Not this time. This is something else.

"You don't owe me anything." His voice is quiet. Rough. "My job has always been to protect you."

I shake my head. "You protected me even when I made it impossible."

Something flickers across his face.

But it doesn't shatter him this time. He just exhales slowly.

Okay. Here we go.

"We need to find Seren."

He nods once. Listening.

"I'm not rushing in recklessly." I hold his gaze. "Not this time. We're healed. You're stable. I'm stable. There's no reason we can't leave tomorrow."

He doesn't argue or try to stall. Just stands there watching me like I'm a puzzle he can't figure out.

"You said you'd follow me anywhere," I say quietly.

Kieran inhales.

I watch it happen—the shift.

His shoulders drop. His magic settles. His eyes go soft in a way that makes my chest hurt.

He steps toward me but stops himself before he gets too close.

Giving me the space I need. Even now.

"I did," he says. "And I meant it. If you're ready... then I'm ready."

I nod. "Then let's go find her."

He gives me a small smile.

It's the first real one I've seen in a long time. It lights up his entire face and does something to my insides I am not ready for.

"I'll alert the others. We leave at dawn."

"Thank you," I whisper.

He hears everything I'm not saying.

Then he turns and walks back toward the house.

I watch him go.

Something settles in my chest.

This time I'm not running scared. I'm not shoving my way forward because I can't stand still.

This time I do it right.

And Kieran's following because he wants to. Not because he feels like he has to.

My shadows curl around my ankles. Quiet and steady.

We're not running toward danger this time.

We're doing what needs to be done. And we're doing it together.

Chapter 18
KAIA

The village hall is warm and smells like bread and woodsmoke.

It's strange how normal it feels. How safe. Like we're not sitting in the middle of a corrupted realm with monsters pressing against the wards. Like this is just... dinner.

Bob stations himself by the door, posture rigid, while Finnick lounges along a ceiling beam pretending this is all normal. Patricia hovers near my shoulder, notebook at the ready like she's expecting minutes to be taken.

I take my seat at the long table, and the others settle around me. Torric on my left, close enough that I can feel the heat radiating off him. Aspen across from me, calm and watchful. Malrik at the far end, eyes already tracking the room.

Finn beside him, present but quiet.

Too quiet.

Finnick, for once, is still — hands tucked behind his head, gaze fixed on Finn instead of me.

That's... not good.

Kieran stands near the head of the table, speaking in low tones with an older woman I haven't met yet.

She's tall, silver-haired, with the kind of face that's seen too much and decided to keep going anyway. When she turns to look at me, her eyes are sharp but warm.

She reminds me of my mother... I think.

Kieran starts to introduce us, but I stand before he can.

"Thank you for taking us in," I say. "For the healing. For the safety. I know it wasn't easy, and I know we've brought trouble to your door."

The woman at the head of the table studies me for a long moment.

"Elda," she says. "I lead what's left of this village."

"Kaia."

"I know who you are." She doesn't look away. "I've heard stories of the last Valkyrie. I'll admit — I didn't have high hopes."

My heart kicks, trying to figure out what she means.

"I was wrong." Her smile is slow, genuine. "Your shadows love you like you're one of them. And you stopped to feed the curiosity and wonder of a little boy. You have a good heart, Kaia." She gestures to the table. "Absentia is lucky to have you."

I don't know what to do with that.

So I sit.

I catch Kieran watching me from across the table. There's something in his expression that looks suspiciously like pride.

Dammit.

I look away before I can think too hard about it.

The door opens behind us.

Bob tightens by my chair, edges sharpening. Mouse flicks his tail once under the table, a low warning only I feel.

Darian slips in, slightly out of breath, like he ran here. He's trying to keep his expression neutral, but there's something at the corner of his mouth. A smirk he can't quite kill.

"Sorry I'm late," he says.

Bob relaxes. Barely.

Darian takes the empty seat at the end of the table — furthest from me, still giving me space — and I catch myself staring.

What the hell is he so pleased about?

He catches me looking. The smirk gets worse.

Then schools his features like a child about to get caught.

I glance at Malrik. He's watching the exchange with that quiet, knowing look he gets when he's three steps ahead of everyone else.

His eyes flick to mine. One eyebrow lifts, barely perceptible.

I look away.

What the hell is going on?

Elda waits for the table to settle before speaking.

"I have information you need before you leave," she says. "Two nights before you arrived, a caravan passed through the village. Traders heading east."

She pauses.

"They reported seeing a young woman with purple hair — with someone hooded beside her. They didn't look like willing companions. Moving fast. Heading toward the mountain."

My heart stops.

Seren.

For half a second the hall blurs — firelight, faces, noise — and all I can see is a kid with purple hair and too-big boots trailing in my shadow.

Patricia appears at my elbow, notebook blazing, then blurs like the ink can't keep up. Mouse presses against my boot.

"Sorrow's Keep," Kieran says quietly.

Elda nods. "That's what they call it. The mountain at the heart of the corruption. They say it holds the gateway to the gods." She shrugs slightly. "Whether that's true or superstition, I couldn't say."

Darian shifts in his seat. "It's not easy to reach. The terrain around it is... wrong. Twisted. Alekir talked about it constantly, but I never saw it myself."

"There's more," Revna says from the doorway. I didn't even notice her arrive. "A separate witness spotted someone else heading the same direction. Hours apart from the caravan."

She steps into the room, her expression grim.

"Callum."

The name lands like a stone in still water.

Carl peels out from beneath the table, halfway through a salute before Bob yanks him back, edges sharp with *don't you dare*.

Torric's rune flares briefly, heat rolling off him before he clamps it down. Aspen goes very still. Kieran's jaw tightens, controlled and focused.

Finn stiffens beside Malrik, something flickering across his face — grief, guilt, fear — before he shoves it down and goes blank.

Darian tenses.

I notice. So does Malrik.

"You know him?" Malrik asks, voice carefully neutral.

Darian hesitates. "I've heard the name. Thorne mentioned him once. Maybe Alekir too. I don't know the details."

Malrik nods slowly, filing that away.

"They weren't traveling together," Revna continues. "The sightings were hours apart. But they're both heading toward the Keep."

Silence settles over the table.

I take a breath.

"We leave at dawn."

Bob snaps into a crisp salute. Behind him the new recruits scramble to copy it, half a step late and wildly uneven. Linda nods approvingly.

Are there more than before?

No one argues. No one hesitates.

Elda nods, unsurprised. "Dawn is ideal. The winds die down just before sunrise — you'll have a window to cross the eastern boundary without fighting the corruption."

She looks around the table, assigning tasks like she's done this a hundred times.

"Torric, I'll need you to reinforce the fire wards at the southern gate before you go. Aspen, Revna — check the outer markers one last time. Malrik, come find me after dinner. We'll go over the route together."

Her gaze lands on Finn, and something in her expression softens.

"And you," she says gently. "Eat. Rest. You'll need your strength."

Finn's jaw tightens, but he nods.

The meeting winds down. People start to move, conversations breaking into smaller groups.

Elda catches my eye before I can stand.

"You're ready, more than you realize," she says quietly. "You're not running anymore."

I meet her gaze. "No. I'm not."

She smiles — warm, approving. "Good. The village stands with you. Whatever waits at Sorrow's Keep, we're behind you."

"Thank you," I say. And I mean it.

Later, as we file out into the cool night air, I let myself feel it.

The steadiness. The certainty.

I'm not running from fear. I'm not acting recklessly. I'm here, with the men I lo... *nope*. I have people behind me are following because they choose to.

And it's terrifying.

Kieran falls into step beside me, Torric's warmth at my back.

Aspen's calm, Finn's uncharacteristically quiet, but he's here. That's what matters.

And Malrik is already planning.

Darian catches my eye one more time. The smirk is gone, replaced by something softer. Something like hope.

Bob settles at my side, Mouse at my heel, Steve dangling upside down from the rafters like this is all just a show. They're... Ready.

We leave at dawn.

Sorrow's Keep is waiting.

And Seren is close.

Chapter 19
DARIAN

I've been standing outside the hall for way too long.

Long enough for my palms to go damp. Long enough to rehearse the same words in my head a hundred different ways.

Hey Kaia? Can we talk?

Too forward.

Can we speak for a moment?

Too formal.

Garden? Outside? Please?

Too pathetic.

I settle on the worst version of them all, because it's the only one that will actually come out of my mouth.

The door opens and she steps into the hallway with Torric at her side, his hand resting on the small of her back. The sight of it twists something in my chest that I refuse to examine.

Her shadows curl around her ankles, and I catch Bob watching me from her shoulder. His edges aren't sharp anymore — not like they were in the beginning — but he's not exactly rolling out the welcome mat either.

Fair enough.

"Hey, Kaia?" My voice cracks like I'm fourteen. Fantastic start. "Can we... talk? For a minute? In the garden?"

Torric's eyes narrow, heat flickering in his gaze. But he doesn't move. Doesn't challenge.

Kaia blinks up at me, and for a second I forget how to breathe. Violet. Her eyes are violet. I spent months in that cell trying to remember, and now I can't look away.

Kieran appears from somewhere — of course he does — and gives me a single, slow nod.

It's ready.

Kaia hesitates. Just a breath.

Then she turns to Torric, touches his arm, and says something too quiet for me to hear. He nods once, presses a kiss to her temple, and walks away.

She follows me.

We walk around the side of the house in silence.

I'm hyper-aware of everything. Her footsteps syncing with mine. The soft rustle of her shadows. The way the bond hums between us — not wrong anymore, just... there. Waiting.

Mouse pads along at her heels, tail swishing. He looks up at me once with an expression that clearly says *I'm watching you.*

I don't blame him.

Patricia drifts near Kaia's shoulder, notebook flickering faintly. Finnick is nowhere to be seen, which probably means he's about to drop out of a tree and scare the hell out of me.

I try to speak once. Fail.

Kaia doesn't push. She just walks beside me, letting me be nervous, and somehow that makes it worse.

She's going to hate this. I shouldn't have tried.

The corrupted magic flickers faintly around the garden corner — tiny lights leaking into view.

Too late to turn back now.

We round the corner, and the lights drift up to meet us.

Dark spheres float lazily through the air, each one carrying a small point of soft light inside. Like stars trapped in ink. They bob gently around the garden, casting shifting patterns across the plants and stones.

Not quite right. Not quite wrong.

Me, underneath it all.

I watch Kaia's face, heart hammering so hard I'm sure she can hear it.

She stops short.

Her breath catches.

Her shadows go still — all of them, even Mouse — and for one terrible second I think I've made a horrible mistake.

Then Bob's edges soften. Patricia's notebook stops flickering. Finnick drops silently from somewhere above and does a slow, curious flip around one of the floating lights.

"You made this?" Kaia's voice is barely a whisper.

"I... yeah." I swallow hard. "I wanted to make something for you. Something that wasn't... hurtful. Or from fear. From any of that."

She steps forward slowly, lifting her hand toward one of the lights. She doesn't touch it — but almost. Her shadows flicker with curiosity instead of fear.

"It's beautiful," she says.

My chest nearly caves in.

"You don't owe me anything," I say quickly, the words tumbling out before I can stop them. "I don't want anything in return. I just... hoped you might like it. That's all."

She turns to look at me, and her eyes — violet, always violet, how could I ever forget — are soft in a way I don't deserve.

"Thank you, Darian."

I don't know what to do with that. Don't know where to put it.

So I just nod, trying not to show how much her reaction means. Trying not to fall apart.

One of the bubbles flickers.

The light inside flares too bright, fracturing, and I feel the corruption surge through the bond like oil through water. Cold and hungry and wrong.

I grab for it instinctively, dispersing the bubble before it can burst, forcing the corruption back down with everything I have. My hands shake. My vision blurs at the edges.

For a second — just a second — I feel like I'm back in that cell. Alenya's key burning in my palm. Choosing fear because it was easier than hope.

Then something else breaks through.

Light.

Not corrupted. Not twisted. Just... light.

It flickers beneath my skin, faint but visible, pushing back against the darkness. Fighting for space.

Kaia sees it. I know she does.

"You're getting better," she says quietly.

I shake my head, still trembling. "I'm trying."

The words echo in my skull. *I'm trying.* The same thing we're both doing — trying to be something other than what we were.

"You don't have to pretend it's easy," she says.

"I'm not." I force myself to meet her eyes. "But I'm not giving up either."

The garden is quiet around us. The lights bob gently, casting soft shadows across her face.

I want to say so many things.

I'm sorry.

I never wanted to hurt you.

I don't deserve any of this.

I think I'm falling in love with you and it terrifies me.

Instead, I settle on something safer.

"I meant what I said. I don't want anything from you." My voice is rough, barely holding together. "Just... this. Just you not being afraid of me."

Kaia is quiet for a long moment.

Then she steps closer.

"I'm not afraid of you, Darian."

She reaches out — slowly, carefully — and wraps her arms around me.

I freeze.

Every muscle in my body locks up, because I don't know what to do with this. Don't know how to hold something this fragile without breaking it.

But then her shadows curl around us both, soft and warm, and something in me shatters.

I wrap my arms around her and hold on like she might disappear. Like this might be the last good thing I ever get to have.

She smells like woodsmoke and magic and... and, Kaia. The bond hums between us — quiet, almost aligned. Not wrong anymore.

Not wrong at all.

She pulls back first.

But she's not cold or distant.

She gives me one last look — soft, unreadable, but not afraid — and then she turns and walks back toward the house.

I watch her go. She looks back once, almost as if she's committing it to memory, and disappears around the corner.

The garden dims around me, the lights fading slowly as my magic settles. I should go inside. Should rest. Should prepare for tomorrow.

But I can't. Because even though she's gone, I can't bring myself to turn away from this beautiful moment.

A flicker of movement catches my eye.

I look up, expecting Finnick or one of the other shadows come to judge me.

Instead, I find Walter.

He bobs lazily near the garden wall, starlight rippling through his form like captured moonbeams. The same impossible little shadow that found me in my cell all those months ago.

"You," I breathe. "You were there. In the dungeons."

Walter just bobs in acknowledgment.

Then he pulses.

The vision hits me like a punch to the chest.

I see myself in the cell. Forehead pressed against cold stone. Alenya's key burning in my palm. My shadow magic surging with victory as I chose fear over hope. Chose to forget her eyes.

The shame of it nearly brings me to my knees.

"I know," I whisper. "I know what I did."

Walter pulses again.

A new vision. Different.

Gates. Massive. Ancient. Stone carved with symbols I don't recognize. Six points of light arranged in a perfect pattern, power flowing between them like rivers of starfire. At the center, a seal. Something stirring behind it. Waiting.

My breath catches.

"What does it mean?" I ask, but Walter just bobs serenely, completely unfazed by my confusion.

He drifts closer, brushes against my hand — the touch feels like sunshine and laughter, just like before — and then floats away into the darkness.

I stand alone in the fading garden, the last of the lights winking out around me.

I remember the color of her eyes.

Violet. Always violet.

I'm not that man in the cell anymore. I don't have to be.

I don't have to forget.

Because maybe tonight was the beginning of forever.

Chapter 20
KIERAN

I wake before dawn.

Not because I'm rested. Because I can't sleep.

The house is quiet around me, the others lost in whatever dreams they've earned. I lie still for a long moment, staring at the ceiling, letting the silence press against my chest.

My thoughts won't settle.

Kaia's steadiness last night. The way she spoke to Elda like an equal. The way she didn't flinch when Seren's name came up.

Torric's hand on her back. His kiss to her temple before he let her walk away with Darian.

Darian's nervous energy. The garden I helped him prepare. The lights blooming as they rounded the corner together.

...Not my finest habit.

Finn's silence at dinner. The grief he's burying so deep I'm not sure even he knows it's there anymore.

Malrik's eyes tracking everything, already ten steps ahead.

And Sorrow's Keep, waiting at the end of this road like a door I'm not sure any of us are ready to open.

I push myself upright and swing my legs over the edge of the bed.

The weight of it settles across my shoulders like armor I never asked to wear.

I don't bother trying to sleep again. I get dressed and go looking for her instead.

I look for her. Not with Torric. Not with Aspen or Finn or Malrik.

Not with Darian, either—huh.

...Efficient. I meant efficient.

I find her in the garden.

Kaia stands near the garden wall, shadows curled around her ankles, staring at the fading lights Darian left behind. They're almost gone now — just a few stubborn sparks drifting lazily through the air.

Does she have any idea how beautiful she is?

Bob is at her shoulder, posture rigid. Linda hovers nearby, radiating quiet energy. Steve is upside down in a bush, apparently stuck.

I don't approach.

Not because she's distant. Because I am.

I watch her from the doorway, and something in my chest aches in a way I don't have words for.

She's stronger than she was when I found her again. Steadier. More certain of who she is and what she's capable of.

I don't know where I fit into who she's becoming.

I don't know if I'm leading her toward something, or just following behind.

"You're too quiet."

Aspen's voice is soft, but it still makes me flinch. I didn't hear him approach.

He leans against the doorframe beside me, arms crossed, watching Kaia with the same quiet intensity I was.

"I'm always quiet," I say.

"Not like this." He tilts his head, studying me. "You're carrying something."

"I'm carrying a lot of things."

"Mm." He doesn't push. Just stands there, steady and patient, waiting for me to break first.

I don't.

After a long moment, he laughs softly — the kind of laugh that says he sees right through me and isn't surprised by what he finds.

"She's stronger than you think," Aspen says. "So are you."

I don't respond.

But something settles, just slightly.

We stand in silence, watching her. The lights Darian made have mostly faded, just a few stubborn sparks drifting through the morning air. Kaia stands at the garden wall, shadows wrapped around her ankles like they're keeping her company.

She doesn't know we're here.

A soft footstep behind us.

Malrik appears first — quiet, inevitable, like he stepped out of shadow itself. He doesn't say anything. Just watches her alongside us, eyes sharp and thoughtful.

Another set of footsteps.

Finn stumbles up beside Aspen, hair a disaster, blanket still half-wrapped around his shoulders.

He takes one look at the three of us lined up like idiots staring dreamily at Kaia and snorts.

"Let me guess," Finn mutters. "Kieran was here first."

Malrik actually laughs — low, quiet, and too amused for my pride.

"Some things never change," he says.

Aspen hides a smile. Finn smirks. Malrik just lifts a brow.

I don't dignify any of them with a response.

But my jaw tightens.

The sun breaks over the horizon as we turn, heading for the front of the house.

Torric is checking gear, adjusting straps when we get there. Finn rubbing sleep from his eyes, dark circles bruising the skin beneath. At least his humor is still there.

Jerk.

Malrik counts heads. Darian stands apart as Kaia makes her way from the garden. She gives him a small smile that looks warmer than yesterday as she steps up beside me.

Her shadows act first. Bob snaps into a crisp salute. Mouse flicks his tail once, a low acknowledgment. Finnick dangles upside down from the eaves, chewing on a stolen pastry. Patricia's notebook flickers to life, already documenting. Linda drifts close, radiating approval. Steve extracts himself from another bush and attempts a salute, wobbling dangerously.

"Ready?" she asks.

One word. Simple. Direct.

But it carries everything.

She's not afraid. She's centered. She trusts me. She sees me.

My chest aches.

"Yes," I say.

It feels like a lie.

Elda steps forward as we approach the gate.

She doesn't offer speeches or blessings. Just looks at each of us in turn, and finally settles on me.

"You'll know when you've done what must be done," she says quietly.

I nod once.

She steps aside.

I turn to the group. My group. My responsibility.

"Let's move."

We cross the threshold of the village, and the world shifts.

The air changes first — heavier, colder, carrying the faint tang of corruption. The wards fade behind us, their protection dissolving into memory.

Ahead, the road stretches toward the mountains. Toward Sorrow's Keep.

I've been there once before. A long time ago, when it was just a relic. A monument to something ancient and forgotten.

It didn't feel like this then.

It didn't feel like it was waiting.

I glance over my shoulder.

Kaia walks in the center of the group, shadows swirling around her like a living cloak. Torric flanks her left, Aspen takes her right, as Finn trails behind, quiet but present. Malrik brings up the rear, eyes scanning the treeline.

Darian walks apart from the others, close enough to matter, far enough to give her space.

They're all watching her.

They're all following her.

Even if they don't realize it yet.

I turn back to the road ahead.

I won't lose you again.

The Keep waits.

Chapter 21
KAIA

Three days out from the village, and the exhaustion is starting to show.

Not just in me—in all of us.

Thinking back, the village disappears behind us like it was never there. Like those few days of rest were just a dream we all woke up from too soon. One second I can feel the wards humming at my back, steady and safe. The next, there's nothing but open road and the faint pull of corruption seeping back into the air.

It's subtle at first. A cold prickle at the base of my spine. The way the trees lean a little too close to the path. But by the second day, it's undeniable—the corruption is returning, creeping in at the edges like mold.

My shadows curl tighter around my ankles.

I glance back once, but there's nothing to see. Just the echo of something that felt, for a few days, almost like home.

Keep moving.

The group is quiet.

Too quiet.

Torric catches my eye and gives me a tight smile, his hand settling briefly on my shoulder as he passes. But his fingers linger a second too long, like he's memorizing that I'm real. That I'm still here.

The tension in his jaw wasn't there three days ago.

Aspen nods when I look at him, hovering closer than usual. Overprotective. Frost clings to the edges of his hair, faint and glittering in the weak sunlight. Like he's been burning through his magic without realizing it.

Finn won't look at me at all.

He's walking near the back of the group, shoulders hunched, hands shoved in his pockets. But his attention isn't on me—it's on the shadows. Small ones, drifting out of the trees, drawn toward us like moths to a flame.

He watches each one arrive.

Counts them.

His jaw tightens when another slips from the underbrush, and he glances at me for half a second before looking away again. He doesn't say anything. Just keeps walking.

Every time I look back, Darian is pretending to study the trees.

He's keeping his distance. Too much distance. Like he's afraid to breathe near me after that night in the garden, afraid that getting too close will shatter whatever fragile thing we built.

And Kieran—

Kieran is watching me like a hawk. Silent. Intense. His eyes track every movement I make, but he hasn't said a word since we left the village.

Bob bristles at my shoulder. Patricia's notebook flickers nervously. Even Mouse seems on edge, his tail twitching like he can feel my anxiety.

Knowing him, he probably can.

They're all carrying something.

And I don't know how to help any of them.

Malrik falls into step beside me.

I smile to myself, because he appears at my side like he was always meant to be there, quiet and steady and grounding.

I exhale.

I didn't realize how tight my chest was until he showed up.

"Where does Revna keep disappearing to?" Torric asks breaking the silence.

"The sanctuary." Kieran doesn't look up. "She reports back. Keeps me informed of what's happening there while we travel."

"That's... a long flight."

"She's done it for hundreds of years. I doubt she notices anymore."

Something about that — the quiet loyalty of it, centuries of the same pattern — settles warm in my chest.

We walk in silence for a while, our footsteps syncing without either of us trying. The jagged road stretches ahead, winding toward the mountains in the distance. Toward Sorrow's Keep.

Toward whatever's waiting for us there.

"We're running low on supplies," Malrik says quietly. "Another day, maybe two, and we'll need to forage or stop somewhere."

My stomach sinks. One more thing I hadn't been paying attention to.

"Tell me what's wrong," he adds, softer now.

"Nothing's wrong."

He gives me a look. Flat. Unimpressed.

"Try again."

I sigh.

"I don't know. Everyone's just... off. And I can feel it, but I don't know what to do about it."

Malrik doesn't respond immediately. He just walks beside me, steady and patient, waiting for me to keep going.

So I do.

"Finn's pulling away. Darian's nervous. Kieran feels…" I struggle for the right word. My hand flails in the air while I try to think. "Strange. Aspen's hovering like he's expecting an attack. Torric's trying too hard to stay calm. And you—"

I look at him.

"You're carrying something too. I can feel it."

Malrik is quiet for a long moment. Something tightens in his jaw—brief, barely there—before he smooths it away.

Then he says, "Finn's hurting. He'll come back to himself when he's ready."

I wait.

"Darian's trying so hard not to mess things up that he's going to accidentally combust."

Despite everything, I almost smile.

"Kieran is terrified of losing you," Malrik continues. "Aspen's on high alert because he loves you. Torric sees danger in every shadow now."

He looks at me, and his voice softens.

"And none of that is your fault."

Something in my chest loosens.

"You are not responsible for their storms, Kaia," he says. "Only for your own."

"And you?" I ask quietly. "What's your storm?"

Malrik's eyes hold mine for a beat too long.

"I'm just trying to give you the happiness you deserve."

I open my mouth. Close it. Open it again.

Nothing comes out.

Malrik doesn't seem to mind. His mouth tilts up, warmth in his eyes, and he just keeps walking beside me, steady as always.

We walk in silence for a few more minutes.

The road curves ahead, disappearing into a stretch of twisted trees. The corruption is stronger here. I can feel it pressing against my skin like cold fingers.

"You're sure he's okay?" I ask quietly. "Finn, I mean."

Malrik exhales slowly.

"No," he says. "But he will be. And when he's ready, he'll come to you."

"But what if he doesn't?"

Malrik glances at me, something unreadable in his silver eyes.

"He already has," he says. "You just didn't see it."

I don't know what that means. My stomach sinks anyway.

But before I can ask, Malrik's hand brushes my wrist, brief but grounding, and I let myself lean into it for just a second.

Finnick settles on Malrik's shoulder like he belongs there. Malrik doesn't even blink.

"Stop trying to carry all of them," he says quietly. "You'll break yourself before we even reach the Keep."

I don't know if I believe him.

But I nod anyway.

The mountain looms larger as the day wears on.

By the time the sun begins to set, we're all dragging. My legs ache. My ribs feel bruised from the inside out. Even my shadows seem sluggish, their movements slower than usual.

Sorrow's Keep.

I've never seen it before, but I know it's there. Can feel it in my bones, a pull that gets stronger with every step. Like something is waiting.

The corruption hums against my skin, and my shadows press closer.

Bob takes point, posture rigid. Mouse pads silently at my heel. Patricia's notebook has gone still, like even she doesn't want to record what's coming.

Behind me, the group spreads out along the road.

I take a breath and let myself relax knowing they're here with me. That we're in this together.

Whatever waits at Sorrow's Keep, it's already watching us.

I can feel it.

We round a bend in the road.

The path narrows. The trees press closer. The mountain looms ahead, dark and jagged against the sky.

My shadows stiffen.

All of them. At once.

Bob's edges go sharp. Mouse freezes mid-step. Patricia's notebook flares to life. Even Finnick, who's been lounging on Malrik's shoulder, goes rigid.

Behind me, the guys react instinctively. All of them suddenly on edge, feeling that something, isn't right.

And then I see him.

Standing in the middle of the road, like he's been waiting for us the entire time.

Callum.

He looks... wrong. Thinner than I remember. Paler. His eyes have a strange, hollow quality that makes my skin crawl.

But he's grinning.

"Hello, Kieran," he says.

My blood turns to ice.

Chapter 22
KAIA

Nobody moves.

For a long, terrible second, nobody even breathes.

Callum stands in the middle of the road like he belongs there, like he's been waiting for us since we left the village. Maybe longer. His grin stretches too wide, his eyes too hollow, his body twitching with an energy that doesn't look human anymore.

"Hello, Kieran," he says, savoring the words. "Miss me?"

Kieran goes rigid beside me. I can feel it through the bond — something cracking, splintering, threatening to shatter completely.

Bob's edges go razor-sharp at my shoulder.

"Say the word." Torric's voice is low, dangerous. "He doesn't get near her again."

But Callum isn't looking at me. He's looking at Kieran like he's the only person in the world.

"Did you miss me?" Callum tilts his head, that wrong grin stretching wider. "Did you look for me? Did you even *care*?"

"Callum." Kieran's voice breaks on the name.

Callum giggles — high, sharp, wrong.

"The Valkyrie opens the Gate," he whispers, almost to himself. "The God devours... devours..." He trails off, blinking rapidly, then refocuses on Kieran with unsettling intensity. "You LEFT me there."

The group shifts uneasily.

I catch Torric taking a step forward — not attacking, just positioning himself between me and Callum. His jaw is tight, heat radiating off him in waves he's barely controlling.

Finn hasn't moved. His face is blank, closed off, but I can see his hands shaking at his sides.

Malrik is quiet. Watching. Trying to assess damage none of us can see.

And Darian—

Darian takes a step back.

I notice because everyone else stepped forward — toward me.

His corruption flickers around his fingers, dark and uneasy, and his eyes are locked on Callum with an intensity that makes my stomach twist.

"There's something else inside him," Darian says. His voice is barely above a whisper. "Something wrong."

Callum's head snaps toward Darian.

He stops twitching. Stops grinning. Goes completely, horribly still.

For one long moment, he just stares. His hollow eyes move from Darian to me. Back to Darian. Back to me.

Then he starts laughing.

High and sharp and utterly unhinged, the sound bouncing off the twisted trees around us. Linda drifts toward Kieran, hovering close like she's trying to offer comfort he can't accept.

"Oh," Callum gasps between laughs, tears streaming down his face. "Oh, that's *precious*. You found him. You actually found him." He doubles over, wheezing. "The last one. The broken one. Does he know what he is yet? Does *she*?"

Darian flinches like he's been struck.

"Shadows bite, shadows bite," Callum sing-songs, wiping his eyes. "The broken one shines brightest before he burns..."

"Callum." Kieran takes a step forward — just one — like he can't help himself.

I grab his wrist.

He freezes. Turns to look at me with eyes that are wet, furious, terrified.

I don't let go.

Callum straightens slowly, his laughter dying into something worse — a soft, broken humming.

"Kieran, Kieran, Kieran," he murmurs. "Always so loyal. Always so *devoted*." His voice cracks. Breaks. Reforms into something sharper. "You left me there. You LEFT me. And *he* found me instead." His grin stretches wrong. "The one behind the Gate. The hunger. He *saved* me."

Finnick is doing jagged somersaults near my shoulder, mirroring the chaos radiating off Callum.

"Who?" Kieran's voice is barely recognizable. "Callum, who found you?"

Callum's grin returns, wrong and stretched.

"The God is coming," he whispers. "The Gate is waking. And you — all of you — you have no idea what's waiting." He laughs again, softer this time. "No idea what he's going to do when it opens."

"Who?" I demand. "Alekir?"

Callum's eyes slide to me, and something shifts in his expression. Something almost like recognition.

"Your unnatural shadows," he breathes. "Your hungry little monsters. Do you think you can stop any of this?"

His head twitches. His eyes unfocus.

"The Valkyrie feeds the Gate... the Gate feeds the God... the God devours the broken one..." He trails off, muttering to himself, then suddenly refocuses with frightening clarity. "He sees everything. He knows everything. He's been inside my head for so long I can't remember what it felt like before."

His voice drops to a whisper.

"It's *hungry*, little Valkyrie. And you're exactly what it wants."

"Enough." Torric's voice cuts through the tension like a blade. "I'm done listening to this."

He steps forward, flames flickering at his fingertips, and I see it — the moment he's about to cross the line.

"NO." Kieran's voice cracks like a whip. He tears forward, putting himself between Callum and Torric. "You don't touch him."

Torric stops. His flames don't die, but they don't advance either.

"Kieran—" Aspen's voice is sharp with worry. "He's compromised. We don't know what he'll do."

"I don't care."

"He betrayed you," Finn says quietly, looking at Kieran. "And her. And all of us."

"I know what he did." Kieran's hands are shaking. "I know. But he's not — he's not himself. Can't you see that?"

The group falls silent.

Callum giggles softly in the background, swaying on his feet. "The broken ones always see clearest... the broken ones always burn first..."

Patricia's notebook has gone dark, like even she can't bear to record this.

Darian speaks quietly. "Whatever Alekir did to him... it's still there. I can feel it. The feeling is..." He swallows. "Familiar. Not him — just the way it moves."

Callum's head snaps toward Darian again. "The broken one," he whispers. "The broken one shines brightest before he burns."

Kieran flinches at that. But he doesn't move.

Slowly — so slowly — he turns back to Callum and kneels.

"Callum." His voice breaks completely. "What did they do to you?"

Callum stops swaying. His hollow eyes focus on Kieran's face with something that might have been recognition, once.

"Everything," he whispers. "They did everything."

His head tips back, eyes rolling toward the sky.

"And it was beautiful."

I move without thinking.

I cross to Kieran and put my hand on his back. I can feel him trembling under my palm — small, constant tremors he's trying desperately to hide.

He leans into my touch. Barely. But real.

The group is watching us. Waiting.

Torric's flames have died, but his expression is murderous. Aspen looks torn between wanting to comfort and wanting to strategize. Finn has turned away entirely, jaw tight, hands still shaking.

Malrik catches my eye. Nods once. *Your call.*

But it's not my call.

I stand and face them.

"We're not killing him."

"Kaia—" Torric starts.

"We're not killing him," I repeat, and my voice is steady even though my heart is pounding. "But this isn't my decision to make."

I turn and look at Kieran.

He's still kneeling, one hand hovering near Callum's shoulder like he's afraid to touch him. Like touching him might confirm that this broken, hollow thing is really all that's left of his friend.

"He's yours," I say softly. "Whatever you decide, we follow."

The silence stretches.

Finn shifts uncomfortably. Torric's jaw works like he's biting back words. Aspen's frost crackles once, then goes still.

But nobody argues.

Because they understand. They were all there when Darian showed up. When everyone wanted to kill him, and I said no. When I claimed him as mine.

Callum is Kieran's.

And none of us have the right to take that choice away from him.

Bob's edges soften. Mouse nudges Kieran's knee, like even they understand.

Kieran's breath shudders.

He looks at Callum — really looks at him. At the hollowed cheeks, the twitching hands, the madness swimming in his eyes. At the ruin of the man he used to know.

"The Gate opens," Callum murmurs, half-conscious now. "The God rises... the Valkyrie bleeds... the broken one burns..."

Kieran closes his eyes.

When he opens them again, something has settled. Not healed — nothing could heal this — but decided.

"We take him with us," Kieran says.

His voice is barely a whisper, but it carries.

Torric swears under his breath. Aspen's expression tightens with frustration. Finn doesn't turn around.

But Malrik just nods.

"Then we need to move," Malrik says. "Whatever broke him, whatever's waiting at the Keep — we can't stay here."

Callum collapses.

One second he's murmuring prophecies to no one, the next his eyes roll back and he crumples like a puppet with its strings cut.

Malrik catches him before he hits the ground, lowering him carefully to the dirt.

"Exhaustion," he says, checking Callum's pulse. "Or something else. Either way, he's out."

He scans Callum's arms, his neck. "No fresh wounds. Just old scars. Whatever broke him — it wasn't physical."

Bob takes point, posture rigid. Mouse pads in a slow circle around us now, no longer frozen — alert, tracking every sound. The small shadows Finn kept counting earlier edge closer, restless with whatever's wrong here.

Kieran hasn't moved.

He's still kneeling where Callum collapsed, staring at the space where his friend used to be. His hands are pressed flat against his thighs like he's afraid of what they'll do if he lets them move.

I crouch beside him.

"Hey."

He doesn't look at me.

"Kieran. Hey."

His eyes finally meet mine. They're red-rimmed. Devastated. Older than I've ever seen them.

"Thank you," he whispers.

"Don't thank me yet." I put my hand on his arm, feeling the tremor still running through him. "We're not out of this."

"I know." His voice cracks. "But you gave me a choice. You didn't take it from me."

"Of course," I say softly. "Because choice matters, Kieran."

Something shifts in his expression. Realizing just what he did taking my choice from me.

He nods.

I squeeze his arm, then stand.

Torric and Malrik lift Callum between them. He's lighter than he should be — I can see it in how easily they carry him, how his bones jut beneath his clothes.

Whatever Alekir did to him, it hollowed him out. Left nothing but madness and what sounds like twisted prophecy.

The mountain looms ahead. Sorrow's Keep. Closer now than it's ever been.

My shadows press close around me. Bob at point. Mouse at my heel. Patricia's notebook flickering back to life, already documenting. Finnick settling on my shoulder, finally still.

The group falls into formation around me. Different now. Heavier.

Finn still won't look at me. Darian is keeping his distance from Callum's unconscious body. Aspen hovers close to my left, frost at his fingertips. Torric's heat near enough I feel it.

And Kieran walks beside Malrik, his eyes fixed on Callum's slack face.

"Let's move," I say.

We start walking toward the Keep.

Whatever's waiting for us there, we're running out of time.

And I can't shake the feeling that something is watching us.

Something hungry.

Something that already knows we're coming.

The trees feel too quiet. Like they're holding their breath.

Chapter 23
KAIA

We walk in silence.

The forest presses in around us, twisted trees reaching overhead like claws. The corruption hums against my skin, stronger now, but I barely notice it anymore. It's just... there. Part of the landscape. Part of Absentia.

Ahead, Torric and Malrik carry Callum between them. He's still unconscious, his head lolling with every step, and I can see the tension in Torric's shoulders every time Callum's body shifts. He keeps flicking glances back at me — protective, pissed and worried all at the same time.

Kieran walks beside them, his eyes fixed on Callum's slack face like he's afraid to look away. Like looking away might mean losing him again.

Bob is on high alert at my shoulder. The small shadows that have been following us since the village drift through the trees, keeping pace. More of them now than before. I don't know where they're coming from.

I hang back from the formation.

I need space. The guys let me have it.

Darian is walking too far from the group.

I notice because I've been watching him since we started moving again. His shadow magic flickers around his fingers — dark, uneasy — like something inside him is unsettled and he can't make it stop.

He sees me looking and straightens. Tries to smooth his expression into something neutral.

He's not fooling anyone.

I slow my pace until I'm walking beside him. He tenses but doesn't move away.

"Are you okay?"

He laughs — short, hollow. "Fine."

"Darian."

He's quiet for a long moment. The magic flickers again, and he stares at his hands like they belong to someone else.

"I've never seen it," he says finally. His voice is rough. "Seen someone be what I could've been. I didn't know what it looked like from the outside."

My chest tightens.

"I never thought I'd see what it looks like. What Thorne did, forcing magic, wrong magic, on someone else." He swallows hard. "Why didn't that happen to me?"

The question hangs in the air between us.

I don't have an answer. I wish I did.

"I don't know, Darian." I keep my voice soft. Honest. "But I'm glad it didn't."

He doesn't cry. But something in his expression cracks — just a little — and he nods without looking at me.

We walk in silence after that. But it's not the heavy, suffocating silence from before.

It's just... quiet.

The forest thickens as we move deeper into the trees.

The shadows drift closer, curious rather than crowding. The small ones that have been following us since the village edge nearer, tentative and watchful.

I notice Finn watching them.

He's walking a few paces behind the main group, hands stuffed in his pockets, shoulders hunched. He looks tired. Worn. Like the weight of everything is pressing down on him and he doesn't know how to carry it anymore.

There's something hollow in his expression, something frayed, and I hate that I don't know how to reach him.

But his eyes are tracking the shadows with something like fascination. Like his brain is clinging to the one thing he can understand right now.

One of the new shadows hovers near his boot, flickering uncertainly.

Finn crouches a little, squinting at it.

"...You're definitely an Ed."

I freeze mid-step. "What?"

He gestures at the shadow like it's obvious. "That one? Ed. Very clear Ed energy."

The shadow flicks its shape — a shy, uncertain movement that almost looks like a shrug.

Finn taps his boot lightly near it. "Come on, Ed. Don't be shy."

The shadow warbles — a soft, pleased little sound — and drifts closer.

Finn surveys the others drifting around me, his expression deadly serious.

"Actually... all of you. Eds. Every last one of you."

"You are *not* naming my shadows Ed."

"Why not?" He looks genuinely confused. "They look like Eds."

"None of them look like Ed!"

"Have you ever met an Ed?"

"No!"

Finn spreads his hands. "Then you can't prove me wrong."

The shadow at his foot warbles again.

Finn looks down at it, then back at me.

"See? Ed approves."

I stare at him. At the shadow. At the absolute absurdity of this moment.

"There are *multiple* Eds now, actually. I've been counting."

Survival Tip #23: Never let Finn name anything. Ever again.

I press my hand over my mouth, shoulders shaking.

And then I laugh.

Really laugh — for the first time since before the village. It bubbles up from somewhere deep and broken, cracking through the heaviness in my chest like sunlight through storm clouds.

Finn's composure cracks too — his mouth betrays him first, then his eyes. It's the closest he's come to smiling since the village.

"You're ridiculous," I manage between laughs.

"Ed doesn't think so."

"There is no Ed!"

"There are multiple Eds. I just told you. Keep up."

Darian glances back at the sound — startled, relieved, and something like grateful.

The shadows drift around us, and I swear some of them are preening.

Bob looks deeply offended.

Patricia's notebook flickers, definitely amused, probably documenting this travesty for the permanent record.

Finnick does a delighted flip, clearly thrilled by the chaos.

After a while, the laughter fades.

Finn's smile softens, then dims. He glances at me — just for a second — with something uncertain in his eyes. Like he's not sure he deserves this moment after everything that happened.

I see it. I don't push.

But that moment of laughter cracked something open in both of us. Something that needed air.

We keep walking.

The shadows drift around us like fireflies.

I take a breath that isn't all pain for the first time in hours.

The group ahead keeps moving toward Sorrow's Keep. Torric's heat. Aspen's frost. Malrik's steady presence. Kieran's grief. Darian's quiet struggle.

And Finn, walking beside me now, not quite smiling but not quite drowning either.

Up ahead, Kieran doesn't turn, but his shoulders ease the smallest amount at the sound of my laugh.

Maybe it won't last. Maybe nothing does.

But right now, Finn is here. The shadows are harmless. And the world isn't falling apart.

Not yet. But the trees feel too quiet. Like they're waiting.

Chapter 24
ASPEN

Something is wrong.

No — not wrong. Different.

I've been walking near the back of the group, tracking Kaia's movements, tracking Kieran's tension, tracking the weight Torric and Malrik are carrying between them. Callum's unconscious body sways with every step, and I keep waiting for him to wake up and start screaming prophecies again.

But that's not what's making my skin prickle.

My ice spikes.

Not a flare of danger. Not fear. Not the oily wrongness of corruption pressing against my senses.

A pull.

A tug beneath my sternum — quiet but undeniable — like something in the land is whispering *here*.

I slow without meaning to.

The ground underfoot has changed. I didn't notice it happening, but now I can't unsee it. The dark, corrupted soil is giving way to something else. A faint blue glimmer beneath the dead leaves. Frost-mist rising in delicate curls. Tiny flecks of pale light drifting through the air like snow motes, like stars fallen to earth.

And flowers.

Blue-luminescent flowers pushing through the rot, their petals soft and glowing, impossibly alive in a land that's been dying for centuries.

I stop walking entirely.

"Aspen?"

Malrik's voice cuts through the haze. I blink, realizing the group has continued on without me. They've stopped a few paces ahead, all of them turning to look at me with varying degrees of confusion.

"You're going the wrong way," Malrik says.

I shake my head slowly, like waking from a trance. "No. We have to go this way."

Kieran tenses immediately. "Aspen, we can't. We have to get Callum somewhere safe—"

"It's not far." The words come out sharper than I intend. I rub my temple, frustrated by the pull I can't explain. "I just... I need to see."

Kieran opens his mouth to argue.

"Please." I don't beg. I never beg. But this is important. I can feel it in my bones, in my blood, in the frost crackling at my fingertips. "Trust me."

Kaia is watching me with that careful, empathetic attention that always makes me feel too exposed. Like she can see past my calm exterior to the chaos underneath.

"We follow him," she says quietly.

No one argues.

When I ask for things, they listen. Because I don't ask lightly.

The corruption thins as we walk.

It's subtle at first — the air less heavy, the wrongness less present. But then the change accelerates.

The blue flowers multiply, opening like they're waking up. Wisps of frost drift upward, glittering in the strange half-light. The ground beneath our feet begins to gleam, dark earth shot through with veins of pale luminescence.

Pink motes of light drift past us like lazy fireflies. The air grows cooler but not biting — gentle winter, soft as a held breath.

Linda drifts closer to Kaia, curious. Carl tumbles past my ankles, nearly tripping me, clearly fascinated by the glowing flowers.

And then we see it.

"What the hell," Finn breathes.

The tree.

It rises from the earth like something from a dream — massive, ancient, withered but beautiful. The trunk is as wide as four people standing arm-to-arm, bark gnarled and pale, shot through with frost that traces delicate fractals like veins of light.

It should be dead. Everything in Absentia is dead or dying.

But this tree... this tree is something else entirely.

No one speaks.

Kaia moves first, stepping closer with wonder written across her face. "How did we not see this?"

"Where the hell did this come from?" Finn echoes his earlier comment, but softer now. Almost reverent.

Torric shifts Callum's weight, staring up at the branches. "Is this... normal Absentia shit, or—?"

Malrik steps forward, his eyes wide, his voice dropping to something low and awed.

"It can't be..."

Kieran inhales sharply beside him. "Are you thinking what I'm thinking?"

Malrik nods once.

"Japti."

The word settles over us like snowfall.

Finn raises a hand. "Okay, so... anyone want to translate the big dramatic word?"

Malrik doesn't look away from the tree. "It's ancient. I didn't think any still existed."

Kaia moves toward the trunk like she's being drawn too.

Her hand reaches out, fingers brushing the bark, tracing the pale frost, the glowing veins beneath. The tree reacts subtly — frost glimmers brighter where she touches, spreading outward in delicate spirals.

The small shadows cluster around her ankles, calm and curious. Walter drifts closer, pulsing faintly with that strange starlight he carries.

A soft hum rises from somewhere deep within the wood. Like distant wind through hollow branches. Like the tree is breathing.

"It's a safe place, isn't it?" Kaia whispers.

Malrik's eyes soften. "Yes. Japti means safety."

The knowing hits me like a wave. I don't know why, but it's a need I can't ignore.

This is why I felt it. This is what was calling me.

"We need to go inside."

Kaia blinks, turning to look at me. "...Inside?"

I rub my forehead. The certainty is giving me a headache — pressing against my skull like something trying to get out. "I don't know how I know. I just do."

I've never felt anything like this before. Not with my ice, not with my connection to Absentia, not with anything. It's like something inside me is waking up. Reaching toward the tree like it recognizes home.

Kaia doesn't question me. She just nods and turns back to the trunk.

She circles it slowly, her hand trailing along the bark. The shadows follow her — Linda hovering at her shoulder, Carl tumbling at her feet.

Then Bob appears.

He materializes at the base of the trunk, posture rigid, edges sharp with purpose. He's not guarding. He's... directing.

He nudges Kaia's hand. Insistent. Specific.

She follows his guidance, her palm sliding across the bark until it finds something beneath the frost.

A rune.

A spiral shape carved deep into the wood, frosted over but faintly glowing. Her palm fits perfectly against it, like it was made for her.

She looks at me.

I nod.

She presses.

The entire trunk shifts.

A seam appears in the bark — hairline at first, then widening. Frost cracks and falls away like shed skin. The wood splits open in a soft gasp of cold air, ancient and clean.

A doorway forms.

Wide. Dark. Descending.

Spiral stairs wind down into the earth, carved from the same pale wood as the tree itself. Blue light flickers along the walls, pulsing gently, alive.

A breath of crisp, winter-clean air rises from within. It smells like snow and stone and something older than memory.

I exhale shakily.

"There," I whisper. "That's why I felt it."

Kaia meets my eyes. There's no doubt in her expression. No hesitation.

"Then let's go."

Chapter 25
FINN

The stairs spiral down forever.

Or at least it feels that way — step after step carved from pale wood, descending into the earth beneath the impossible tree. Lanterns flare to life as we pass, soft pink light blooming like flowers waking up, and I can't shake the feeling that the walls are watching us.

Definitely creepy.

I trail my fingers along the wood as we descend. It hums faintly beneath my touch, warm despite the frost that edges everything, and my chaos magic stirs in response. Not the usual "you're about to explode something" feeling. Weirder. Like my magic is wagging its tail.

I pull my hand back.

Nope. Don't like that.

Ahead of me, Aspen leads like he's being pulled by an invisible thread. He hasn't hesitated once since we entered the tree — just keeps moving forward with that quiet certainty that makes the rest of us follow without question.

Must be nice, having instincts that don't mostly get you in trouble.

Kaia walks near him, her shadows gliding alongside her like purposeful pets. Bob is on high alert, but even he seems... calmer here. Less murder-y. Like the tree convinced him we're not all about to die.

Torric and Malrik carry Callum between them, his unconscious body slack and too light. Kieran hovers close, jaw tight, eyes never leaving Callum's face.

The rest of us just follow. Story of my life, really.

The stairs end.

We step into a wide hallway, the walls curving gently ahead so I can't see where it leads. The air is different here — cooler, cleaner, like winter without the bite.

And the walls are covered in carvings.

Berserker warriors etched in glowing frost-lines, caught mid-battle, mid-ritual, mid-transformation. The detail is insane. I can see individual muscles, individual expressions, individual moments of "I'm about to ruin someone's day."

The tree's already picking favorites, apparently.

Aspen stops dead.

His breath catches — a small, sharp sound that makes everyone freeze. He's staring at the carvings like they just spoke his name.

Torric almost walks into him. He shifts Callum's weight, mouth opening to say something — and then he sees the walls.

His face goes slack. Eyes wide. Jaw loose.

I've never seen Torric look like that. Like the ground just disappeared under his feet and he's still falling.

"I got him," I say, moving forward before I can think about it. I duck under Callum's arm, taking Torric's place. Malrik adjusts without a word, and suddenly I'm half-carrying an unconscious traitor through a magic tree.

Not how I saw today going, but fine.

Torric doesn't even notice. He's already at the wall, one hand reaching out like he can't stop himself.

The carvings glow brighter where his fingers touch the wood. Gold threads through the frost-lines — fire meeting ice.

Aspen moves to stand beside him. They don't speak. They don't have to.

I watch them trace the carvings with their eyes, with their hands. Watch Torric's shoulders shake once before he locks them down. Watch Aspen press his palm flat against a carving of two warriors standing back to back — twins, I realize. Twins like them.

And then Aspen goes still.

"Torric," he breathes. "Look."

He's pointing at a larger carving near the end of the hall. Berserkers in formation — dozens of them — flanking a central figure. A woman with wings spread wide, something that looks suspiciously like shadows curling at her feet. A Valkyrie.

The berserkers aren't just warriors. They're protectors. Shields. Standing between the Valkyrie and whatever's coming for her.

"We were her guard," Torric says roughly. His voice cracks on the words. "That's what we were. That's what berserkers were for."

"Our father never told us," Aspen adds, quieter. "He branded us with runes we didn't understand. Trained us like weapons. And he never—" He stops. Swallows. "He knew. He had to have known what we were."

Torric's hand finds his brother's shoulder. Grips hard.

"Maybe he was afraid," Aspen says quietly. "Of what we'd become if we knew the truth."

"Then he was a coward."

Aspen doesn't argue. He just stands there, steady and solid, while Torric breathes through whatever's breaking inside him.

Kaia moves closer. She doesn't touch them — doesn't intrude — but she's there. Present. Her shadows curl around the edges of the hallway like they're standing guard.

"This is your history," she says softly. "Not his. Whatever he did with it, whatever he kept from you — this belongs to you now."

Torric's jaw works. He doesn't look at her, but I see his shoulders drop. Just a little. Just enough.

"No," he says roughly. "It belongs to *us*."

She smiles softly, but it doesn't meet her eyes, like she doesn't know what to do with that idea.

"Of course you two get the murder-hallway," I mutter, because someone has to break the tension before we all start crying.

Aspen's mouth twitches. Almost a smile.

Torric snorts. "Shut up, Finn."

Good enough.

We keep moving.

The hallway curves once more, and then the world opens up.

"Holy shit," I breathe.

The cavern is massive — bigger than anything I expected, bigger than should be possible beneath a single tree. The ceiling arches overhead like the inside of a cathedral, studded with glowing stones that pulse like heartbeats. Bioluminescent plants climb the walls in soft blues and pinks and silvers, their leaves unfurling toward some invisible light source.

A bathing spring dominates the center of the space, crystal-clear water swirling with pink and white motes. A smaller pool feeds into it — drinking water, maybe. Fresh and clean and impossible.

Fruit-bearing trees cluster near the edges, their branches heavy with things I've never seen before. Probably shouldn't eat those until someone confirms they won't kill us. My stomach growls.

Please don't kill us.

Soft wind stirs from nowhere, carrying the scent of winter and growing things.

And everywhere — everywhere — motes drift like fallen stars.

Everyone goes silent. Even me. That's how you know it's serious.

Five tunnels radiate outward from the cavern walls. Dark. Silent. Waiting.

Behind us, the Berserker hallway glows softly — the only one lit.

Kaia is wide-eyed, her hand pressed to her chest like she's trying to keep her heart inside her body. Carl tumbles past her ankles, fascinated by the glowing plants, while Linda drifts toward the spring like she's checking if it's safe.

"Over here," Malrik says, nodding toward the warm side of the spring.

We lay Callum down gently. He doesn't stir — still unconscious, still broken, still a problem we don't know how to solve. Kieran kneels beside him immediately, one hand hovering over Callum's chest.

The rest of us gather near the center, catching our breath. Shadows drift to the perimeter — Bob taking point, Mouse pacing a slow patrol. The Eds cluster near Kaia like nervous puppies.

For a moment, nobody speaks. We just... exist. In this impossible place that shouldn't be real.

"What is this?" Kaia finally asks. Her voice echoes slightly in the vast space. "How can any of this exist?"

"It shouldn't," Malrik says quietly. "But it's beautiful. I thought they were myth. Something my mother made up to make me feel better when my father traveled."

"Clearly not," Torric mutters.

We all seem to focus on the dark tunnels. They're spaced evenly around the cavern walls. Waiting for something. Waiting for someone.

"Should we...?" Kaia gestures vaguely.

"Carefully," Kieran says, rising from Callum's side. His voice is rough. "We don't know what else might be—"

He stops mid-sentence.

His head turns toward one of the dark tunnels. Slowly. Like something is pulling him.

Kieran moves before any of us can react.

He drifts toward the tunnel on the far side of the cavern, his steps slow and measured, like he's walking through a dream. Like he can't stop even if he wanted to.

"Kieran?" Kaia calls.

He doesn't answer.

The moment he crosses the threshold, gold light floods the passage.

Dragons.

Etched into every surface, circling carved mountains, breathing fire that streaks through the wood like living flame. The craftsmanship is breath-taking — individual scales showing, wings spread wide, eyes that seem to track you as you move.

Kieran stops in the center of the hall. His whole body goes rigid.

Kaia is already moving. She crosses the cavern quickly, shadows trailing behind her, and stops at the entrance to his hall. She doesn't step inside — doesn't intrude on whatever this is — but she's close enough that he knows she's there. We all follow, hanging back.

"Kieran," she says softly. "What do you see?"

His voice comes out broken. "The dragon riders. My mother used to tell me stories about them. I thought…" He presses his palm flat against the wall. The dragons glow brighter under his touch. "I thought she was making them up. Fairy tales to help me sleep."

He traces one of the carvings — a massive dragon in flight, wings spread wide, scales etched in golden light. And on its back…

A figure with wings of her own. A Valkyrie.

Kieran goes very still.

"They were real," Kaia breathes, stepping closer. She sees it too.

"They were real." His voice is barely a whisper. "And they… we…" He can't finish. His hand trembles against the wall.

Kaia stares at the carving. At the Valkyrie astride the dragon. At the ancient partnership etched into the wood.

Her shadows curl around her ankles, restless.

Neither of them says what we're all thinking. But the implication hangs in the air like smoke.

Kieran isn't meant to carry a rider.

He's meant to carry *her*.

His fist clenches at his side. His jaw works like he's fighting something.

Kaia reaches out and touches his arm. Just that. Just a touch. But I see his shoulders drop. See some of the tension bleed out of him.

"You don't have to figure it out right now," she says. "We're here. Whatever this means, you're not carrying it alone."

Kieran doesn't respond. But he doesn't pull away either.

They stand there for a long moment, gold light washing over them, while the rest of us watch from the cavern. Aspen and Torric exchange a look — they understand this. The weight of discovering something about yourself you never knew. The way it cracks you open.

Eventually, Kieran nods. Once. Small.

Kaia squeezes his arm and steps back, giving him space to breathe.

"Okay," I say, because someone has to move us forward. "So that's... dragons. Cool. Terrifying. Very on-brand for Kieran."

Torric snorts. Aspen almost smiles.

Malrik is already moving.

He walks toward one of the remaining dark tunnels — not drifting like Kieran, not pulled. Walking with purpose. Like he knows what he'll find and he's dreading it.

"Malrik?" I call.

He doesn't stop.

I follow. I don't know why. Maybe because everyone else is still processing Kieran's moment. Maybe because Malrik shouldn't have to face whatever this is alone. Maybe because I'm nosy.

Probably that last one.

The tunnel blazes to life the moment Malrik approaches. Deep blue light pulses through the passage. Royal sigils. Swords held upright. A coronation scene carved in excruciating detail — a crown being placed on a bowed head, subjects kneeling, a kingdom being born.

And standing beside the throne, hand resting on the shoulder of the newly crowned king — a Valkyrie. Wings folded. Eyes watchful. Blessing the line.

Malrik stops at the entrance. His expression goes carefully blank.

"The royal line," he says quietly. His voice is flat. Controlled. The voice he uses when he's feeling too much and refuses to show it.

I step up beside him. "Heavy."

"You have no idea."

He traces one of the sigils with his finger. The carving glows brighter, humming softly.

"These are the founding sigils," he says. "The ones in the palace are copies. Poor ones. This..." He shakes his head. "This predates everything. The monarchy. Absentia as we know it. All of it."

His eyes linger on the Valkyrie beside the throne.

"The royal line didn't just rule," he murmurs. "They ruled because *she* chose them. The Valkyrie legitimized the crown."

I don't know what to say to that. So I just stand there. Present. The way Kaia was there for Kieran.

Malrik glances at me. Something flickers in his expression — surprise, maybe. Gratitude.

"Thank you," he says quietly.

"For what?"

"For not making a joke."

"Give me a minute. I'm working on one."

His mouth twitches. Almost a smile.

I kiss him before I can talk myself out of it.

It's brief — barely more than a brush, my hand catching his jaw for half a second before I pull back. Impulsive. Stupid. Completely worth it.

Malrik blinks. Once. Twice. His expression doesn't change, but something in his eyes does.

"That wasn't a joke," he says quietly.

"No," I manage. "It wasn't."

We stand there for a beat too long, the Royal Hall glowing blue around us, and I have no idea what my face is doing but it's probably embarrassing.

And then I notice Darian.

He's standing at the edge of the cavern, but he's not where I left him. He's closer now. Closer to the Royal Hall. Like something dragged him forward against his will.

His magic twitches at his fingertips — dark, uneasy. His whole body is tense, vibrating with something that looks a lot like fear.

He takes a step toward the hall. Stops. Takes another half-step. Stops again.

His eyes are fixed on the sigils. On the coronation scene. On the Valkyrie blessing the king.

On whatever truth is carved into those walls.

And then he turns away. Deliberately. Forcefully. Like it takes everything he has.

He retreats to the far side of the cavern, arms wrapped around himself, shoulders hunched.

I don't understand it. But I clock it.

File that away for later. Probably important.

Kaia drifts toward one of the remaining dark tunnels.

She doesn't seem to realize she's doing it. Her shadows are guiding her — swirling around her ankles, nudging her forward, pulling her toward the passage like they know something she doesn't.

Bob takes point, posture rigid. Walter floats alongside her, pulsing with that strange starlight.

Are there more Eds than before?

The moment she crosses the threshold, silver light explodes through the passage.

Winged figures. Valkyries carved in ice-lines, fierce and beautiful and ancient.

The carvings tell a story.

On the left wall — their rise. Valkyries in their glory, wings spread wide, shadows swirling at their feet. Leading armies. Blessing kings. Riding dragons. Standing at the center of everything, the axis around which the world turned.

On the right wall — their fall. A figure standing over them. Their homes crumbling. Wings broken. Shadows scattered. One by one, the Valkyries disappearing, until only emptiness remains.

And at the far end, where both walls meet—

A single figure. Standing alone. Wings folded. Shadows gathering at her feet.

The last one.

A massive statue dominates the center of the hall — a woman with her hand outstretched, wings spread wide, eyes soft but powerful. Waiting.

Kaia stops. Her breath catches.

"Oh," she whispers. Just that. Just *oh*.

The rest of us gather at the entrance, drawn by the light, by the gravity of the moment. Even Darian edges closer, though he keeps his distance.

Kaia walks toward the statue like she's in a trance. The shadows follow, clustering at her feet, climbing the walls, filling the hall with living darkness that somehow doesn't feel dark at all.

She stops in front of the statue and looks up at its face.

"She looks like you," I say before I can stop myself.

Kaia doesn't answer. She just reaches up and touches the statue's outstretched hand.

The entire cavern responds.

Every tunnel brightens for a heartbeat — all of them, all at once.

This cannot be good. Right?

Like Japti itself is acknowledging something. Acknowledging her.

The shadows curl around Kaia's feet more content than I've ever seen them.

"It can't be." Kaia whispers.

Malrik's voice is soft. Reverent. "Kaia, you don't have to be anything but who you are. This doesn't change anything."

We stand there in silence, watching the light pulse and fade, watching the shadows settle, watching Kaia at the center of something none of us fully understand.

Aspen moves first. He steps into the Valkyrie hall and stands beside Kaia. Doesn't say anything. Just... present.

Torric follows. Then Kieran. Then Malrik.

They form a loose circle around her. Protective. Supportive. A family that chose each other.

Even Darian edges closer, though he stays at the threshold. Watching. Wanting. Afraid.

And me?

I'm still standing in the cavern. Looking at the one tunnel that's still dark.

The symbols flare.

What the... Did anyone else see that?

I blink, but they're still there. Flaring violently — blazing to life like they've been waiting centuries for me to show up and finally something interesting is happening. Pink and white and crackling, pulsing wild and untamed. A low hum builds in the air, vibrating through the wood beneath my feet.

Everyone turns.

"What the—" Torric starts.

I stumble back a step. "Okay... nope. Nope. That feels illegal."

Kaia exhales softly — not quite a laugh, but close. She's already moving toward me, shadows trailing behind her.

One of the Eds drifts closer to the tunnel, curious, then immediately retreats like it got zapped. Fair enough, little guy.

The violent flare settles into something steady, rhythmic, matching my heartbeat exactly. Which is creepy as hell, by the way.

But I can't look away.

The group circles me instinctively. Kaia reaches me first, standing close enough that I can feel the warmth of her. Aspen and Torric flank her. Malrik hangs back, observing. Kieran watches with something like understanding in his eyes.

Darian stays at the edge. Watching from a distance.

"Finn?" Kaia says softly.

I don't answer. I'm already moving.

The air crackles as I step into the tunnel. My magic surges in response, rising to meet whatever the hell is calling to it.

The carvings are different from the others.

Where Malrik's hall is ordered and regal, mine is... chaos. Literally. Swirling patterns that never repeat, symbols that seem to shift when I blink, energy captured in wood that feels like it's about to burst free at any moment.

And at the center of it all — a Valkyrie.

She stands in the eye of the storm, chaos swirling around her but never touching her. Not controlling it. Not fighting it. *Wielding* it. Like chaos was always meant to be hers.

It should be weird.

It's not.

For the first time in my life, my magic doesn't feel like a glitch in the system. It feels like a key.

I reach out before I can talk myself out of it, and the wall reaches back. The wood is warm under my fingers, thrumming with power that echoes the chaos in my blood. The carvings pulse brighter, welcoming, and something in my chest does something uncomfortable.

Because the thing I've never talked about? I've never belonged anywhere.

Not really. Not completely. I've always been too much — too loud, too chaotic, too likely to accidentally set something on fire or say the wrong thing or make a joke when everyone else is being serious. Even with Kaia, even with the others, there's always been a part of me that wondered if I was really wanted or just... tolerated. The comic relief. The one they keep around because someone has to lighten the mood.

But this place...

This place was waiting for me. Specifically me. Chaos and all.

"Finn?"

I blink, and Kaia is there. Right beside me, inside my hall, her shadows curling around both of us.

She doesn't ask if I'm okay. She just stands near me, close enough that I can feel the warmth of her, and lets me have this moment. It's annoying. And also the reason I'm probably in love with her, but we're not thinking about that right now.

"You feel it too," I say quietly. "Don't you?"

She nods.

Behind her, the others have gathered at the entrance to my hall. Aspen and Torric, shoulder to shoulder. Kieran, raw but steady. Malrik, watching with that quiet intensity.

They're all here. For me.

Something cracks in my chest. Something I've been holding together for a very long time.

Kaia turns to face me fully. Her violet eyes are soft, steady, certain.

"I see you, Finn," she says quietly. "I always have." She pauses, something flickering across her face — regret, maybe. Recognition. "Even when I didn't know it."

She holds out her hand.

I stare at it. At her. At the offer sitting there between us like it's the simplest thing in the world.

It's not. It's everything.

My brain cycles through a dozen deflections — a joke, a shrug, a *thanks but I'm fine* that would let me keep my walls exactly where they've always been.

But my hand is already moving.

Her fingers close around mine. Warm. Real. Hers.

We walk back to the center of the cavern together. Hand in hand. And I don't let go.

The others fall in around us — Aspen and Torric, Kieran, Malrik. Even Darian edges closer, though he keeps his distance.

"This place isn't just safe," I say slowly.

Everyone looks at me.

I meet Kaia's eyes. Then Malrik's. Then each of them in turn.

"It knows us," I say.

The motes swirl overhead, brightening in response.

A soft wind stirs Kaia's hair.

Shadows curl at her feet.

And I finish, quiet but certain:

"All of us."

Chapter 26
KAIA

The motes settle slowly around us, the cavern still humming with whatever just happened.

We stand there in the soft glow — Finn's hand still warm in mine — and I don't want to move. Don't want to break whatever this is.

But then Aspen tilts his head.

"There's one more," he says quietly.

I follow his gaze. On the far side of the cavern, half-hidden in shadow, there's a sixth tunnel. I didn't notice it before — too caught up in the halls that were blazing to life, too overwhelmed by everything we were learning.

But it's there. Waiting.

We drift toward it together, the group moving as one without anyone saying a word. Finn's fingers slip from mine as we walk, but the warmth lingers.

It's not dark like the others were before they woke up. It's not waiting. It's just... nothing. Smooth walls. Bare wood. No carvings. No light. No hum.

We stand in front of the blank hall for a long moment.

I move toward it, curious, and my shadows refuse to follow. They pool at my feet, tense, unwilling. Bob's edges sharpen like he's warning me. Mouse chirps once — short, clipped. *Don't.*

"What's in there?" I ask.

Nobody answers. Nobody knows.

Finn steps closer. His chaos magic goes quiet — I can feel it through the bond, the sudden stillness where there's usually static. Like it's listening. Waiting for something.

A single mote drifts toward the tunnel. Hovers at the threshold. Then retreats.

"It's not empty," Aspen says quietly. "It's dormant."

We all stare at it for a long moment. The blank space where something should be. The unwritten hall.

Whatever it's waiting for, it's not us. Not yet.

I turn away first. There's nothing for us there — not tonight.

And honestly? I'm exhausted. We all are. Days on the road, sleeping in shifts, eating whatever we could find. The corruption pressing against us constantly. Callum's broken prophecies. The weight of everything we just learned in these halls.

I look at the bathing spring in the center of the cavern. Crystal-clear water swirling with pink and white motes. Steam rising gently from the surface.

Gods, I want to be clean.

"I'm getting in," I say.

Every head turns toward me.

Torric's eyebrows rise. Aspen's mouth twitches. Kieran goes very still. Malrik's expression doesn't change, but something shifts in his eyes — something heated, something hungry.

And Finn—

Finn grins. Wide and shameless and so completely *him* that my chest aches.

"Finally," he says. "I was starting to think you'd forgotten what water was for. You know, besides drinking. And crying. And—"

"Finn."

"—dramatic reveals where someone emerges glistening and backlit like a—"

"*Finn.*"

He holds up his hands, still grinning. "I'm just saying. The view's about to improve significantly."

My face burns. "Turn around. All of you."

They do.

But not before I catch the smirks. Every single one of them. Even Darian, though his is more uncertain — like he's not sure he's allowed to want this but can't help it anyway.

Kieran is the last to turn, his gold eyes lingering on mine for a beat too long before he gives me his back.

I wait until they're all facing away. Six broad backs. Six sets of shoulders. Six men who have seen me fight, bleed, break, and rise. Who have held me. Kissed me. Loved me in ways I'm still learning to accept.

And now they're *all* going to see me naked. All at once.

Great. Fine. This is fine.

I strip quickly — or try to. My fingers fumble with the laces of my shirt, clumsy with exhaustion and something else. Nerves. Anticipation. The knowledge that the moment I say they can turn around, everything changes.

The cool air hits my skin as I pull off my shirt. Then my pants. Then everything else.

I don't look at them. I don't let myself.

I slip into the water.

It's perfect. Warm without being hot, silky against my skin, the motes swirling around me like curious fireflies. The tension in my shoulders starts to unwind immediately. I sink lower, letting the water rise to my collarbone, and finally let out a breath I didn't know I was holding.

"Okay," I say. "You can turn around."

They do.

And the heat in their eyes nearly drowns me.

Torric turns first. His gaze rakes over me — what he can see above the waterline — and his jaw tightens. The fire rune on his chest pulses once, bright and hungry even through his shirt.

Aspen is next, his ice-blue eyes softening even as something darker flickers beneath the surface. His attention lingers on my shoulders, my throat, the wet hair clinging to my neck.

Kieran's gold eyes find mine and hold. He doesn't look anywhere else. Just my face. Like he's memorizing me. Like he's afraid to look away.

Malrik's gaze is slower. More deliberate. He takes his time, letting his eyes travel from my face to my shoulders to the water where it meets my skin. His expression stays controlled, but I can feel the want radiating through the bond like a banked fire.

Finn is grinning again, but it's softer now. Less joke, more wonder. Like he can't believe he gets to be here. Gets to see this.

And Darian—

Darian looks like he's about to combust. His cheeks are flushed, his magic flickering at his fingertips, and he's very carefully not looking directly at me while also absolutely looking directly at me.

"Well?" I manage, my voice coming out rougher than intended. "Are you getting in or just going to stand there?"

Finn's grin widens. "Oh, we're getting in. But fair's fair, Trouble."

I blink. "What?"

"You made us turn around." He reaches for the hem of his shirt. "We're not turning around for you."

Oh.

Oh no.

Finn goes first.

Because of course he does.

He pulls his shirt over his head in one fluid motion, and I forget how to breathe.

I've seen Finn shirtless before. Caught glimpses. Stolen glances when I thought no one was looking. But there's something different about watching him strip with full intention, knowing I'm watching, *wanting* me to watch.

He's lean — not bulky like Torric, not carved like Malrik. But there's strength in the lines of him, definition in his arms and shoulders and the planes of his stomach. Freckles scattered across his chest like constellations.

He catches me staring and winks.

"Like what you see?"

I don't answer. I can't. My mouth is too dry.

He kicks off his boots, shoves down his pants, and—

Gods.

I look away. I try to. But my eyes have other ideas, and I catch a glimpse of narrow hips, strong thighs, and— and—

Linda drifts to the edge of the pool. If shadows could fan themselves, she would be.

I sink a little lower in the water.

Finn laughs, low and warm, and slides into the water beside me. Close enough that I can feel the heat of him even through the warmth of the spring.

"Your turn to be red, Trouble," he murmurs near my ear. "I like it."

Two Eds settle at the pool's edge. Watching.

Great. We have an audience.

Torric goes next.

He doesn't make a show of it like Finn did. He just... strips. Efficient. Practical. Like he's done this a thousand times and can't be bothered with modesty.

But there's nothing practical about the way he looks.

He's *huge*. I knew that. But seeing all of him, bare and golden in the soft light of the cavern — the breadth of his shoulders, the thick muscles of his arms and chest, the fire rune blazing over his heart — it's different. More.

His body is a weapon. Built for violence. Scarred from a lifetime of it.

Bob puffs up at the pool's edge, posture going even more rigid than usual. Like he's trying to match Torric's energy. It's both adorable and terrifying at the same time.

"Competition, Bob?" Finn murmurs beside me. "Bold move."

I choke on nothing.

When Torric's eyes meet mine, there's something soft underneath all that ferocity. Something that's just for me.

He steps into the water, and the level rises noticeably. He settles next to me, close enough to touch if I reached out.

"Breathe, sunshine," he rumbles. "You're turning purple."

I exhale shakily. He smirks.

Four more Eds drift to the pool's edge. The audience is growing.

I sink lower.

Aspen is quieter about it.

He undresses with his back half-turned, like he's giving me the choice of whether to look. But I look. Of course I look.

He's beautiful in a way that's almost unfair — lean and pale, his white-blond hair still perfectly styled even after days on the road, the water rune on his arm pulsing soft blue. There's a stillness to him even now, a calm that makes me want to curl into him and never move.

When he turns, I see the scars on his chest. Old ones. From their father. From the brands that made them what they are.

Patricia's notebook flickers. Documenting. Always documenting.

"She's taking notes," Finn whispers. "On all of us. For posterity."

"Shut *up*, Finn."

But then Patricia turns — *turns* — like she wants me to see.

My eyes catch the edge of the page.

Tick marks.

Evenly spaced.

Perfectly straight.

Like a ruler.

Like a *measuring stick.*

My brain supplies the horrifying implication a full second before my face goes nuclear.

"Patricia," I whisper, scandalized, "*no.*"

Patricia's notebook flickers again.

Oh gods. She is. She's literally measuring them.

Aspen steps into the water beside Torric, catching my expression. He glances at Patricia. Glances at me. Glances back at Patricia.

"...Should I be concerned?" he asks.

Finn nearly chokes trying not to laugh.

Finnick does a little flip near Linda, clearly showing off. More Eds gather. I've lost count now.

The pool's edge is starting to look crowded.

Kieran takes longer.

He stands at the edge of the pool, golden eyes fixed on some middle distance, and I watch his throat work as he swallows.

"Kieran," I say softly. "You don't have to—"

"I want to," he says. His voice is rough. "I just..."

He doesn't finish. He doesn't have to.

He's been alive for centuries. Loved me for most of them. And somehow, this moment — stripping down in front of me, vulnerable and bare — feels like more than any of that.

He undresses slowly. Deliberately. Like he's giving himself to me piece by piece.

And I watch every second of it.

His body is lean, elegant, built for speed rather than brute strength. Pale skin marked with faint silver lines — old scars, old battles, old lifetimes.

Mouse settles at the pool's edge, tail curling around his paws. Watching with ancient, knowing eyes. The Eds part for him like he's royalty.

Because he is. Shadow royalty. Obviously.

When Kieran finally steps into the water, there's a tremor in his hands that he can't quite hide.

I reach out without thinking and catch his fingers under the surface.

He squeezes once. Doesn't let go.

"This is very romantic," Finn stage-whispers. "I'm not crying. You're crying."

"Finn," Torric growls.

"What? I'm supportive."

Malrik goes next to last.

He meets my eyes as he reaches for his shirt, and there's a challenge in his gaze. *Watch me*, it says. *I dare you.*

So I do.

He pulls the fabric over his head, and I stop breathing again.

He's carved from marble. That's the only way to describe it. Every muscle defined, shadows pooling in the hollows of his hips, his chest, his stomach. Dark hair falls across his forehead as he moves, and I want to push it back. Want to trace every line of him with my fingers. My tongue.

He takes his time with his pants. Knows exactly what he's doing to me. Knows and *enjoys* it, the bastard.

Walter drifts lazily overhead, pulsing with starlight, completely unbothered.

Every other shadow at the pool's edge has gone still. Even Bob. Even Finnick.

The Eds are practically vibrating.

Finn leans in, his breath warm against my ear. "You're drooling, Trouble."

"I am *not*—"

"You absolutely are. It's okay." He pauses. "I am too."

My face burns hotter. Finn just grins and settles back, looking far too pleased with himself.

When Malrik finally steps into the water, he positions himself directly across from me. Close enough that our knees could touch if either of us moved.

"Enjoying the show?" he asks, voice low enough that only I can hear.

"Shut up," I manage.

He smiles. Slow and devastating.

I sink so low in the water my chin touches the surface.

Darian is last.

And he looks like he's about to die.

His face is bright red, his magic crackling at his fingertips, and he's staring at the water like it personally offended him.

"Darian," Finn calls, still grinning. "The water's not going to bite."

"I know that," Darian snaps. But he doesn't move.

"Do you want us to turn around?" I ask gently.

He hesitates. Then shakes his head, jaw tightening with something like determination.

"No," he says. "No, I— I can do this."

He undresses with his back to us, which is somehow worse because now I'm watching the muscles of his shoulders flex, the curve of his spine, the way his hands shake slightly as he pushes down his pants.

Carl tries to sneak closer to investigate and gets yanked back by Steve, who immediately trips into Carl and sends them both tumbling into a heap at the water's edge.

When Darian finally turns and steps into the water, he's flushed all the way down his chest.

He sinks low immediately, water up to his chin, and refuses to meet anyone's eyes.

"See?" Finn says cheerfully. "That wasn't so hard."

Darian makes a sound like a dying animal.

And then I finally take stock of the pool's edge.

It's *packed*.

Bob stands at attention, still puffed up from his Torric-competition moment. Patricia hovers beside him, notebook flickering — I refuse to look at that page again. Finnick is doing lazy victory laps in the air. Linda radiates smug approval. Carl and Steve are still in a heap, arguing silently. Mouse sits at the head of the formation like a disappointed king surveying his chaotic subjects.

Walter bobs lazily at the far end, pulsing with starlight, completely un-bothered by everything.

And the Eds—

The Eds are *everywhere*.

Dozens of them. Maybe more. Crowded along the waterline like specta-tors at a sporting event. Some of them are floating *on* the water now, little dark shapes drifting closer, clustering at the edges of our group.

"Are they..." Torric squints at them. "Are they *watching* us?"

"They're always watching," Finn says, sounding far too delighted. "Hey, Eds. Enjoying the show?"

Several of them bob enthusiastically.

"I hate this," Darian mutters, sinking even lower.

"I don't," Finn says. "This is the best day of my life."

I drop my face into my hands.

The water is warm. The company is... a lot. The shadows are judging us.

And somehow, impossibly, I start to laugh.

Chapter 27
MALRIK

The water is perfect.

I sink lower, letting the warmth seep into muscles I didn't realize were knotted. Days on the road. Nights of broken sleep. The constant pressure of leading without being asked to lead. It's all been building in my shoulders, my neck, the space between my ribs where tension lives.

For the first time in what feels like weeks, I breathe.

Around me, the others are finding their places. The pool is larger than it looked from the edge — big enough for all of us to spread out, though no one seems inclined to spread far. We've been pressed close for so long, I'm not sure any of us remember how to do distance.

Torric groans like a dying animal as he sinks deeper. "Gods. *Gods.* Why didn't we find this place sooner?"

"Because we were busy almost dying," Aspen says mildly. He's settled beside his brother, shoulders finally dropping from their usual tension. His eyes are already moving — cataloging everyone's state, tracking who's relaxed and who's faking it.

I do the same thing. Always have.

Kaia floats near the center, her golden hair fanning out around her like a halo. She looks... peaceful. Actually peaceful. Her shadows drift lazily through the water around her, loose and content in a way I haven't seen since before the sanctuary.

Finn is beside her — close but not touching. He's practically vibrating with energy, even in the water. His chaos magic hums beneath the surface, a low static charge I can feel against my skin.

Kieran has positioned himself near the far edge. Close enough to be present, far enough to maintain that careful distance he's been keeping. His gold eyes drift to Kaia every few seconds — quick glances he probably thinks no one notices.

I notice.

And Darian...

Darian has sunk so low that only his face is visible above the waterline. His cheeks are still flushed, his eyes darting everywhere except directly at anyone. His magic flickers nervously at his fingertips beneath the surface.

He looks like he wants the water to swallow him whole.

The pool's edge is already crowded with shadows.

Bob has taken up position near Kaia's discarded clothes, standing at rigid attention like he's guarding state secrets. His posture radiates *I am watching everything and judging all of it.*

Patricia hovers beside him, notebook flickering at a leisurely pace. Documenting. Always documenting.

Finnick does a lazy flip through the air — showing off for no one in particular. Linda drifts nearby, radiating quiet approval.

And the Eds...

Two of them sit at the water's edge. Then three. They bob gently, attention fixed on the pool. On us.

Walter floats overhead, pulsing with soft starlight, completely unbothered by everything.

"Your shadows are staring," Torric says to Kaia.

She glances at the pool's edge and sighs. "They always stare. You get used to it."

"Do you though?" Finn asks. "Because Bob's been giving me a look since I got in, and I'm starting to take it personally."

Bob's posture somehow becomes more rigid.

"He's protective," Kaia says.

"He's *terrifying*. In an adorable, I-could-end-you kind of way."

Patricia's notebook flickers faster. Recording.

"Great," Finn says. "Now I'm being documented. By shadows, that I named. This is fine. Everything is fine."

The conversation drifts into safer waters.

Finn makes a crack about Japti's architecture — something about the cavern looking like "someone's very specific fever dream." Torric argues with Aspen about whether the berserker carvings in their hall were "badass" or "overdramatic." Aspen maintains they were historically accurate. Torric maintains they were *metal as fuck*.

Kieran offers quiet context — how Japti was built before the first Valkyrie walked, how the halls have been dormant for millennia. His voice carries the weight of someone who's seen centuries unfold, and I find myself listening more closely than I expected.

"So we just... woke them up?" Kaia asks.

"You woke them up," Kieran corrects gently. "The rest of us just followed."

Something flickers across her face — uncertainty, maybe. Or the weight of being the center of something ancient and enormous.

Finn bumps her shoulder with his. "Don't get a big head about it, Trouble. We're still not letting you pick restaurants."

She laughs — the right kind of laugh. Surprised. Real.

I feel something in my chest loosen at the sound.

I can't help but pay close attention. Watch the dynamics, track the undercurrents, notice what people reveal when they think no one's paying attention.

Kaia is more relaxed than I've seen her in days. Her shoulders have dropped from their usual defensive hunch. A few Eds circle around her like excited children.

She's beautiful like this. Unguarded. Present.

Finn keeps glancing at her — quick looks followed by quicker deflections. He's been doing that for months. Looking and then looking away, like he's afraid of being caught wanting something he doesn't think he's allowed to have.

I know that feeling intimately.

Torric has stretched out like a cat in a sunbeam, his massive frame taking up more than his fair share of space. The tension he's been carrying since his father has finally unwound. He looks younger like this. Less like a weapon waiting to fire.

Aspen watches everything with those ice-blue eyes, cataloging and calculating. But there's something softer in his expression tonight. Something almost hopeful.

Kieran's gaze keeps drifting to Kaia like she's a star he's spent centuries orbiting but never quite reaching. The longing in his face is ancient. Patient. The kind of want that's learned not to push.

Ironic, considering.

And Darian's magic keeps flickering under the water. Nervous. Uncertain. Like he doesn't know how to exist in a space where no one's demanding anything from him.

An Ed drifts past his shoulder.

He flinches.

The Ed bobs past Darian's arm, then floats away.

He watches it go with obvious suspicion.

"They're curious," Kaia says, noticing his tension. "They won't hurt you."

"I'm not worried about them hurting me," Darian mutters. "I'm worried about them... existing. Near me. Constantly."

"Welcome to my life," Finn says cheerfully.

Darian sinks a little lower.

I stretch, adjusting my position in the water. Casual. Natural.

My calf brushes against Kaia's ankle.

She goes still.

It could be an accident. The pool is crowded. Bodies in close proximity. These things happen.

But I don't move away. I let the contact linger — light, barely there, but unmistakable.

Her ankle presses back. Just slightly. A question, maybe. Or an answer.

I keep my face neutral. Above the surface, nothing changes.

Below it, everything does.

"The berserker murals were definitely the most dramatic," Finn is say-ing. "All that fire and ice and *raw masculine energy*—"

"Are you mocking us?" Torric asks.

"I would never."

"You're absolutely mocking us."

"I'm *appreciating*. There's a difference."

Aspen sighs — the long-suffering sigh of someone who's spent his entire life managing his brother's intensity and Finn's chaos. "Can we not?"

"We can never 'not,'" Finn says solemnly. "It's against my religion."

Kaia laughs again, and I feel the vibration of it through the water. Through the place where our legs are still touching.

She doesn't move away.

Neither do I.

Three Eds drift across the water toward Darian.

Then four.

They cluster near his shoulder, bobbing gently, their attention fixed on him with what I can only describe as fascination.

"Um," Darian says.

"They really like you," Finn observes, delighted.

"I don't want them to like me."

"Too late. You've been chosen."

Kaia is watching with obvious amusement. "They're harmless. Mostly."

"*Mostly?*"

"Well, Carl once got stuck in someone's hair for three hours. But that was an isolated incident."

Darian looks like he wants to cry.

I shift again.

This time, I extend my other leg.

It finds Finn.

He startles — a barely perceptible jerk beneath the surface. His chaos magic flickers once, a spark of surprised energy that dissipates quickly.

He doesn't look at me. Doesn't acknowledge it.

But he doesn't move away either.

I hold the contact. Light but deliberate. My calf against his, my other leg still pressed to Kaia's ankle.

Both of them. At once. Intentional.

I see you, I think. *Both of you. I want you both here.*

Kaia's ankle presses more firmly against mine. Her breath doesn't change, but I feel the shift in her — awareness sharpening, attention focusing.

Finn's chaos magic settles into something almost calm. The nervous hum beneath his skin goes quiet.

Under the water, we're tangled together. Above it, no one can tell.

Almost no one.

Aspen's gaze sharpens.

He's not looking at Darian and his Ed problem. He's looking at *us*. At the space between the three of us that's somehow gotten smaller. At the way Kaia's shoulders have angled toward me. At the way Finn has gone unusually still.

He doesn't speak. Just files it away.

But I see the flicker of understanding in his ice-blue eyes.

Six Eds now. Maybe seven.

They've formed a loose semicircle around Darian, bobbing at the surface like cheerful little sentinels.

"This is getting out of hand," Darian says, his voice pitched higher than normal.

"On the contrary," Finn says, "I think this is the perfect amount of hand. The exact right number of hands. Shadow hands. Ed hands. Whatever they have."

"They don't have hands."

"That's what makes it special."

Torric is staring at the Ed formation with growing confusion. "Why are they doing that?"

"Unknown," Aspen says. But he's smiling now — actually smiling, not just the controlled twitch of amusement. "Perhaps they sense his discomfort."

"They're *feeding* on my discomfort?"

"That seems dramatic."

"I'm being swarmed by shadow creatures and you're calling *me* dramatic?"

Patricia's notebook is flickering rapidly. Documenting every moment of Darian's descent into madness.

I let my foot trace along Kaia's calf. Slow. Deliberate. Unmistakable now.

Her breath catches — a soft hitch that she covers by shifting position.

At the same moment, I tap my other foot lightly against Finn's leg. Once. Twice. *I'm here. I'm not forgetting you.*

He makes a sound low in his throat. Barely audible. Quickly swallowed.

His hand moves under the water.

Finds Kaia's.

I watch their fingers intertwine beneath the surface. Watch Finn's whole body shudder at the contact — such a small thing, but for him it might as well be a declaration.

Kaia squeezes his hand. Doesn't let go.

Aspen's smile has become a full grin.

I've known him for months. He doesn't grin. He offers controlled almost-smiles. Careful expressions of mild amusement.

This is different. This is a real grin, spreading across his face like he can't contain it.

Torric notices. Follows his brother's gaze. Studies me, then Finn, then Kaia. Studies the way we're positioned — closer than we were. Angled toward each other.

"Oh," he says.

Aspen makes a sound that's definitely a laugh, quickly smothered.

"*Oh,*" Torric repeats, understanding dawning.

He starts grinning too.

Kieran registers the shift.

His expression shutters — that careful blankness he uses when he's feeling something he doesn't want to show. His gold eyes move from Kaia to Finn to me, tracking the invisible lines between us.

Something flickers in his gaze. Not jealousy, exactly. Something else. More complicated.

Loved her since she was six years old centuries ago.

And he's watching her choose someone else. Again.

But he doesn't reach. Doesn't push. Just withdraws a little further, that patient ache settling deeper into his features.

I see all of it.

I don't know how to fix it.

The Eds have multiplied.

They're up to Darian's chest now — a thick ring of small dark shapes, bobbing and clustering and apparently having the time of their lives.

"No," Darian says. "No no no—"

More arrive. They float across the water from all directions, converging on him like he's the most interesting thing they've encountered in centuries.

"What the *fuck*," Torric says, staring.

"Language," Aspen murmurs, but he's still grinning.

"The shadows are swarming him and you're worried about my language?"

The Eds pile higher. Shoulders now. Creeping toward his neck.

"I can't— They won't— *Why is this happening—*"

Carl tries to join the swarm from the left. Steve tries to intercept him. They collide, tangle, and crash into the water with a splash that sends ripples across the entire pool.

Patricia's notebook is strobing now. Flickering so fast it's practically a light show.

Bob observes the chaos with the expression of a general watching his troops descend into anarchy.

"Should we help him?" Kaia asks, but she's laughing too hard to be serious.

"I don't know how," Finn admits. "This is unprecedented. Historic. I'm witnessing shadow history."

"I hate you," Darian says, muffled by Eds. "I hate all of you."

"That's fair," Finn says cheerfully.

Torric uses the chaos.

He stands — water streaming off his massive frame — and stretches like he's been in the pool for hours instead of twenty minutes.

"I think it's time to get out."

"What?" Kaia looks up at him. "Why?"

"Because we've been in here a while." His eyes flick to me. To Finn. To the way we're arranged around Kaia like planets around a sun. "And some of us probably want some privacy."

"Privacy for what?"

Aspen chokes on nothing.

Finn goes very still.

Torric just grins — wide and knowing and completely unsubtle. "Figure it out, Kaia."

Aspen is already moving, following his brother toward the pool's edge. "We should check on Callum anyway. Make sure he hasn't done anything stupid."

"I can check on Callum," Kieran offers, but he's already standing. His gold eyes find Kaia's one last time — a long, soft look that says *not tonight, but someday.*

She meets his gaze. Something passes between them. Understanding, maybe. Or a promise.

Then he turns and follows Aspen out of the pool.

Torric reaches down and physically hauls Darian out of the water. The Eds come with him — clinging to his shoulders, his arms, his chest like a living cloak.

"They won't let go," Darian says miserably.

"They'll let go eventually."

"You don't know that."

"I'm choosing to believe it. Come on."

Carl attempts to follow and trips over Steve. They both go down in a heap of shadowy limbs.

Finn watches the whole thing with obvious delight. "Ten out of ten. Perfect dismount. The judges are impressed."

"*Finn*," Darian hisses.

"What? I'm being supportive."

Torric pauses near the pool's edge, glancing down at Callum's unconscious form. He's still out cold, propped against the rocks where we left him.

"We should move him," Kieran says quietly.

"I've got his legs," Torric grunts.

Kieran takes his shoulders without argument. Between them, they lift Callum like he weighs nothing — which, compared to what they usually carry, he probably doesn't.

"Berserker hall," Aspen says. "There's space to lay him down properly."

The twins' hall. Of course. Somewhere Callum can be monitored without being in the way.

Darian trails after them, still draped in Eds, looking like a man who has accepted his fate but resents it deeply.

Aspen pauses at the cavern's edge. Looks back.

His eyes meet mine.

"Malrik," he says. Just that. My name. But it's loaded with meaning — approval, understanding, a hint of *finally*.

I nod once.

He smiles and disappears into the shadows.

"Don't break anything," Torric calls over his shoulder.

"That's not—" I start.

"I'm talking to Finn."

"Rude," Finn says, but he's grinning.

And then they're gone.

All of them.

Just the three of us left.

The silence is deafening.

The motes drift lazily around us. The water laps gently at our skin. Bob has turned his back at the pool's edge, posture rigid with forced nonchalance — though I suspect he's monitoring through some shadow-sense I don't fully understand.

Kaia looks at me. At Finn. At their hands still intertwined beneath the water. At my legs still tangled with theirs.

"Oh," she breathes. "Oh."

Finn's laugh is shaky. "So."

"So," I agree.

"They, uh." He swallows. "They weren't subtle about leaving."

"No."

"Like, really not subtle."

"No."

Kaia's blush has spread down her neck, across her shoulders. Her shadows are curling in slow, lazy spirals around the three of us — possessive and approving and completely uninterested in giving us space.

"I didn't—" She stops. Starts again. "I wasn't sure if—"

"Kaia." I keep my voice steady. Certain. "We're sure."

Finn nods rapidly beside her. "So sure. Very sure. The surest."

"That's not a word."

"It is now. I'm making it a word. For this moment. Because I'm—" He exhales shakily. "I'm really fucking sure, Trouble."

She looks between us. The man she's already chosen. The man who's been waiting.

And the one who wants them both.

"Well," she says, her voice steadier than I expected. "I guess we should stop pretending we came here to talk."

Finn makes a sound somewhere between a laugh and a prayer.

And I finally let myself reach for what I've wanted.

For *both* of what I've wanted.

Chapter 28
FINN

Malrik moves first.

Not fast. Not urgent. Just... certain. The way he does everything.

His hand finds my jaw, tilting my face toward his, and for a second I forget how to breathe. We've kissed before. Stolen moments in dark corridors. Heat and tension and always, *always* pulling back before it went further.

This isn't pulling back.

His mouth covers mine, and I make a sound I'm going to pretend never happened—something between a groan and a whimper that vibrates through my whole chest. His kiss is slow, thorough, like he's been planning exactly how he wants to take me apart and now he finally has permission.

Finally.

The word ricochets through my skull. Finally finally finally.

Kaia's breath hitches beside us. I feel it more than hear it—the sharp little intake that means she's watching. My chaos magic sparks under my skin, responding to the heat building between all three of us.

Malrik breaks the kiss just enough to speak against my mouth. "Breathe, Finn."

"I'm breathing," I manage. "I'm definitely breathing. Breathing is happening."

"You're vibrating."

"That's just my personality."

He laughs—low, warm, barely more than an exhale—and then his other hand reaches past me. Toward her.

Kaia's fingers find his, and I watch them intertwine. Watch the way her whole body shudders at the contact. Watch her violet eyes go dark with want.

Gods, look at her.

She's so fucking beautiful it hurts. Water droplets clinging to her shoulders, golden hair plastered against her neck, lips parted just enough to show she's as wrecked as I am. Her shadows curl lazily around all three of us—Bob has very pointedly turned his back, Patricia's notebook is dark for once, and the Eds have retreated to a respectful distance.

Smart shadows.

"You two," Kaia breathes, her voice rough. "You're—"

"Yes," Malrik says simply.

"Together?"

"Yes."

She stares at us. At the way I'm still pressed close to Malrik, his hand on my jaw, mine somehow on his chest without me remembering putting it there. At the way he's reaching for her at the same time, like he can't imagine having one of us without the other.

"Both of you?" Her voice cracks slightly. "At the same time?"

"That's generally how threesomes work, Trouble."

I regret the joke immediately. Not because it's wrong, but because her eyes snap to mine with something so raw and vulnerable that my heart does something painful in my chest.

"I've never—" She stops. Swallows. "I don't know how to—"

"You don't have to know anything." Malrik's voice is steady. Anchoring. The calm center in a storm we're all feeling. "Just tell us what you want."

What she wants.

Such a simple question. Such a loaded one.

I watch her process it—the way her brow furrows, the way her teeth catch her lower lip, the way her shadows flutter with nervous energy. She's not confused. I know that. She knows exactly who she wants, has known for longer than any of us admitted.

She's just... overwhelmed.

Join the fucking club.

"I want—" She exhales shakily. "I want to stop thinking so much."

Something cracks in my chest. A feeling so big I can't name it. Want and relief and desperation and a protective fury that she's ever had to worry at all, that the world hasn't been kinder to her, that we haven't been—

"Finn."

Malrik's voice cuts through the spiral. Steady. Present.

I blink. Realize my chaos magic is sparking visibly now, little crackles of light dancing across my skin.

"Sorry," I manage. "I'm just—"

"I know." He does. He always does. His hand settles on my shoulder, grounding. "Go to her."

Not a command. Permission.

I don't hesitate.

I close the distance between me and Kaia, and for a heartbeat we just look at each other. Her violet eyes. My green ones. All the history between us—the first day we met, the moments we stole, the almost-kisses and interrupted touches and the way I've been in love with her since before I knew what to call it.

"Hey, Trouble."

"Hey, chaos boy."

My hand shakes when I lift it to her face.

She notices. Of course she notices.

"Finn—"

"I'm fine," I say quickly. "I'm great. I'm fantastic. I'm about to kiss you properly for the first time in months and I'm definitely not having a minor emotional crisis about it."

Her lips twitch. "Minor?"

"Okay, moderate. Significant. Potentially catastrophic." I lean closer, my forehead nearly touching hers. "Please shut me up."

She kisses me first.

And everything else dissolves.

Her mouth is soft and warm and tastes like the spring water, and I make another embarrassing sound against her lips because I can't fucking help it. I've wanted this so badly for so long that actually having it feels like a fever dream, like I'm going to wake up any second and find out none of this was real.

But her hands are real on my shoulders. Her body is real against mine under the water. The little moan she makes when I finally, *finally* let myself kiss her the way I've been imagining—

That's definitely real.

Malrik's hand settles on my lower back. Warm. Grounding. Reminding me he's still here. Still part of this.

I break the kiss just long enough to gasp for air, and Kaia makes a sound of protest that goes straight to my cock.

"Eager," I manage.

"You're one to talk." She's breathless. Pink-cheeked. Absolutely devastating. "You've been looking at me like that for months."

"Like what?"

"Like you're starving."

I laugh—raw, honest. "Because I am. Have been. For a really fucking long time, Trouble."

"Then stop talking," she says, "and do something about it."

Gods, yes.

I kiss her again, harder this time. Let myself be messy about it. Let my hands slide from her jaw to her shoulders to the curve of her waist under the water. She arches into my touch like she's been waiting for it, and the knowledge that she *wants* this—wants *me*—is so overwhelming I have to pull back before I combust.

Malrik's there when I do. His mouth finds the side of my neck, teeth grazing my pulse point, and I choke on air.

"Oh fuck—"

"Still with us?" His voice is low. Amused.

"Barely. Definitely. Possibly dying."

He laughs against my skin, and the vibration of it sends sparks down my spine. Then his hand—the one that was on my back—slides lower. Under the water. Across my hip.

I go very, very still.

"Okay?" he asks.

"If you stop now I'll kill you."

"Noted."

Kaia watches us with eyes that have gone darker than I've ever seen them. Her lips are swollen from kissing me. Her chest rises and falls with unsteady breaths. And the expression on her face—

She likes watching us.

The realization hits me like lightning. She *likes* it. Not jealousy. Not uncertainty. Just pure, undiluted want.

"See something you like?" I manage, aiming for cocky and landing somewhere around desperate.

"Yes." No hesitation. "I see two of you. Together. And I—" She stops, swallows. "I want to be in the middle of it."

Fucking hell.

Malrik moves before I can respond. His hand leaves my hip—I make a sound of protest I'm not proud of—and reaches for Kaia instead. He pulls her closer, positioning her between us, and suddenly I understand exactly what he's doing.

He's not taking over.

He's *arranging* us.

Like pieces of a puzzle. Like he knows exactly where everyone fits.

Kaia's back presses against my chest. Malrik faces her, close enough that their noses nearly touch. And I'm behind her, arms automatically wrapping around her waist, chin resting on her shoulder.

"Oh," she breathes.

Yeah. That's about right.

"Better?" Malrik asks, and I can hear the smile in his voice even though I can't see it.

"I—" Kaia's hands find mine where they rest on her stomach. Our fingers intertwine. "Yes. Better."

"Good."

He kisses her.

I can't see it properly from this angle, but I feel it—the way her whole body softens against mine, the little sounds she makes into his mouth, the way her grip on my hands tightens like she needs something to anchor her.

I press my lips to her shoulder. Trace a path up her neck. Let myself do all the things I've been imagining for months—the spot behind her ear that makes her shiver, the hollow of her throat where her pulse flutters, the curve where her neck meets her shoulder that I've wanted to sink my teeth into since the first time I saw her.

She moans. Actually moans. Loud enough that I feel it vibrate through her whole body.

"Sensitive there," I note against her skin.

"Shut—" She gasps against his lips as I do it again. "Shut up, Finn."

"Never."

Malrik breaks their kiss, silver eyes finding mine over her shoulder. There's heat there. Want. But also something softer. Something that says *this is right* and *thank you* and *I've been waiting too.*

I lean forward, catching his mouth over Kaia's shoulder, and for a moment we're all tangled together—her between us, him kissing me while my hands are still laced with hers, everything overlapping and messy and absolutely fucking perfect.

"You're going to kill me," I say when we break apart. "Both of you. This is how I die."

"Dramatic," Malrik murmurs.

"It's a valid concern."

Kaia turns her head, catching my mouth in an awkward angle that somehow works. "If you die," she says against my lips, "I'll find a way to resurrect you just so I can do it again."

"Kinky."

She bites my lower lip in retaliation.

Gods, I love her.

The thought crashes through me with the force of a tidal wave, and for a second I can't breathe around it. I've known for a while. Maybe since the beginning, if I'm being honest with myself, which I rarely am. But knowing it and *feeling* it are different things, and right now I'm feeling it so intensely that my chest actually aches.

"Hey." Kaia's voice goes soft. Her hand lifts to cup my cheek. "Where'd you go?"

"Nowhere." I swallow past the sudden tightness in my throat. "I'm here. I'm so fucking here, Trouble."

She studies my face for a moment—really studies it, with those violet eyes that always see too much—and whatever she finds there makes her expression shift into something tender.

"Good," she says simply. "Stay."

"Always."

Malrik's hands are moving. I can feel them through the water—one tracing up Kaia's side, the other reaching past her to rest on my hip again. He doesn't rush. Doesn't push. Just touches us both with the same steady certainty he does everything.

"Finn."

"Yeah?"

"I'm going to touch her. And I want you to watch."

My brain short-circuits.

"That—" My voice cracks. I clear my throat. Try again. "That works. That's—yes. Watching is good. I'm excellent at watching. Gold star observer over here."

Kaia laughs—actually laughs, bright and surprised—and the sound breaks something open in my chest.

"You're ridiculous," she says.

"You love it."

"Unfortunately."

Malrik's hand slides lower under the water, and Kaia's breath catches. Her fingers tighten on mine. Her head falls back against my shoulder.

"Oh—"

I watch her face. Watch the way her lips part, the way her eyes flutter closed, the way color spreads down her throat. Watch her mouth his name like a prayer or a curse or both.

She's beautiful. She's always beautiful. But like this—coming undone between us, letting us see her—she's something else entirely.

"Finn," she gasps. "Finn, I need—"

"Tell me."

"Touch me. Please. I need—" Her hips roll against Malrik's hand, chasing whatever he's doing to her. "I need more."

More.

The word echoes in my head as I let my hands finally, *finally* move from her waist. I've been so good. So patient. Keeping my hands where she put them like it was a test I couldn't fail.

But she said more. She said *please.* And I'm only human.

My palm slides up her stomach. Over her ribs. Finds the curve of her breast, and—

Oh.

She gasps, arching into my touch, and I have to press my forehead against her shoulder to keep from making sounds that would embarrass us both.

"Okay?" I manage.

"Yes—" Her voice breaks. "Yes, don't stop—"

I don't stop.

I learn her with my hands the way I've imagined doing hundreds of times. The weight of her. The way she responds to pressure here versus softness there. The spot that makes her moan and the one that makes her whimper and the one that makes her grind back against me so hard I see stars.

Because she's not just pressed against me anymore. She's *moving*. Rolling her hips in a rhythm that matches what Malrik's doing to her, and every motion brings her ass against my cock, and I'm harder than I've ever been in my life.

"Fuck," I choke out. "Kaia—"

"I know." She sounds wrecked. Destroyed. Perfect. "I can feel you."

"Sorry, I can't—"

"Don't apologize." She rolls against me again, deliberate this time. "I *want* to feel you."

Malrik makes a sound—low, approving. His silver eyes are molten when they meet mine. "She's close."

"Already?"

"It's been a while." Kaia's voice is breathless. Desperate. "And you're both—you're everywhere, and I—"

"Let go." Malrik's voice is steady. Anchoring. Even now. "We've got you."

"I don't—"

"You do." I press a kiss to her neck. "Come for us, Trouble. We want to see it."

Something in her expression cracks open.

And then she's falling.

Her whole body shudders between us, her back arching against my chest, my name and Malrik's tangling together on her lips. I feel it through every point where we're touching—the tremor in her thighs, the clench of her hands, the ragged sob of breath.

Beautiful. She's so fucking beautiful.

Malrik works her through it, murmuring things I can't quite hear against her throat. I hold her steady, pressing kisses to her shoulder, her neck, anywhere I can reach. The Eds have clustered at the far edge of the pool now—definitely watching, definitely judging, definitely getting an eyeful they'll never unsee.

I should care about that. I really don't.

When Kaia finally comes down, she's trembling. Limp against me. Breathing like she's run a marathon.

"Holy shit," she whispers.

"Good holy shit or—"

"Finn." She turns her head to look at me. Her eyes are glassy, soft, completely wrecked. "Shut up and let me enjoy it."

"Shutting up. Enjoying. These are things I can do."

She laughs weakly. "You're incapable of shutting up."

"Valid point."

Malrik withdraws his hand slowly—I watch Kaia's face flicker with the loss—and brings his fingers to his mouth. Holds my gaze as he tastes her.

Fuck.

"You're going to kill me," I say again. "Confirmed. Cause of death: whatever the fuck that was."

"Worth it?" he asks.

"Ask me after I recover the ability to think."

Kaia twists in my arms until she's facing me. Her wet hair falls around her shoulders. Her eyes are determined now, focused in a way that makes my stomach flip.

"Your turn," she says.

"My—what?"

"You watched me." She presses closer, and I feel the soft weight of her against my chest. "Now I want you."

The words hit my brain and promptly shatter it.

"I—" My voice comes out strangled. "That's—yes. Obviously yes. Enthusiastic yes. All the yeses."

Malrik's hand settles on my shoulder. Steadying. "There's a ledge," he says. "Behind you. Easier."

I turn my head and see it—a natural shelf of stone at the pool's edge, covered in soft moss that looks almost deliberately placed. Like Japti knew what we'd need before we did.

Ancient sex cavern. Cool. Normal. Definitely not weird at all.

"Come on." Malrik guides us both toward it, his movements unhurried but certain. The water grows shallower as we go, the warmth of it giving way to cooler air against my skin.

Kaia reaches the ledge first. She hoists herself up, sitting on the mossy stone, and for a moment I just... stare.

Water streams down her body. Her skin glows in the soft light of the motes. Her legs dangle in the pool, parted just enough that I can see—

Gods.

"Finn." Malrik's voice is low. Amused. "You're staring."

"I'm appreciating. There's a difference."

"Is there?"

"Shut up."

Kaia laughs—that bright, surprised sound I'd kill to keep hearing—and reaches for me. "Get up here."

I don't need to be told twice.

The moss is soft under my palms as I pull myself up beside her. Cool against my heated skin. She immediately reaches for me, pulling me closer, and then we're kissing again—desperate and messy and nothing like the careful kisses we've stolen before.

This is claiming. Finally.

I ease her back against the moss, my body covering hers, and the feeling of her bare skin against mine from chest to hip is so overwhelming I have to stop and just *breathe.*

"You okay?" she asks softly.

"I'm great. I'm fantastic. I'm about to—" I swallow hard. "Kaia, I need you to know that I've wanted this for so long that I might actually embarrass myself."

"Finn—"

"I'm serious. Like, mortifyingly fast. There's a very real possibility here."

She cups my face in both hands. Her violet eyes are soft. Steady. "I don't care."

"You say that now—"

"I mean it." She pulls me down for another kiss. "I just want you. However long it takes. However it happens. I just want *you*."

Something cracks open in my chest.

I'm going to tell her I love her. Right now. I can feel the words building in my throat—

Malrik's hand settles on my lower back.

I'd almost forgotten he was there. Almost. But now I feel him behind me—still in the water, leaning against the ledge between my legs—and his touch is grounding. Present.

"Take your time," he says quietly. Just for me. "She's not going anywhere."

I exhale shakily. Nod.

Kaia's legs wrap around my hips, and the movement shifts me against her, and—

Oh fuck.

I'm right there. Pressed against her entrance. One movement away from being inside her.

"Yes?" I manage.

"Yes." No hesitation. "Please, Finn."

I push forward.

And the world narrows to the feeling of her around me.

Tight. Warm. *Perfect.*

I choke on a groan, my forehead dropping to her shoulder. "Holy—fucking—*gods*—"

She gasps beneath me, her nails digging into my shoulders. "Finn—"

"I know. I know. Just—give me a second—" I'm shaking. Actually shaking. Trying desperately to hold still, to not move, to not end this embarrassingly fast the way I warned her I might. "You feel—I can't—"

Malrik's hand slides up my spine. "Breathe."

"I'm trying—"

"You're holding your breath."

He's right. I force myself to exhale. Then inhale. Then exhale again.

Kaia's hand finds my cheek, turning my face toward hers. "Hey. Look at me."

I look.

Her eyes are huge. Soft. Full of something that makes my chest ache.

"We have time," she says quietly. "We have all the time we need."

"I know. I just—" My voice cracks. "I've wanted this so badly. For so long. And now you're here and you're *real* and I'm inside you and it's—"

"A lot?"

"Everything." The word slips out before I can stop it. "You're everything, Trouble."

Her breath catches.

And then she moves.

Just a slight shift of her hips, but it's enough to remind me that we're still connected, that I'm still buried inside her, that this is actually happening.

"Move with me," she whispers. "Please."

I do.

Slow at first. Careful. Learning the rhythm of her body, the angle that makes her gasp, the depth that makes her moan. She rises to meet every thrust, her fingers tangling in my hair, her mouth finding mine between ragged breaths.

"There—" she gasps. "Right there—"

I repeat the movement. Watch her eyes flutter closed. Feel her tighten around me.

"Again—"

I give her again. And again. And again.

Malrik's hands are still on me—my back, my hip, my thigh. Guiding without taking over. His mouth presses kisses to my shoulder blade, my spine, the small of my back. Everywhere he touches feels like fire.

"You're doing so well," he murmurs against my skin. "Both of you. Look at her, Finn."

I look.

Kaia is flushed and breathless beneath me. Her hair spreads across the moss like spilled gold. Her lips are parted, sounds spilling from them that I want to record and replay forever.

"She's beautiful," Malrik says.

"I know." My voice is wrecked. "Gods, I know."

"Tell her."

"You're beautiful." The words tumble out without thought. "You're fucking beautiful, Kaia. I've thought so since the first moment I saw you. Before I knew your name. Before I knew anything. Just—*you*. Standing there with your shadows. Looking at me like I was crazy for jumping off a tower."

She laughs—broken, gasping, somehow perfect. "You *were* crazy."

"I was trying to impress you."

"It worked."

I thrust harder, and her laugh cuts off into a moan.

"Yeah?" I manage. "Impressed now?"

"Getting there—" Her nails rake down my back. "Don't stop—"

I couldn't stop if I wanted to. Every part of me is focused on her—the sounds she makes, the way she moves, the way she feels clenched around me like she never wants to let go.

Malrik shifts behind me. His hand slides around my hip, lower, and suddenly he's touching us both—his fingers finding where we're joined, circling Kaia's clit while I'm still moving inside her.

She nearly screams.

"*Fuck*—Malrik—"

"Too much?" he asks.

"No—don't you dare stop—"

His laugh is dark. Satisfied. His fingers keep moving, matching the rhythm I've set, and Kaia's whole body starts to shake.

"Close," she gasps. "I'm—again—*already*—"

"Good." I thrust harder, chasing that sound. "Don't fight it. I want to feel you come around me."

She looks at me—really looks, violet eyes burning into mine—and something breaks open in her expression.

"Finn—"

"I've got you, Trouble. Fall. I'll catch you."

She does.

Her whole body arches off the moss, her inner walls clamping down around me so tight I see stars. My name rips from her throat, tangled with Malrik's, and the sound of it—the *feeling* of it—

I have to stop moving.

Everything in me is screaming to chase my own release, to follow her over that edge, to let go the way she just did. But I don't want this to end. Not yet. Not when I've waited so long for exactly this moment.

I hold still inside her, trembling with the effort, while she comes down from the peak.

Malrik's hand leaves where we're joined and settles on my hip instead. Steadying.

"Good," he says quietly. "Take a breath."

I take three.

Kaia's eyes flutter open. Dazed. Wrecked. The most beautiful thing I've ever seen.

"You stopped," she whispers.

"Didn't want it to be over yet."

Understanding dawns in her expression. Something soft. Something wondering.

"Finn..."

"I know." I lean down, pressing my forehead to hers. "I know, Trouble. Just—give me a second. Let me have this. Let me—"

I don't finish the sentence.

I don't need to.

She reaches up, threading her fingers through my hair, and pulls me down for a kiss so gentle it makes my chest ache.

And I stay exactly where I am—buried inside her, trembling with want, surrounded by the two people I love most in any realm—and let myself *feel* it.

All of it.

Finally.

"Finn." Kaia's voice is soft against my mouth. "You don't have to hold back."

"I know. I just—"

"I want to feel you." She shifts beneath me, and the movement sends sparks up my spine. "I want all of it. All of you."

All of me.

Something in my chest cracks wide open at the words.

I start moving again.

Not slow this time. Not careful. Just *honest* — desperate and messy and everything I've been holding back for months. She meets me thrust for thrust, her legs tightening around my hips, her nails leaving marks I'll wear like badges of honor.

Malrik's hand stays steady on my hip. Grounding me. Reminding me he's here, that this is real, that I'm not dreaming this.

"That's it," he murmurs. "Let go, Finn."

"I'm—" My voice breaks. "I can't—"

"You can." His mouth presses against my shoulder. "She wants it. Give it to her."

Kaia's hands find my face, pulling my gaze to hers. Violet eyes burning with something that looks like—

Love.

It looks like love.

"Finn." My name on her lips like a prayer. "Stay with me."

"Always," I choke out. "I'm always—"

The pressure builds at the base of my spine. Everywhere we're touching ignites. My chaos magic sparks and crackles across my skin, reaching for her, reaching for *them* —

And then something shifts.

Not just pleasure. Something deeper. Something that hooks behind my ribs and *pulls*.

The bond.

I feel it snap into place like a key turning in a lock. Like a missing piece I didn't know I was carrying suddenly finding where it belongs. It floods through me — warmth and want and *her*, Kaia, everywhere at once. In my blood. In my bones. In the chaos magic that's always felt broken until this exact moment.

I cry out — her name, maybe, or just sound — and bury myself as deep as I can go.

Everything whites out.

I'm aware of her arms around me. Malrik's hand on my back. The pulse of the bond threading through all of us, connecting what was always meant to be connected.

When I come back to myself, I'm shaking.

Not the fun kind of shaking. The kind that says something fundamental just rearranged itself inside me and I'm still catching up.

"Finn?" Kaia's voice is worried. Her hands stroke through my hair. "Finn, are you—"

"I felt it." The words come out raw. Wrecked. "The bond. I felt it—"

"I know." She presses her forehead to mine. "I felt it too."

"It's real." I'm not sure why I'm saying it. Maybe because I need to hear it out loud. "We're actually—"

"Real," she confirms. "Finally real."

I kiss her. Slow and deep and completely different from everything that came before. This isn't desperate. Isn't frantic.

This is *ours*.

When I finally pull back, I realize I'm still trembling. Still inside her. Still trying to process the enormity of what just happened.

Malrik's hand traces soothing patterns on my back. Patient. Present.

"You okay?" he asks quietly.

"I don't know." I laugh, and it comes out wet. "I think I just felt my soul rearrange itself. Is that normal? That doesn't feel normal."

"It's normal." His voice is warm. "It happened with each of us."

"Well, someone could have warned me."

"Would you have believed us?"

"...No. Probably not."

Kaia laughs softly beneath me, and the vibration of it travels through the bond — through *our* bond — and settles somewhere deep in my chest.

I ease out of her carefully, already mourning the loss of connection. She makes a small sound, her fingers tightening on my shoulders.

"Sorry," I murmur. "I just—"

"Don't apologize." She pulls me down beside her on the moss, curling into my side immediately. "Stay close."

"Wasn't planning on going anywhere."

Malrik pulls himself up onto the ledge on her other side. The moss is big enough for all three of us, barely, and we end up tangled together — Kaia in the middle, me pressed against her front, Malrik solid and warm at her back.

"What about you?" Kaia asks, twisting to look at him. "We didn't—"

"Shh." He presses a kiss to her shoulder. "Tonight wasn't about me."

"But—"

"Kaia." His voice is gentle but firm. "I got exactly what I wanted."

She frowns. "Watching us?"

"Being here." He meets my eyes over her shoulder, and something passes between us. Understanding. Gratitude. A promise for another time. "Being part of it. Seeing you two finally stop dancing around each other."

"We weren't dancing," I protest weakly.

"You were waltzing. Very badly. For months."

Kaia snorts. "He's not wrong."

"Whose side are you on?"

"The side that just gave me two orgasms."

"That's—" I pause. "Okay, fair."

Malrik's arm drapes over both of us, his hand finding mine across Kaia's hip. Our fingers intertwine.

"This is okay?" I ask quietly. Meaning all of it. Meaning *us*.

"More than okay." He squeezes my hand. "This is what I wanted. What I've wanted for a long time."

"Both of us?"

"Both of you." No hesitation. No uncertainty. Just truth.

Something loosens in my chest that I didn't know was tight.

The motes drift lazily overhead, painting soft patterns of light across our skin. The Eds have retreated to a respectful distance — though Bob is definitely still watching from his post near our clothes, posture radiating *I am choosing to pretend I saw nothing*.

At the edge of the Berserker hall, a flicker of gold catches my eye. Kieran. Standing in the shadows, watching — then gone before I can blink.

Of course.

"We should probably go back eventually," Kaia murmurs. She doesn't sound like she means it.

"Eventually," I agree.

"The others will wonder."

"Let them wonder."

Malrik huffs a laugh against her hair. "They know exactly what we're doing."

"They know what they *think* we're doing."

"Finn." Kaia twists to look at me. "Torric literally said 'don't break anything.' They know."

"In their defense," I say, "I did almost break several things. Internally. My brain, specifically. Multiple times."

She laughs — tired and warm and completely content — and the sound travels through the bond like sunlight.

Our bond.

I still can't quite believe it's real.

"Hey," I say softly.

"Hey."

"I love you."

The words slip out before I can stop them. Before I can wrap them in jokes or deflection or any of the armor I usually wear.

Just truth. Bare and simple.

Kaia's breath catches. Her eyes go wide. Behind her, I feel Malrik go still.

"You don't have to say it back," I add quickly. "I just—I needed you to know. After everything. After *this*. I couldn't not say it."

She stares at me for a long moment.

Then she kisses me.

Soft. Sweet. Full of everything she's not quite ready to say out loud.

When she pulls back, her eyes are bright. "Finn Veylan."

"Yeah?"

"You're ridiculous."

"That's not—"

"And I love you too."

My heart stops.

Starts again.

Starts hammering so hard I'm pretty sure they can both feel it.

"You—"

"I love you," she repeats. Steadier this time. Like she's testing out how it feels. "I've loved you for a while, I think. I just didn't—I wasn't ready to—"

I kiss her before she can finish.

She laughs against my mouth, and it's the best sound I've ever heard. Better than chaos. Better than magic. Better than anything.

Malrik's hand squeezes mine, and when I look at him over her shoulder, he's smiling. Actually smiling. The real kind, not the controlled almost-smiles he usually offers.

"Finally," he murmurs.

"Yeah." I grin back at him, probably looking completely unhinged. "Finally."

We lie there in the soft light, tangled together on the mossy ledge, listening to the water lap at the stone below us.

The blank hall waits in the shadows across the cavern. Callum is still unconscious in the berserker hall. Tomorrow we'll have to deal with Seren, with Lira, with whatever trap Alekir has laid for us.

But right now, in this moment, none of that matters.

Right now there's just this:

Kaia's heartbeat against my chest.

Malrik's hand in mine.

A bond that finally feels complete.

And for the first time in my life, the chaos inside me is perfectly, impossibly still.

Chapter 29
TORRIC

The bond snaps into place like a door slamming shut.

We all feel it — the ripple through the magic, the vibration in the air. Something clicking. Something becoming *whole*.

Finn's bond. Finally locked.

I exhale slowly, a smile tugging at my mouth despite myself. "About damn time."

"Took them long enough," Aspen agrees. There's warmth in his voice. Real warmth, not his usual controlled calm.

Darian nods, something complicated flickering across his face. The Eds are still clustered around him — dozens of them clinging to his shoulders, his arms, drifting in lazy orbits around his head. He's stopped trying to shake them off. "They deserve it."

A few more Eds have wandered toward the Berserker chamber where Callum lies unconscious, hovering near him like tiny, judgmental nurses.

Footsteps echo from the side corridor.

Kieran walks back in like he was never gone.

I don't even bother pretending I didn't notice where he came from.

"You're impossible," I say. "You know that?"

He doesn't flinch. Doesn't have the decency to look guilty. "I wasn't hiding."

"You were literally in the shadows. Watching them."

"That's where shadows go."

Aspen snorts beside me. Darian suddenly finds the cave wall very interesting.

I should be annoyed. I *am* annoyed. But there's something different in Kieran's expression tonight — a softness around the edges that I've never seen before. Like whatever he saw in that cavern didn't hurt him the way *he* expected it to.

Maybe it even helped.

"You're a creep," I tell him, but there's no heat in it.

"Noted."

But he's gone very still. Those gold eyes are fixed on some middle distance, and for a moment I see everything he's feeling written across his face — longing, hope, something that might be peace.

Then it's gone. Shuttered behind that ancient mask he wears.

But I saw it.

"You good?" I ask quietly.

"Yes." The word comes out softer than I expected. Not defensive. Almost... relieved.

I don't push. Some things don't need words.

The moment stretches. Settles.

Then I roll my shoulders and shift back into practical mode. Someone has to.

"So what's the plan?"

Kieran answers immediately — which means he's been thinking about it the whole time he was lurking in shadows like a lovesick dragon.

"We leave at first light," he says. "The mountain pass won't wait, and every day we delay gives Alekir more time to prepare."

"Food?" Aspen asks.

"There's a grove in the cavern in the center. The fruit there must be magically sustained — it should hold for travel."

I remember seeing it on our way in. Strange trees with glowing fruit that smelled like summer despite being underground. Japti provides, apparently.

"The climb itself," Darian says slowly. "I've studied the maps Kieran showed us. It's... not easy."

"Define 'not easy.'"

"Up to a week of travel. Narrow passes." He pauses. "Avalanche risk."

"Fantastic."

"The footing is unstable in several sections. One wrong step—"

"I get it." I crack my neck. "Deadly mountain. Noted."

Aspen is already calculating — I can see it in the way his eyes go distant. Planning routes, assessing risks, figuring out what we need. That's his gift. Mine is simpler: hit things until they stop being problems.

Mountains are harder to punch than most of my problems.

"What about Callum?"

The question comes from Aspen, but we're all thinking it. The unconscious man a few feet away from us. The traitor who might also be a victim. The weight we'll have to carry — literally.

Kieran's answer is immediate. "He comes with us."

"He can't walk," I point out. "He can barely breathe."

"Then we carry him."

"For a *week*? Up a *mountain*?"

"If necessary."

I exchange a look with Aspen. Classic Kieran. Protective even when he's pretending not to care. Even for someone who betrayed us.

"We'll need something to transport him," Aspen says, already problem-solving. "A sled. Drag-board. Something we can pull."

"Can you build it?"

"If I can find the right materials." He's already looking toward the curved staircase that leads to the upper levels. "I saw workable wood earlier. Fallen branches, some structural pieces that looked salvageable."

Darian leans forward. "We'll need to stabilize it for uneven terrain. Runners wide enough not to catch on rocks, but narrow enough for the passes."

"Padding for Callum," Aspen adds. "Something to keep him secured when the angle shifts."

"Rope," I say. "Lots of it."

They both nod.

Look at us. Actually functioning like a team. Finn would make a joke about it if he were here.

But Finn is... otherwise occupied.

The thought makes me smirk.

"I'll gather materials," I say, pushing off the wall. "Aspen builds, Darian advises. Kieran—"

"I'll check the route," Kieran finishes. "Make sure the path is still clear."

"And brood mysteriously?"

"If time permits."

That might actually be a joke. Hard to tell with him.

Aspen heads for the staircase, his footsteps echoing off the stone. He moves with purpose now — finally something concrete to do after hours of.... listening.

I watch him go, then turn back to Kieran.

He's staring toward the hot spring cavern again. Not moving. Just... looking.

"Hey."

He blinks. Focuses on me.

"You sure you're good?"

For a long moment, he doesn't answer. Then something in his expression shifts — not quite a smile, but close.

"I've waited centuries," he says quietly. "A few more won't kill me."

"That's not what I asked."

"I know." He meets my eyes. "I'm good, Torric. Truly. Seeing them happy..." He trails off. Swallows. "It helps."

I nod slowly. "Okay."

"Okay."

The word hangs between us. An understanding. A truce, maybe, between two men who love the same woman in different ways.

I clap him on the shoulder — probably harder than necessary, but he doesn't flinch. "Don't stay up all night brooding. We need you functional tomorrow."

"I don't brood."

"You absolutely brood."

"I contemplate."

"Same thing. Fancier word."

He almost smiles. Almost.

I head for the stairs, already cataloging what we'll need. Rope. Something soft for padding. Something to bind the frame together. The fire rune on my chest pulses with warmth as I walk.

We're really doing this. Leaving Japti. Climbing a mountain. Chasing Seren and Lira into whatever trap Alekir has set.

And somehow, despite everything, it feels right.

The group is finally aligned. Finn and Kaia, bonded. Malrik steady at the center. Me and Aspen are finding our footing. Even Kieran, for all his ancient baggage, feels more *here* than he has since we arrived.

We're not whole yet. There are still cracks. Still wounds that haven't healed.

But we're closer.

"TORRIC!"

Aspen's voice echoes down from above. "I NEED SOMEONE TALL!"

I sigh.

"Coming," I call back, already moving faster up the stairs.

Some things never change.

Behind me, a low rumble trembles through the stone. Distant. Faint. The kind of sound you feel more than hear.

I pause. Look back.

Darian is frowning at the ceiling. "The mountain's shifting."

"Settling," Kieran corrects. But there's tension in his shoulders that wasn't there before.

"We leave at dawn," I say. "No later."

No one argues.

I take the stairs two at a time, following my brother's voice toward whatever ridiculous task requires my height.

The Eds watch me go, their small dark shapes tracking my movement like a silent audience.

"Stop staring," I mutter at them.

They don't stop.

Of course they don't.

Chapter 30
KAIA

We leave at an ungodly hour.

And by "we leave," I mean Aspen physically drags me out of a warm pile of blankets while Torric stands in the doorway nodding like a drill sergeant who's been waiting for this moment his entire life.

"We have to go now," Aspen says. Calm. Reasonable. Completely unsympathetic to the fact that I got approximately three hours of sleep.

Behind him, Kieran nods solemnly. Agreeing.

I stare at the three of them — the frost twin, the fire twin, and the ancient dragon shifter — standing in a unified front of *we're leaving right this second and you have no say in it.*

"When the hell did all three of you start agreeing on anything?" I demand. "Is this a new form of magic? Did you practice this? Is there a secret meeting I wasn't invited to?"

Nobody answers.

Because they know I'm stalling.

I groan, dragging myself upright. Every muscle in my body aches in ways that are entirely Finn and Malrik's fault. Good ways. *Excellent* ways. Ways that make me want to crawl back to that hot spring and refuse to leave for approximately a century.

Instead, I'm stumbling through Japti's halls at whatever horrible hour this is, trying to remember how my legs work.

Finn falls into step beside me, disgustingly awake. "Morning, Trouble."

"Don't."

"Sleep well?"

"*Don't.*"

He grins. That stupid, beautiful, infuriating grin that makes my chest do things it has no business doing at this hour.

Malrik appears on my other side. Says nothing. Just smirks.

I sigh loudly enough to echo off the stone walls.

"I hate all of you."

"No you don't," Finn says cheerfully.

He's right. I don't. That's the worst part.

Bob drifts alongside me, posture radiating silent judgment. Even my shadows think I'm being dramatic.

The path out of Japti winds upward through tunnels I don't remember from the way in. Kieran leads, because of course he does. The rest of us follow in a loose cluster that's less "tactical formation" and more "barely conscious stumbling."

Behind us: *thump... thump... thump...*

I turn to look.

Kieran is dragging Callum.

Not carrying. *Dragging.* On a makeshift sled of bound wood and vines used as rope, padded with—

I squint.

Is that the moss from the hot spring ledge?

It is. It absolutely is. The same soft, green moss that was under my back while Finn—

Nope. Not thinking about that right now.

Definitely not a keepsake anymore, I decide firmly. *I don't want souvenirs that smell like unconscious traitor and male bonding sweat.*

Aspen catches me looking and straightens with obvious pride. "The runners distribute weight evenly across uneven terrain. Should hold for the full climb."

"I carried the frame," Torric adds, because he can't let his brother have anything without commentary.

"I supervised," Darian mutters. The Eds are still clustered around him — dozens of them clinging to his shoulders, drifting in lazy orbits around his head. He's stopped trying to shake them off. One of them keeps bumping against his ear like an affectionate, shadowy gnat.

Kieran says nothing. Just keeps dragging Callum with the grim determination of a man who refuses to acknowledge he has feelings about any of this.

Thump. Thump. Thump.

The sound follows us up the stairs like a heartbeat.

We emerge from Japti's entrance into cold, gray dawn.

The mountain rises ahead of us — massive, jagged, wreathed in mist that clings to the peaks like it's trying to hide something. The path forward is narrow, carved into the stone at an angle that makes my stomach clench just looking at it.

This is going to be a very long week.

"So," Darian says, clearing his throat. "We should discuss what to expect."

Nobody responds.

He tries again. "The elevation will increase significantly over the next few days. Temperatures will drop. There are sections where the path narrows to single-file, and several areas with avalanche risk—"

Finn's shoulder brushes mine.

Accidentally.

I glance at him. He's looking straight ahead, expression innocent.

His shoulder brushes mine again.

Less accidentally.

Heat pools in my stomach despite the cold air. The bond between us — new, fresh, still settling — pulses with warmth under my skin. I can feel him through it now. His amusement. His want. The way he's deliberately trying to distract me.

"—and we'll need to stay alert for loose footing," Darian continues. "One wrong step on some of these ledges—"

Malrik steps closer behind me. Not touching. Just... *there*. Close enough that I can feel his heat through my clothes.

I lose track of whatever Darian is saying.

"—the cold at higher elevations can be dangerous if we're not prepared. Hypothermia sets in faster than most people—"

Aspen is watching me instead of Darian. There's a knowing glint in his ice-blue eyes that makes me want to throw something at him.

Torric keeps glancing between me and Kieran with an expression that clearly says *I know exactly what happened and I'm going to be insufferable about it.*

Kieran refuses to make eye contact with anyone. He just keeps dragging Callum with more force than strictly necessary, jaw tight, golden eyes fixed on the path ahead.

"—and the structural integrity of the southern pass has been questionable since the last major—"

"Am I talking to myself?" Darian interrupts himself. "Is anyone actually listening?"

Silence.

A few Eds drift past his head like tumbleweeds.

"No," Finn admits. "Sorry. Got distracted."

"By *what*?"

Finn doesn't answer. His shoulder brushes mine again.

Darian pinches the bridge of his nose. "Wonderful. We're all going to die because nobody can focus."

"To be fair," I say, "you picked a really bad morning for a briefing."

"There's no good morning for—" He stops. Processes my words. Looks at me. Looks at Finn. Looks at Malrik, who is still hovering behind me like an anchor with a pulse.

"Ah," he says flatly. "Right. The hot spring."

"We don't need to talk about it," I say quickly.

"We absolutely need to talk about it," Torric says.

"We really don't."

"Kaia." Aspen's voice is mild, but his smirk is devastating. "Everyone knows."

Great.

I look around at them — at Torric's raised eyebrow, Aspen's barely-contained amusement, Darian's aggressively neutral expression, Kieran's refusal to acknowledge anyone exists.

Mouse has somehow migrated to Finn's shoulder. The smug little shadow is practically glowing. Patricia hovers near Darian, notebook flickering — probably documenting everyone's lack of attention for future reference. Finnick does a lazy loop around my head, and I swat at him.

"I hate all of you," I repeat.

"Still no you don't," Finn says.

We walk.

The path climbs steadily, winding along the mountainside in switchbacks that make my thighs burn. The air gets colder. The mist gets thicker. Behind us, the steady *thump-thump-thump* of Callum's sled provides a rhythm that's almost hypnotic.

I should be paying attention to my surroundings. Watching for danger. Staying alert, like Darian said.

Instead, I'm thinking about last night.

About Finn's hands. Malrik's mouth. The way the bond snapped into place like it had been waiting for exactly that moment.

It didn't confuse anything.

That's what I keep coming back to. I expected to feel overwhelmed in a bad way — guilty, uncertain, stretched too thin between too many people who want pieces of me I'm not sure I know how to give.

But I don't feel any of that.

I feel... clarified.

Like puzzle pieces clicking into place. Like the picture was always there, and I'm just now seeing it clearly.

I want all of them.

Not in spite of each other. Not as competition or compromise.

All of them.

And last night — with Finn inside me and Malrik's hands on both of us and the bond blazing to life between us — that want finally made sense. Finally felt possible.

Finn glances at me, catching my expression. "You're thinking loud."

"Shut up."

"Your face is doing the thing."

"What thing?"

"The soft thing. The 'I'm having feelings' thing." He grins. "It's cute."

"I'm not cute."

"You're a little cute."

"I will push you off this mountain."

"Worth it."

Malrik's hand brushes the small of my back. Brief. Grounding. A reminder that he's here. That he sees me, even when I'm spiraling.

The bond with Finn pulses warm. The older bonds, hum steadily beneath my skin.

I want to keep them safe.

All of them.

Whatever's waiting for us at the end of this path — Seren, Lira, Alekir, whatever it is — I want to face it with them beside me. With all of them whole and alive and *mine*.

The ferocity of the feeling catches me off guard.

Bob materializes at my side, edges sharp. Like he felt that surge of protectiveness and approved.

Mine.

When did I start thinking of them like that?

When did it stop feeling like a question?

Kieran stops.

The sudden halt ripples through the group — Aspen nearly walking into Torric, Finn grabbing my arm to keep me from stumbling.

"What?" Torric asks. "What is it?"

Kieran doesn't answer immediately. His golden eyes are fixed on the path ahead, narrowed against the mist.

Then I feel it.

A rumble. Low. Deep. The kind of sound you feel in your bones more than hear with your ears.

The stone beneath my feet vibrates.

"That normal?" Aspen asks quietly.

Kieran's jaw tightens.

"...No."

"Fantastic," Torric says.

The rumble fades. The mountain settles. But the tension doesn't leave Kieran's shoulders, and I see his grip tighten on the rope attached to Callum's sled.

"We keep moving," he says. "Stay close. Stay quiet."

My shadows cluster tight — Bob at point, Patricia and Linda flanking, the Eds swirling in a nervous orbit around Darian. Even Finnick has gone still.

Nobody argues.

We walk.

The mist swallows the path behind us.

And I want the hot spring back.

Chapter 31

KIERAN

Four days.

Four days of climbing. Four days of wind that cuts through every layer. Four days of narrow ledges and loose stone and cold so deep it settles into bone.

We're a little past halfway. I can feel it in the thinning air, the way the mountain's magic presses against my skin. The sanctuary at the peak is close enough now that its pull is unmistakable.

Close enough to feel.

Not close enough to reach.

I take point because I refuse to let anyone else risk the edges. The path here is barely a path at all — more suggestion than structure, crumbling stone that shifts under every footfall. One wrong step and the mountain will swallow you whole.

Behind me, the group moves in exhausted silence. No one has the energy for conversation anymore. Even Finn has gone quiet, his usual chaos muted by cold and fatigue.

I check on her without meaning to.

It's become reflexive. A glance over my shoulder every few minutes to confirm she's still there, still upright, still breathing. I tell myself it's tactical. That I'm monitoring the group's weakest points.

I'm lying.

Kaia walks a few paces behind Torric and Finn. Her gait is stiff — exhaustion she won't admit to, wearing at muscles that have been pushed too hard for too long. Bob prowls at her side, edges sharp. Mouse scouts the ledges ahead, darting between shadows with predatory focus.

Her shadows are wrapped close today. Tighter than normal. Protective in a way that tells me she's more strained than she's letting on.

Her breath fogs in the air. She keeps rubbing her arms.

I hate that I can't give her my coat anymore. That she wouldn't accept it if I tried.

The boulder came two days ago.

Loose stone, weakened by frost. It broke free without warning — a crack, a rumble, and then half the mountainside was falling toward Darian.

I moved first.

Her shadows moved faster.

The Eds swarmed — dozens of them, throwing themselves between Darian and the crushing weight of stone. The impact was brutal. When the dust cleared, several of them were just gone. Crushed. Unmade.

Kaia gasped. Her hand went to her chest — to the bond, I realized. The one she shares with all of us. The one that includes him now, whether any of us like it or not.

That's when I understood.

She won't let Darian die. Even now. Even after everything.

Not forgiveness. Not yet.

But connection.

And connection is what terrifies me.

I've started noticing the pattern.

It's subtle. The kind of thing you'd miss if you weren't watching. If you weren't cataloging every movement, every glance, every unconscious shift of weight.

But I am watching. I always am.

Every time Darian stumbles, Kaia glances back.

Every time the air thins or the footing gets treacherous, he moves closer to her. Automatically. Like gravity.

Every time she slows, his pace matches hers.

She tries to ignore it. Pretends she doesn't notice the way their orbits keep intersecting.

Her shadows do not pretend.

Patricia's notebook flickers with pointed light whenever Darian drifts too near. Bob inserts himself physically between them more than once — but not aggressively. A wall of shadow and silent judgment.

Mouse growls each time Darian crosses some invisible threshold. Low. Warning.

Darian ignores all of it. Or doesn't notice. Or doesn't care.

The Eds still cluster around him, despite losing several of their number to the boulder. Loyal to a fault. Protective in ways I don't fully understand.

I watch Kaia almost laugh at something Finn says.

I look away immediately.

We stop when the mountain finally forces us to.

The wind is brutal here — cutting sideways across the path with enough force to stagger. There's no shelter. No caves. No convenient overhangs. Just exposed stone and open sky and cold that seeps through everything.

Everyone is staggering.

Kaia tries to insist we keep going. "We're so close. We can push through—"

"We can't." Finn's voice is gentle but firm. "Trouble, look at yourself. Look at all of us. We need to rest."

She opens her mouth to argue.

Closes it.

Nods, once.

Bob circles the perimeter aggressively, bristling at shadows that aren't there. Mouse curls at Kaia's feet, a small warm weight against the cold. Finnick attempts to imitate Aspen's shivering — an exaggerated, full-body convulsion — and Bob shoves him into a snowdrift without breaking patrol stride.

Aspen snorts. It's the closest thing to laughter we've had in days.

I approach her while the others are settling.

"You should take this." I hold out my coat.

She doesn't look at me. "I'm fine."

"You're freezing."

"I said I'm fine."

I let a beat pass. "The path gets worse ahead. You should rest while you can."

She nods. Still doesn't look at me.

Her shadows stiffen between us — not aggressive, but watchful. Wary. Like they're not sure what I'm going to do next.

Neither am I.

I step back. That's what I do now.

As the group settles in for the night, I find a position at the edge of our makeshift camp. Close enough to respond if needed. Far enough to give her space.

I watch without meaning to. Again. Always.

Darian shifts closer to the group for warmth. His movements are stiff with cold, his face pale.

Kaia shifts to give him room.

She doesn't seem to realize she's doing it.

Mouse growls once — low, disapproving — but doesn't stop her.

Finn watches from across the camp, biting his cheek. His chaos magic sparks faintly in the darkness, restless.

Malrik pretends not to notice. His silver eyes are fixed on the path ahead, but his jaw is tight.

Torric is simmering. I can feel the heat radiating off him, anger he's barely containing.

And Darian just... settles. Accepts the space she gave him. Doesn't acknowledge what it means.

I see it all with brutal clarity.

Darian is a gravity well.

Kaia is orbiting without realizing it.

And I am losing the one thing I've been pretending I didn't want anymore.

Halfway up a goddamn mountain, and somehow he's still the one she gravitates toward.

I hate how unsurprised I am.

Chapter 32
KAIA

Mouse finds the cave.

One moment he's scouting ahead, a dark streak against the white. The next, he's back at my feet, tail flicking toward a shadow in the rock face I would have walked right past.

"There?" I manage through chattering teeth.

He flicks his tail again. *Obviously.*

The entrance is narrow — barely wide enough for Torric to squeeze through sideways — but it opens into a space large enough for all of us. Dry. Sheltered from the wind. Cold, but not the killing cold of the exposed mountain.

It's the closest thing to salvation we've found in days.

"Thank the gods," Finn breathes, stumbling in behind me.

Nobody argues. Nobody has the energy.

Torric gets a fire going with a flick of his wrist — his rune flaring bright before settling into steady flames. The warmth spreads slowly, pushing back the worst of the chill. We cluster around it like moths, drawn to the heat with a desperation that would be embarrassing if we weren't all feeling it.

My shadows settle around us. Bob takes position near the cave entrance, a dark sentinel against whatever might try to follow us in. Patricia's notebook dims as she drifts toward the fire. Linda hovers near Aspen, who's already half-asleep against the cave wall. The Eds cluster around Darian, as always — fewer of them now, after the boulder.

I try not to think about that.

Mouse curls at my feet, a warm weight against my frozen toes. Finnick attempts to burrow into my coat pocket and gets batted away by Walter, who's taken up residence there without asking permission.

"We should set watches," Kieran says.

"We should sleep," Finn counters. "All of us. For once."

"The mountain—"

"The mountain will still be there in the morning." Finn's voice is exhausted. "And we'll be useless if we're dead on our feet when whatever's waiting at the top."

Kieran's jaw tightens. But he doesn't argue.

We settle.

Torric and Aspen take one side of the fire, gravitating toward each other the way they always do. Finn sprawls nearby, chaos magic crackling faintly as he finally lets himself relax. Malrik positions himself where he can see everyone — always watching, always steady.

Kieran takes the spot nearest the entrance. Even now, he can't stop guarding.

And Darian...

Darian hovers.

I can feel him through the bond — that strange thread that's been humming wrong since the moment he kneeled in beside my bedroll the night he found us. Found me. He wants to be close. He's terrified to be close. He's caught between the pull and the guilt, and I can feel every inch of his hesitation.

My shadows make the choice for him.

Bob shifts, creating a gap beside me. Not an invitation — more like a command.

Darian freezes. Stares at the space. Stares at me.

"Just lie down," I mutter, too tired to navigate whatever emotional minefield is happening inside his head. "You're letting the heat out."

He lies down.

Stiff as a board. Arms at his sides. Barely breathing.

Like he's afraid any movement will be the wrong one.

I'm too exhausted to deal with it. The fire is warm. The cave is dry. My muscles ache in ways I didn't know muscles could ache.

I close my eyes.

The bond hums between us — wrong at the edges, but not threatening. Not anymore.

I fall asleep.

I wake because I'm warm.

Not fire-warm. Not Torric-rune warm.

Body warm.

A slow, steady heat pressed against my spine, radiating through frozen muscles I didn't realize were still clenched.

It takes me a breath to understand why.

Darian.

At some point during the night, he must have shifted. Or I did. Or both. But now his chest is flush against my back — one long, solid line of heat.

And his arm—

His arm is around my waist.

Just resting there. Fingers grazing the fabric of my shirt like he didn't dare hold on. Like even in sleep he was trying not to take too much space.

My breath catches.

The bond answers. A low hum deep under my ribs, warmer than it's ever felt. Not right. Not whole. But quiet.

Mouse lifts his head from where he's curled against my shins, blinks slow violet eyes at the scene, then settles again — tail flicking in what looks a lot like approval.

Traitor.

I should move. I should pull away. I should—

A small, frustrated sound slips out of me instead.

Too many days.

Too many nights freezing, fighting, running. Too many moments replaying the hot spring in my head — Finn's hands, Malrik's mouth, the way they took me apart between them. Too much tension coiled under my skin with nowhere to go.

I've been wound tight for days. Aching. Wanting. And now there's a warm body pressed against mine, and I'm too tired to pretend I don't feel it.

My hips shift before I can think. Just a little. Just enough to ease pressure.

Except easing anything is a lie.

Darian makes a sound — low, rough, unguarded. His fingers flex on my waist.

I go still.

His breath hitches against the back of my neck. And he's—

Oh gods.

He's hard.

It's not intentional. He's still asleep. His breathing is slow and uneven in the way people breathe when dreaming. But his hips have molded to mine, and he's warm everywhere, and I—

I should stop.

I don't.

I roll my hips back again, slower this time, deliberate in a way that only happens when I'm too tired to lie to myself.

A sharp exhale ghosts over my neck.

The arm around my waist tightens — reflex, not choice.

"Kaia..." Barely a whisper. Barely awake. Broken at the edges.

Something hot coils low in my stomach.

The bond sparks — once, bright enough I almost gasp. Shadows stir around us. Patricia's notebook flickers like she's scribbling frantic commentary in her sleep. Bob's posture shifts, not disapproving — watching.

I should stop.

I push back again instead.

This time, the sound he makes is wrecked. Uncontrolled. Pure instinct.

His hand slides — slow, hesitant — up the line of my stomach, fingers curling as if asking a question he doesn't dare voice.

His nose brushes the shell of my ear. His breath stutters like it hurts to want.

I bite my lip. Hard.

Months of tension unravel in the space of a heartbeat.

I grind back once more, deliberately, a long drag of pressure that pulls a curse from his throat.

His forehead drops to my shoulder. His grip on my waist tightens. His body shudders against mine.

"Don't—" he breathes. "I— gods, Kaia, I can't—"

He's awake now. Barely. Fighting himself.

I should stop.

"Please..." he whispers, like he's begging me to stop or begging me not to — he doesn't even know.

Neither do I.

But I know what I want.

Chapter 33

DARIAN

"Please…"

The word escapes before I can stop it. Before I'm even fully awake.

But I'm awake now.

Consciousness crashes through me like cold water — and with it, the horrifying awareness of exactly what's happening.

Kaia is pressed against me. My arm is around her waist. My hand is sliding up her stomach like it has any right to be there. And I'm hard against her, grinding into her like a man who's forgotten every reason this is wrong.

The arena. My corrupted magic. Thorne's voice in my head, telling me exactly how to break her—

I freeze.

Every muscle locks. My hand stops moving. My hips go still despite the ache, the need, the desperate want clawing at my chest.

Don't hurt her. Don't scare her. Don't be what he made you.

"Darian." Her voice is rough with sleep. With want. "Don't stop."

My heart slams against my ribs.

"Kaia, I—" The words come out fractured. "I can't. I shouldn't. The bond between us is— it's not real, it's not—"

"It feels real."

She shifts against me, her ass grinding back against my cock, and the movement drags a sound from my throat I can't control.

"That's the corruption," I manage. "That's Thorne's magic making you think—"

"No." She twists in my arms. Faces me. Her violet eyes are dark in the firelight, pupils blown wide. "That was Thorne's magic. This is me."

I stare at her.

She's so close. Close enough that her breath mingles with mine. Close enough that I can feel the heat radiating off her skin.

"I've been thinking about this for days," she whispers. "About being touched. About wanting. And I kept telling myself it was just— Finn and Malrik got under my skin, and I couldn't stop replaying it, and—" She stops. Swallows. "But it's not just them. It's you too. It's been you for longer than I wanted to admit."

Something cracks in my chest.

"You don't want me." The words hurt coming out. "You want what the bond makes you feel. You want—"

"I want *you*." Her hand finds my face. Cups my jaw. Forces me to look at her when every instinct is screaming to look away. "The real you. Not the bond. I don't care about the corruption. I want you."

"Kaia—"

"Tell me to stop." Her voice is steady. Certain. "Tell me you don't want this, and I'll stop. I'll pull away. We'll pretend this never happened."

I should tell her to stop.

I should be strong enough to do that.

But she's looking at me like I'm something worth wanting. Like the broken, corrupted, ruined thing I've become might still deserve to be touched.

And I am so tired of fighting.

"I can't." The confession tears out of me. Raw. Wrecked. "I can't tell you to stop. I've wanted you for so long it feels like dying, and I—"

She kisses me.

The taste of her floods my senses — soft and desperate and *real*, nothing like the forced intimacy of the arena. This is her choice. Her want. Her mouth moving against mine like she's been waiting for exactly this moment.

I'm lost.

My hands find her hips. Pull her closer. She swings a leg over me, straddling my waist, and the heat of her pressed against my cock makes every thought in my head dissolve.

Around us, I feel the shadows shift.

They're not hostile. They're watching.

I can feel it.

Mouse makes a sound that might be approval.

They're not stopping this.

They're not stopping this.

"Are you sure?" I manage against her lips. "Kaia— I need you to be sure—"

"I'm sure." She rocks against me, grinding down on my cock through the thin fabric separating us, and stars explode behind my eyes. "I've been sure. I just didn't know how to tell you."

"We have to be quiet," I breathe. "The others—"

"I know." She's already tugging at my shirt. "I know, I'll be quiet, just—"

Her hands find bare skin and she gasps. Not quiet.

"Shh—" I clamp a hand over her mouth, but I'm laughing despite myself. Despite everything. "You're terrible at this."

She bites my palm. I yank it back.

"Your fault," she whispers. "You're the one who—"

I kiss her to shut her up.

Her shirt comes off. Then the rest. Layers shed in clumsy, urgent movements until there's nothing between us but skin and heat and the bond humming in my chest.

The wrongness is still there — that sour twist I've carried since Thorne first gave me corrupted magic. But it's quieter now. Muted. Like something inside it is waiting to see what happens next.

I kiss my way down her body. Slow. Deliberate. Memorizing every sound she makes, every hitch of breath, every place that makes her gasp.

"Darian—" She's squirming. "You don't have to—"

"I want to." I press my mouth to her stomach. Lower. "I want to taste you. I've thought about it for months. Let me."

The sound she makes is not quiet.

Someone across the cave shifts in their sleep.

We both freeze.

A long moment. Breathing. Waiting.

Nothing.

"You need to be quieter than that," I murmur against her thigh.

"Then stop being so—" She gestures vaguely at me. At my mouth. "*That.*"

"No."

I spread her open with my fingers.

She's soaked. The scent of her arousal hits me and my cock throbs painfully.

"Gods, Kaia." The words come out reverent. Broken. "You're so fucking wet."

"I told you." Her voice is strained. "Days. I've been like this for days."

I drag my tongue through her folds.

Her hips buck against my face. A moan escapes — too loud, way too loud.

I pull back just enough to nip at her inner thigh. "Shh."

She whimpers.

I don't stop.

I work her with my tongue — long, slow strokes that have her writhing. Quick flicks against her clit that make her thighs shake around my head. I push two fingers inside her, curling them, finding that spot—

She bites her lip to muffle her scream.

Somewhere across the fire, Torric shifts. Mutters something in his sleep.

I fuck her with my fingers while I suck her clit, and she comes apart in under a minute. Clenching around me, soaking my hand, trembling so hard I feel it through every point of contact.

The bond *flares*.

Not the cold, corrupted pulse I'm used to. Something warmer. Brighter. Like light breaking through cracked glass.

I crawl back up her body before she's finished trembling.

"I need—" She reaches for me, fingers fumbling at my pants. Her hands wrap around my cock and I have to bite my own tongue to keep from groaning. "I need you inside me. Now."

"Kaia—"

"Now." She strokes me — once, twice — and my hips jerk into her grip. "Please, Darian. I need to feel you."

I kick off my pants. Position myself at her entrance. The head of my cock slides through her wetness and we both shudder.

One last breath.

One last chance to stop this.

She looks up at me — flushed, wrecked, beautiful — and says, "Choose me."

I push inside her.

Fuck.

She's so tight. So wet. So impossibly perfect around me that I have to stop moving or this will be over before it starts.

"Oh gods—" Her nails dig into my shoulders. "You're— you're so—"

"I know." I'm trembling. Buried to the hilt inside her and barely holding on. "I know, just— give me a second—"

"Don't want a second." She rolls her hips, taking me even deeper, and a groan rips out of me that's far too loud.

Across the fire, Finn makes a sound in his sleep. Torric shifts again.

I go still.

Kaia doesn't.

She clenches around me deliberately, inner walls squeezing my cock in a way that makes my vision blur.

"Kaia—" It comes out strangled. "We're going to wake—"

"Then fuck me fast and make me come before they do."

Gods help me.

I pull back. Thrust in. Hard.

Her mouth falls open in a silent scream. Her back arches off the ground. Her legs wrap around my waist and pull me deeper.

I set a punishing pace — fast, deep strokes that have the obscene sound of wet skin slapping against wet skin filling the cave. There's no way the others are sleeping through this. No way anyone could miss the sounds she's making, the sounds *I'm* making.

"Yes—" She's gasping with every thrust. "Right there— don't stop— *Darian*—"

I shift the angle. Drive into her harder. Feel her tighten around me every time I bottom out.

"You feel so good." The words spill out without permission. "So tight, so wet— I've wanted this for so long— wanted *you*—"

"Harder—"

I give her harder.

The cave floor is cold against my knees but I don't care. Nothing matters except the clench of her around my cock, the sounds she's making, the way the bond is blazing between us.

And then I feel it.

Eyes on us.

I look up without stopping.

Kieran.

He's awake. Propped on one elbow near the cave entrance. Gold eyes gleaming in the firelight as he watches me thrust into her.

Our gazes lock.

I should stop. Should feel shame, embarrassment, something other than this dark, possessive heat that floods my chest.

Instead, I hold his stare and drive into her harder.

Mine, the look says. *Right now, in this moment, she's mine.*

Something flickers across Kieran's face. Not anger. Not jealousy.

Hunger.

Heat coils low in my stomach — and not just from Kaia clenching around me. Something about his eyes on us, on *me*, the weight of his attention while I'm buried inside her—

I don't let myself examine it.

I just thrust harder.

He doesn't look away.

Neither do I.

I fuck her while he watches. Let him see exactly how she responds to me — the way her back arches, the way she clenches around my cock, the way his name isn't the one falling from her lips.

"Darian—" She's close. I can feel it through the bond, building like a wave. "I'm going to—"

"Come for me." I tear my gaze from Kieran's. Look down at her. "Give me what I want, Little Shadow. I want to feel it."

She shatters.

Her whole body convulses beneath me, inner walls clenching so tight around my cock I see stars. My name rips from her throat — loud enough to wake everyone, and I don't fucking care.

Aspen jerks upright across the fire. Finn's eyes fly open. Malrik is already awake, watching with an expression I can't read.

I don't stop.

The orgasm crashes through me like a wave — and with it, something else. Something deeper.

Whatever Thorne did to me — whatever twisted magic he forced into my veins — I feel it *shatter*. A pressure I've carried so long I forgot it was there suddenly releases, like a fist unclenching around my heart. Something snaps, dissolves, burns away.

I bury myself as deep as I can go and spill into her with a groan that echoes off the stone walls.

What's left feels... different.

Clean.

Real.

Mine.

Light pulses under my skin. Actual light — warm and golden, the way my magic used to feel before everything went wrong. It flows through the bond, into Kaia, around us both.

Her shadows react.

Walter flares bright, absorbing something from the air. I feel Patricia's frantic energy, Bob's posture shifting from guarded to accepting. Mouse makes a sound of satisfaction.

When I finally look back toward the cave entrance, Kieran's eyes are closed.

Feigning sleep.

We both know he isn't.

The cave is silent except for our ragged breathing. Everyone is awake. Everyone saw. Everyone *heard*.

I should feel shame.

I don't.

"Darian." Kaia's voice is wrecked. Her hands find my face. "What was—"

"The bond." I'm still trembling. Still inside her. Still trying to remember how to breathe. "The corruption. It's— I felt it break. I felt—"

I can't explain it.

But she feels it too. I know she does. Through the connection that's finally, *finally* clean.

"It doesn't hurt anymore," she whispers. Wonder in her voice.

"No." I press my forehead to hers. "It doesn't."

The cave floor is cold. The air is freezing where sweat has cooled on my skin. My knees ache from the stone. And I'm still buried inside her, softening now, our combined release slick between us.

None of it matters.

"Stay," she says quietly. Echoing what she said to Finn. The same word. The same weight.

Across the fire, Finn clears his throat. "So. That happened."

"Shut up, Finn," multiple voices say in unison.

Despite everything — the awkwardness, the exposure, the fact that I just fucked Kaia in front of all of them — I laugh.

She laughs too.

I don't deserve this. I don't deserve her.

But I stay anyway.

Chapter 34
KAIA

The silence is deafening.

My body is still buzzing — pleasure, exhaustion, something electric I don't recognize humming under my skin. Sweat cools on my bare shoulders. The cave floor is cold beneath me. Darian is still inside me, softening, his weight a warm anchor against the chill.

But I don't regret it, not even a little bit.

Everyone is awake.

I know this without looking. I can feel their eyes on us like physical pressure. Finn's shock. Malrik's steady calm. Torric's embarrassed heat. Aspen's stunned confusion. Kieran's—

Kieran's *hunger*.

It hits me like a wave, and I gasp.

"Kaia?" Darian shifts, concern flooding his voice. "Are you—"

He pulls out of me, and the world tilts.

It's not pain. It's not pleasure. It's *everything* — sensation flooding in from six different directions at once, crashing through me like a dam breaking.

Darian.

Warmth. Guilt dissolving. Awe. Devotion. Relief so overwhelming it steals my breath.

Finn.

Shock. Jealousy tangled with pride. Concern. His chaos magic sparking at the back of my skull like static electricity.

Malrik.

Steady, heavy calm. Protective tension. Something sharp and dark beneath it — possession, maybe.

Kieran.

Hunger. Restraint. A deep, primal thrum I've never felt from him before. The weight of his attention even with his eyes closed.

Torric.

Embarrassed amusement. Heat he doesn't want to acknowledge. Awe at something shifting.

Aspen.

Pure shock. Emotional overwhelm. Empathy so heightened it bleeds into my own panic.

All of them. All at once.

Too much.

My breath stutters. My chest tightens. My fingers go numb against the stone floor. My shadows ripple around me — frantic, disorganized, like leaves in a windstorm.

I try to sit up.

The cave tilts sideways.

"Kaia—" Darian's hand finds my arm.

Another wave crashes through me. His guilt, his fear, his desperate need to know he didn't hurt me — all of it flooding the bond so intensely I flinch.

He yanks his hand back like I burned him.

"I'm sorry—" His voice cracks. "I didn't mean to— I shouldn't have—"

"No, that's not—" I can't finish. Can't explain. The words won't come because everything is *too loud*.

The fire crackles. Too loud.

Someone shifts on stone. Too loud.

Breathing. Heartbeats. The rustle of fabric.

Too loud.

Heat rises in my face — humiliation and want tangling until I can't tell them apart. Every single one of them saw. Heard. Watched Darian take me apart on the cave floor. And now I'm falling apart in a completely different way, and I can't even hide it.

"Something's wrong." Finn is already moving, chaos magic sparking around him as he scrambles toward me. "Kaia, what's—"

His hand brushes my shoulder and I *feel* him — panic, love, guilt, the chaotic swirl of his magic reaching for mine — and a sound tears from my throat.

"Don't—"

I don't know if I'm talking to him or to all of them or to the bonds themselves.

"Everyone stop." Malrik's voice cuts through the chaos. His voice reaches me before his emotions do — calm, commanding, an anchor in the storm. "Give her space. Now."

Finn freezes mid-reach. His magic spikes again, crackling visibly in the firelight. He looks like he's been gutted. Torric and Aspen go still. Even Kieran, propped on his elbow with those gold eyes finally open, doesn't move.

But it doesn't help.

I can still feel them. All of them. Pressing against my mind like hands reaching through fog.

"I can't—" My voice comes out broken. "It's too much. I can feel— *all* of you. Everything. I can't—"

My heart is racing. Vision tunneling. Hands shaking against the cold stone.

The bonds are pulling in six directions at once, and I'm going to fly apart.

Bob surges forward.

He plants himself between me and the others — a wall of shadow and silent fury. Steve stumbles into position behind him, trips over his own edges, but stays there anyway. Determined.

And Mouse.

Mouse climbs onto my chest.

His small, warm weight settles against my sternum, and he *vibrates*. A low, steady purr that I feel more than hear. The rhythm syncs with my heartbeat — or maybe my heartbeat syncs with him. Either way, it's grounding. Real. Something to focus on that isn't the overwhelming flood of everyone else's emotions.

Walter pulses somewhere above us. Slow. Steady. The chaotic static screaming through my skull starts to dim, and I don't know if that's him or the breathing or Mouse or all of it together.

My shadows wrap around me like a cocoon.

The sensory input starts to fade. Just slightly. Just enough.

"Kaia." Malrik's voice, from a few feet away. He hasn't moved closer. He's kneeling, hands visible, posture deliberately non-threatening. "Breathe with me. In for four. Hold for four. Out for four."

I try.

My breath stutters. Catches.

"Again," he says. Steady. Patient. "In for four."

I breathe in. One. Two. Three. Four.

"Hold."

I hold.

"Out for four."

I breathe out. Shaky. But real.

"Good." There's no judgment in his voice. No frustration. Just that steady, anchoring calm. "Again."

We breathe together. In. Hold. Out.

The panic starts to loosen its grip on my chest.

But the bonds are still *there*. Still pressing. Still too loud, too much, too raw.

"It was never supposed to feel like this," I gasp out. "The bonds. They were— before, they were—"

"Muted," Kieran says quietly.

I look at him. He's still by the cave entrance, still maintaining distance, but his gold eyes are sharp with understanding.

"The corruption," he continues. "It wasn't just affecting Darian's magic. It was dampening your connections to all of us. You weren't feeling the bonds as they truly are."

"And now?" My voice cracks. "Now I feel *everything*. I feel Darian's guilt and Finn's panic and Malrik's— whatever that is— and you—"

I stop.

Because I can feel what Kieran is feeling.

Hunger. Want. A restraint so iron-clad it must be painful.

And beneath it all, a desperate, aching hope he doesn't want me to see.

Heat pools low in my stomach — unbidden, unexpected, entirely inappropriate given I'm lying naked on a cave floor in the middle of a panic attack. My body doesn't seem to care about timing.

Not now. Gods, not now.

"Yes," Kieran says softly. "Now you feel us as we truly are."

Finn is at my side before I register him moving.

"Hey. Hey, look at me." His hands find my face, tilting it toward him. His green eyes are bright, a little wild. "What do you need? Tell me what to do."

"I don't—" The words tangle. "I can't make it quieter. I can feel *all* of you and it's—"

"Okay." He's nodding, thumbs brushing my cheekbones. "Okay. We'll figure it out. We'll—"

But he doesn't have an answer. None of them do.

And I can feel his frustration through the bond now — hot and sharp and directed entirely at himself for not being able to fix this with sheer force of will.

I love him for trying. Even when there's nothing to try.

Darian hasn't moved.

He's still beside me, close but not touching, and his guilt is the loudest thing in the room. It pounds through our newly purified bond like a drum — shame, self-loathing, the absolute certainty that he's broken something irreparable.

"Stop." The word comes out sharper than I intend. "Darian, please— I can feel your guilt and it's— I can't—"

"I'm sorry—" He pulls back further. "I'll go. I'll leave. I'll—"

"No." I grab his wrist before he can flee. Force myself to hold on even though the contact sends another wave of emotion crashing through me. "I *chose* you. I chose this. Whatever broke— it needed to break. I just—"

I don't know how to explain it.

I don't know how to make any of them understand that this isn't rejection. This is the opposite of rejection. This is feeling them so completely, so intensely, that I can't process all of it at once.

"She needs rest," Malrik says quietly. "Whatever just happened— whatever shifted— she needs time to adjust."

"The bond purified." Kieran's voice is distant. Almost reverent. "She's feeling a true Valkyrie connection for the first time. It will be overwhelming until she learns to regulate it."

"Can you?" Aspen asks softly. "Regulate it?"

"I don't know." Honesty. All I have left. "I don't know how to make it quieter. I don't know how to not feel all of you all the time."

The cave goes silent.

Then Finn laughs. Broken. Wet.

"Well," he says, "guess we all need to work on our emotional hygiene."

"Shut up, Finn," I whisper. But I'm almost smiling.

Mouse purrs louder against my chest. Linda drifts close, her presence soft and worried, hovering near my shoulder. Carl drops from somewhere near the ceiling to patrol the perimeter, giving Bob permission to finally ease his rigid stance.

"Sleep," Malrik says. It's not a suggestion. "We'll figure the rest out in the morning."

But I can't.

Every time I close my eyes, the bonds press harder. Six heartbeats that aren't mine. Six sets of emotions bleeding into my skull. Darian's guilt. Finn's chaos. Malrik's steady thrum. Torric's heat. Aspen's overwhelming empathy.

And Kieran.

Always Kieran.

That ancient hunger, coiled tight beneath centuries of restraint.

"It's not working." My voice comes out thin. Desperate. "I can't— they won't quiet down. I can't make them—"

"I can."

Kieran's voice cuts through the noise.

Everyone goes still.

He's standing now, though I didn't see him move. Gold eyes fixed on me with an intensity that makes my breath catch.

"I can quiet them," he says. "If you let me."

Malrik glances at me. Not suspicious — just checking. *Your call.*

"How?" I manage.

"Dragons are cold-blooded." Kieran doesn't look away from me. "Our internal rhythms are slower. Steadier. I've had centuries to learn how to still my mind. How to create silence inside myself." He pauses. Swallows. "I can share that with you. Through the bond. But I have to be close. I have to—"

He stops.

The unspoken words hang in the air.

I have to hold you.

Nobody objects.

That's what gets me. A month ago, Torric would've burst into flames. Finn would've made a sharp joke to deflect. Malrik's shadows would've shifted protectively.

Now they just... wait. Watch me. Let me decide.

Because somewhere between Japti and the hot springs and four days of climbing this frozen hellscape together, Kieran stopped being the enemy.

He's just the one I haven't forgiven yet.

"Can you really make it stop?" I ask. "The noise?"

"I can quiet it." His voice is rough. Careful. "Not forever. But long enough for you to rest. Long enough for your mind to adjust."

I should say no.

Not because I'm afraid of him. Not because the others would stop me. But because letting him hold me means something. Means cracking open a door I've kept firmly shut since I learned what he did.

But I'm so tired.

And the bonds are so loud.

Finn catches my eye across the dim cave. His expression is unreadable, but he gives me the smallest nod.

It's okay. We've got you either way.

"Okay," I whisper.

Something cracks open in his expression. Hope. Disbelief. A vulnerability I've never seen him show.

Darian squeezes my hand once, then pulls back. Giving space. His guilt still hums through the bond, but it's quieter now — tempered by something that might be relief.

Kieran moves.

It's nothing like the others. No urgency. No hesitation. Just that ancient, deliberate grace — a predator who's learned patience over centuries of hunting.

He settles behind me. Close. So close I can feel the heat of him through my bare skin.

"May I?"

His voice is barely a murmur. Asking permission for something he could just take. Something he *has* taken before, in other ways.

But not this time.

"Yes."

His arms wrap around me.

And the world goes quiet.

Not silent — not completely. I can still feel the bonds, still sense the others at the edges of my awareness. But it's like someone turned down the volume. Muffled the chaos. Wrapped everything in thick, heavy wool.

Kieran's presence bleeds through the bond — not emotion, not thought, just *stillness*. Ancient and vast and impossibly calm. Like sinking into deep water. Like the moment before dawn when the world holds its breath.

"Breathe," he murmurs against my hair. "Match my rhythm."

I try.

His chest rises and falls against my back. Slow. Steady. Slower than any human could manage. The rhythm of something old. Something patient. Something that has learned to wait for centuries.

My breathing syncs with his.

The bonds quiet further.

"That's it." His voice is barely audible. "Let me carry it. Just for now. Just until you can rest."

I should be tense. Should be wary. Should be holding myself stiff and separate, maintaining the distance I've kept since he forced the bonds on me.

Instead, I melt into him.

My body remembers this. Remembers the safety of him, the steadiness of his presence, the way he used to make me feel like I was precious. Like I was everything.

A blanket slides over me as I let out a breath.

The betrayal is still there. The hurt. The broken trust.

But so is this.

Mouse settles against my chest, purring in that low, resonant way that matches Kieran's breathing. Linda drifts close, her worry finally easing. Somewhere near the cave entrance, Bob's rigid posture softens — just slightly.

"I'm sorry." Kieran's words are so quiet I almost miss them. "For all of it. For everything I took from you. For every choice I made without asking."

I don't respond.

I'm not ready to forgive him. Not yet. Maybe not for a long time.

But I don't pull away either.

And beneath the quiet — beneath the ancient calm he's pouring through the bond — I feel something else.

His want.

Leaking through despite his control. That same pull I've been ignoring for weeks, now pressed against my bare back, wrapped around me in the dark. He's trying to hide it. Trying to keep it locked down beneath centuries of discipline.

But the bond doesn't lie.

He wants me. Has wanted me this whole time. And even now — even shielding me, protecting me, asking nothing in return — that want bleeds through like heat through cracked stone.

Something stirs low in my stomach. Inappropriate. Undeniable.

Not now, I tell myself firmly. *Not yet.*

But my body files it away. Remembers it. Stores it somewhere I'll have to deal with later.

"Sleep," Kieran whispers. "I've got you."

For the first time since the bond purified, I believe it.

I close my eyes.

The bonds hum softly — six threads of warmth and want, muted now, bearable. Darian's guilt. Finn's complicated love. Malrik's steady presence. Torric's banked heat. Aspen's gentle concern. And Kieran — Kieran's ancient patience, wrapped around me like armor.

I'm not ready to forgive him.

But maybe I'm ready to stop running.

The thought follows me into darkness, and for once, it doesn't feel like surrender.

It feels like the beginning of something centuries old.

Chapter 35
MALRIK

The fire crackles.

For the first time in days, nobody is panicking.

Kaia is asleep in Kieran's arms, her breathing steady, Mouse purring on her chest. Bob has settled near the cave entrance — still on guard, but his edges have softened into something almost relaxed. Patricia's notebook is dim. Even Finnick has stopped his constant fidgeting, draped across a rock like a shadow-shaped cat.

And Callum is still unconscious.

Kieran hasn't moved in over an hour. His eyes are open, faintly glowing, fixed on nothing — the vigilance of someone who's decided sleep is optional when something precious is in his arms.

But the rest of us?

We're finally breathing.

Finn is the first to break the silence.

"So." He stretches his legs toward the fire, groaning dramatically. "That happened."

Torric snorts. "Which part?"

"All of it?" Finn gestures vaguely. "The sex. The screaming. The bond explosion. The part where Kieran became a living weighted blanket."

"I am providing a service," Kieran says without looking up.

"You're cuddling. It's cuddling. Just admit it."

The corner of Kieran's mouth twitches. He doesn't deny it.

I feel something loosen in my chest. Not everything — we're still on a frozen mountain with something wrong waiting at the top — but enough. Enough to remember that we're not just soldiers marching toward disaster.

We're also... this. Whatever this is.

Darian shifts against the cave wall.

He's been quiet since Kaia fell asleep, after he hurried back into his clothes. Pale. Shoulders too tight. I've been watching him spiral for the last hour, waiting for the moment he cracks.

Here it comes.

"I shouldn't have—"

"Try finishing that sentence and I'll hit you with a rock," Finn says.

Darian blinks. "What?"

"Seconded," Torric adds.

"You're fine, Darian." Aspen's voice is gentle but firm. "She's fine."

Darian's jaw works. "But she—"

"Chose you." I keep my voice steady. Grounded. "She didn't break because of you. She broke because she finally felt all of us at once. That's not your fault. That's just... a lot."

"Six bonds hitting her at full volume," Finn mutters. "Honestly, I'm impressed she only had one panic attack."

Darian stares at me. At Finn. At the others.

Something shifts in his expression. The guilt doesn't vanish — I don't think it ever will, not completely — but it stops strangling him.

His shoulders drop.

"She was... loud," he says finally. Almost to himself.

Finn's grin spreads across his face like sunrise. "Oh, we *know*."

Torric groans. "We were trying not to mention it."

"Why?" Finn spreads his hands. "It's not like we didn't all hear. These cave walls aren't exactly soundproof."

Aspen has gone slightly pink. "Can we not—"

"She sounded happy," Finn continues, ignoring him completely. "That's the important thing. Very, very happy. Repeatedly."

Darian flushes. But there's something else there now — something that looks almost like pride.

"She was loud because I'm talented, Finn."

The cave goes silent.

Then Torric laughs — a real laugh, not the sharp bark he uses when he's angry. Aspen makes a choked sound that might be a giggle. Even Kieran's mouth curves into something that's almost a smile.

Finn clutches his chest dramatically. "He's *back*. The arrogant bastard is back."

"I'm not arrogant." Darian's chin lifts. "I'm accurate."

"You cried earlier," Aspen points out. "You don't get to be confident yet."

Darian throws a pebble at him. Aspen catches it without looking, frost crackling across his fingers.

"Alright, but seriously—" Finn's voice softens. "She's okay because of you. The bond purified. The corruption broke. That's not nothing."

Darian looks at Kaia's sleeping form. Something complicated moves across his face.

"She chose me," he says quietly. "Even knowing what I was. What I did."

"She chose all of us," I correct. "That's the point."

The fire pops. Shadows dance across the cave walls. And for a moment, we're not six men with complicated histories and tangled loyalties and a Valkyrie who's rewriting everything we thought we knew about bonds.

We're just... us.

"So." Finn stretches again, settling more comfortably against the cave floor. "Since we're apparently having feelings around the campfire — who wants to compare notes?"

Torric stiffens. "Compare *what*?"

"You know." Finn waggles his eyebrows. "Notes. Observations. Kaia-related data."

"Absolutely not," Aspen says.

"I'm genuinely curious though." Finn props himself up on one elbow. "She's different with each of us, right? I felt it through the bond. Like she... shifts. Adapts."

The question hangs in the air.

I should shut this down. It's inappropriate. Invasive. The kind of conversation that could go wrong in a hundred different ways.

But Torric speaks first.

"She's softer with Aspen." His voice is rough. Almost grudging. "Gentler. Like she's afraid of breaking him."

"I noticed that too," Aspen admits. "She holds back. Worries about my control."

"With me, she's—" Torric stops. His jaw works. "Wilder. Like she doesn't have to be careful."

"Because you can take it," Finn says. No teasing this time. Just observation.

Torric nods once.

"She laughs with Finn." Darian's voice is quiet. "Even when things are terrible. He makes her laugh."

Finn's expression flickers. Something vulnerable underneath the performer's mask.

"She trusts Malrik to catch her," Aspen adds. "When she falls. When she breaks. She looks for him."

I don't know what to say to that. So I don't say anything.

"And Kieran?" Finn glances toward where Kieran is holding her. "What's she like with you?"

Kieran is silent for a long moment.

"Guarded," he says finally. "Wary. She watches me like she's waiting for the next betrayal."

The words land heavy.

"But tonight she let you hold her," I point out.

"Tonight she was desperate." Kieran's voice is carefully neutral. "That's not the same as trust."

"It's a start," Darian says.

Kieran's gold eyes shift to him. Something passes between them — not friendship, not yet. But maybe the beginning of understanding.

"Perhaps," Kieran allows.

Finn yawns dramatically, breaking the moment. "Cool. Great talk. Very emotional. Now can we acknowledge that I had sex in a magical hot spring and it was incredible and I deserve recognition?"

"You deserve a rock to the head," Torric mutters.

"Malrik was there too," Finn adds. "In case anyone was wondering."

"We weren't," Aspen says.

"He's very good with his hands."

"*Finn.*"

I pinch the bridge of my nose. "Is there a version of this conversation where you have some dignity?"

"Absolutely not." Finn grins at me, unrepentant. "Dignity is for people who didn't just have a threesome with the love of their life in a sacred healing spring while her shadows watched."

Torric chokes on nothing.

"The shadows watched?" Aspen looks horrified.

"Bob turned around," Finn says. "Eventually. Patricia took notes."

"Of course she did," Darian mutters.

"Speaking of watching—" Finn's grin turns predatory as he swivels toward Kieran. "Want to explain why you were lurking at the edge of the Berserker hall? Again?"

Kieran's expression doesn't change. "I was patrolling."

"You were *watching*."

"I was ensuring her safety."

"From behind a pillar. While she was between me and Malrik. Very safe. Very noble."

Torric snorts. "He watched you two at the sanctuary, too. Back when we first came to Absentia."

"I remember," I say dryly. "I called him out then as well."

"And tonight." Darian's voice is quiet, but there's something almost amused underneath it. "During... us. He was at the cave entrance."

Every head turns toward Kieran.

He remains utterly still. Ancient. Dignified.

"I was standing guard."

"You were *watching*," Finn repeats gleefully. "You're always watching. At this point it's basically a hobby."

"A very dedicated hobby," Aspen adds, and even he's smiling now.

"Centuries of discipline," Torric says, "and you still can't look away."

Kieran's jaw tightens almost imperceptibly. "I take my responsibilities seriously."

"Uh-huh." Finn leans back, utterly delighted. "And which responsibility requires you to watch Kaia get railed, exactly? Is that in the ancient dragon handbook?"

"Finn," I warn, but I'm fighting a smile.

"What? I'm genuinely asking. Is it a protective instinct? A mating thing? Do dragons just... like to observe?"

Kieran's gold eyes finally shift to Finn. There's something dangerous in them — but also, beneath it, the faintest flicker of embarrassment.

"I will end you," he says calmly.

"You won't." Finn's grin is incandescent. "Because then Kaia would be sad. And you'd rather die than make her sad. So I get to mock you forever."

The laughter that follows is real. Warm. The kind of sound I didn't know I needed until I heard it.

Even Kieran's mouth twitches.

We sit in it for a while. Letting the fire burn low. Letting the tension drain out of muscles that have been clenched for days.

Then Kieran speaks again.

"Something in the air changed."

The warmth doesn't vanish, but it... shifts. Sharpens.

"When?" I ask.

"A few days ago. Halfway up the ridge." His eyes are distant. "I thought it was just the mountain at first. The corruption. But it's not."

I frown. He's right — I've felt it too. That wrongness that started pressing harder three days back. I assumed it was exhaustion. Stress. The bonds straining under everything we've been through.

But now that he says it...

"I noticed it too," I admit. "Thought it was my imagination."

"Same," Torric says. "Figured it was the elevation."

Darian is quiet for a moment. Then: "It feels like Absentia. But wrong. Like the magic is... curdling."

"Curdling," Finn repeats. "Great. Love that. Very comforting."

Aspen's frost crackles unconsciously. "Whatever's at the top of this mountain — it knows we're coming."

"Probably." Kieran's voice is calm. "But that's a problem for tomorrow."

Finn waves a hand. "Seconded. Spooky mountain vibes noted. We'll deal with it when we deal with it. Right now I'm trying to enjoy the fact that Kaia isn't screaming."

"Romantic," Torric deadpans.

"Realistic," Finn counters. "I've got low standards at this point. 'Everyone is alive and no one is on fire' is basically a win."

"No one is on fire *yet*," Torric says.

"See? Optimism."

The fire crackles. Mouse's purring is the only sound for a long moment.

I let my gaze drift across the cave.

Finn has sprawled out completely now, one arm flung over his eyes. Torric is still tense, but it's the normal tension — watchful, not wound to breaking. Aspen has tipped sideways, his head resting against his brother's shoulder, eyes half-closed.

Darian is lying on his side, finally, *finally* breathing normally. The tight coil of guilt that's been wrapped around him for weeks has loosened.

And Kieran...

Kieran is holding Kaia like she's the most precious thing in existence. His ancient stillness wrapped around her. His gold eyes soft in a way I've never seen from him before.

She didn't break because she doesn't want us.

She broke because she finally felt how much we all want her.

I close my eyes.

Tomorrow, we face whatever's waiting at the gate.

Tonight, we rest.

All of us.

Together.

Chapter 36
ASPEN

I wake to the wrongness before I see her.

The air in the cave has shifted. Colder. Sharper. The kind of cold that doesn't come from weather — the kind that comes from magic pressing against the edges of a space that should be safe.

My eyes snap open.

She's standing three feet inside the cave entrance.

Platinum hair. Flawless posture. Gold insignia gleaming at her throat even in the dim morning light.

Alenya Virath.

"Well." Her smile is a knife wrapped in silk. "Isn't this *cozy*."

My frost crackles to life before I'm fully conscious, spreading across my fingertips in sharp crystalline patterns. Beside me, Torric jerks awake, heat flaring instinctively.

But it's Darian who reacts like he's been stabbed.

He's on his feet in a heartbeat — no, faster than a heartbeat — positioning himself between Alenya and Kaia with a snarl that doesn't sound human. His corruption flickers around his hands, then stutters, then blazes into something else entirely.

Light.

Pure, golden light.

Something has shifted. I'd almost forgotten, in the chaos of last night — the bond purified. The corruption broke. And now Darian is burning with the power he was always supposed to have.

Alenya's eyes widen for just a fraction of a second.

Then her composure snaps back into place.

"Oh, that's *adorable*." She tilts her head, studying him like a specimen. "You actually think you're a threat now. How precious."

"What the fuck are you doing here?" Torric's voice is a growl. Fire coils up his arms.

"Language." Alenya tsks. "And here I thought the Berserker twins were supposed to be the civilized ones. Relatively speaking."

Finn is awake now too, chaos sparking around him as he scrambles upright. Malrik is already on his feet, shadows writhing, expression carved from stone.

And Kieran—

Kieran hasn't moved.

He's still holding Kaia, who's only just stirring, blinking awake with confusion clouding her violet eyes. His gold gaze is fixed on Alenya with an intensity that could level mountains.

"You should not be here," he says. Quiet. Absolute. Ancient.

"And yet." Alenya spreads her hands. "Here I am."

"How did you find us?" Malrik's voice is controlled, but I can hear the edge underneath. "We weren't followed."

Alenya's smile sharpens. She glances toward the back of the cave — toward the unconscious form of Callum, still strapped to the makeshift sled Torric's been dragging up the mountain.

"Kieran's love for his people has always been his weakness." Her voice drips with false sympathy. "So loyal. So devoted. So *predictable*." She looks back at Kieran, something cruel in her eyes. "His little tracking spell led us right to you. Every step of the way."

Kieran goes very, very still.

I feel it through the bond — not from him directly, but from Kaia. The shock. The realization. The horrible understanding that Callum wasn't just broken.

He was bait.

"You used him," Kaia whispers. She's fully awake now, pulling herself upright, shadows bristling around her like hackles rising. "You broke him and then you *used* him to find us."

"I didn't break him." Alenya examines her nails. "That was Alekir's work. I simply... repurposed what remained."

Mouse growls from Kaia's chest — low and dangerous and ancient.

Bob materializes between Kaia and Alenya at Darian's feet, edges razor-sharp. Patricia's notebook flares to life, documenting everything with furious intensity.

"You're going to regret coming here," Finn says. His voice is light, but there's nothing light in his eyes. "There's six of us and one of you."

"Seven," Kaia corrects quietly. "Seven of us."

Something flickers across Alenya's expression. Fear? No — anticipation.

"Seven," she repeats. "Yes. That's rather the point, isn't it?"

She lets her gaze drift across us. Taking inventory. Taking *aim*.

"The Berserker twins." Her eyes land on Torric, then me. "Fire and ice. How poetic. How *tragic* — branded by your own father, forced into power you never asked for. Does it still hurt? The runes?"

Torric's flames flare higher. I put a hand on his arm — not to stop him, just to steady him.

"The Shadow Prince." She turns to Malrik. "Playing at leadership while your kingdom crumbles. Your father would be so disappointed. Oh wait — he's dead, isn't he? Such a shame."

Malrik's shadows writhe, but his expression doesn't change.

"The Chaos Boy." Finn gets a pitying look. "Still desperate for approval. Still performing. Still hoping that if you're funny enough, charming enough, *enough* enough, someone will finally choose you first." She pauses. "How's that working out?"

Finn's jaw tightens. His chaos magic sparks erratically.

"The Dragon." Alenya's voice drops, almost reverent. "Centuries of power and wisdom, and still you couldn't protect the one thing you actually care about. How many times has she almost died under your watch, Kieran? How many more until you admit you're not enough?"

Kieran doesn't respond. But I feel Kaia's fury spike through the bond.

"And *you*." Alenya finally turns to Darian. Her smile goes sharp. Cruel. "The broken one. The traitor. The boy who let himself be used because he was too weak to say no." She steps closer, ignoring the way his light magic blazes brighter. "I visited you in that cell, remember? After the arena. Gave you a key and a choice."

Her voice drops, saccharine sweet.

"And you *chose*, Darian. Chose fear. Chose to crawl back to us like a good little weapon." She tilts her head. "How does it feel, knowing she trusted you anyway?"

"Don't." Darian's voice is barely human.

"She should have let you die."

The light around Darian's hands explodes outward — but Alenya is faster. Her own magic flares, golden and precise, and the blast deflects harmlessly against the cave wall.

"Temper, temper." She brushes dust from her sleeve. "You'll need that fire where you're going."

Kaia pushes to her feet. Thank gods we dressed her while she was asleep. Her shadows surge around her, Bob and Mouse flanking her like sentinels, the rest of the squad falling into formation.

"We're not going anywhere with you."

"Oh, but you are." Alenya's smile is triumphant. "You see, the Gate is waiting. The alignment is nearly complete. And Alekir has been *so* patient."

She looks at each of us in turn. Seven bonds. Six bloodlines. One Valkyrie.

"You thought you were hunting Seren and Lira. You thought you were the ones in control." She laughs — bright and brittle and wrong. "You were never hunting them. You were being *led*. Every step. Every choice. Every mile up this mountain."

My frost spreads across the cave floor. Torric's heat pushes back against it. My ice knows the truth before I do — we aren't ready for what's at the top.

"Well." Alenya claps her hands together. "This has been fun. But we have somewhere to be."

She snaps her fingers.

The world *lurches*.

One second we're in the cave — cold stone, dying fire, the smell of smoke and sweat and too many people in too small a space.

The next—

Wind. Biting, brutal wind.

I gasp, lungs seizing against the sudden cold. Not my cold — mountain cold. The kind that kills.

We're standing on a plateau. Snow whipping around us. The sky above is wrong — too dark, too churning, shot through with veins of sickly green light.

And in front of us...

A structure. Ancient. Massive. Built from black stone that seems to drink the light.

The Gate.

It's already glowing.

Figures move around it — robed, hooded, their magic pulsing in rhythm with the structure's thrum. And at the center, standing before the Gate like he's been waiting for us all along—

A hooded figure.

Dark robes that seem to drink the light. The hood pulled low, obscuring everything but the faint gleam of pale fingers clasped in front of him. The air warps around him — bends wrong, like reality itself is trying to lean away.

I can't see his face. Can't make out anything beneath that hood.

But I feel him.

Ancient. Patient. *Wrong*.

The snow avoids him. The wind dies where he stands. Even the sickly green light pulsing from the Gate seems to curve around him like it's afraid to touch.

"Ah." His voice carries across the plateau like it's being spoken directly into my skull. Calm. Almost warm. "The Key arrives at last."

His hood shifts — just slightly — as his attention moves to Kaia.
"Hello girl, our meeting is long overdue."

Chapter 37
KAIA

The world snaps back into focus like a rubber band to the face.

Cold. Wind. Snow biting through clothes that are nowhere near warm enough for wherever the hell we are now.

My lungs seize. The altitude is wrong — too high, too thin, the air scraping my throat like broken glass.

And in front of me—

Him.

The hooded figure. The one who makes reality bend away like it's afraid to touch him.

"Hello girl," he says. "Our meeting is long overdue."

My shadows explode outward before I can think.

Bob surges in front of me, edges razor-sharp, positioning himself like a shield made of pure fury. Mouse leaps from my shoulder to my feet, growing larger, darker, his growl vibrating through my bones. Patricia's notebook blazes to life. Walter pulses overhead like a warning flare.

And the bonds—

Gods, the *bonds*.

Six voices screaming through my chest all at once. Finn's chaos crackling like static. Torric's heat blazing at my back. Aspen's frost spreading across the ground beneath my feet. Malrik's shadows sharpening around him like blades. Darian's light — pure, golden, *new* — burning so bright it hurts to look at.

And Kieran.

Kieran is a wall of ancient stillness behind me, his presence pressing against the bond like a hand bracing for impact.

None of them speak.

None of them have to.

The hooded figure — Alekir, it has to be Alekir — tilts his head. Studying us. Studying *me*.

I can't see his face beneath that hood. Can't make out anything except the faint gleam of pale fingers clasped in front of him, too still, too deliberate.

But I feel him.

It's like standing at the edge of a cliff and feeling the drop before you see it. Like the moment before lightning strikes, when the air goes heavy and wrong.

My senses are *screaming*.

"Six bloodlines." His voice carries across the plateau like it's being spoken directly into my skull. Calm. Almost amused. "Seven bonds. One Valkyrie."

He spreads his hands.

"At last."

The robed figures around the Gate shift. Adjusting. Watching. Their magic pulses in rhythm with the structure behind them — that massive, ancient thing built from black stone that drinks the light.

The Gate.

It's already glowing. Sickly green veins of power threading through the stone, pulsing like a heartbeat. Like something alive and waiting.

"You have no idea how long I've waited for this." Alekir's voice is soft. Patient. The kind of patience that comes from centuries of planning. "How many pieces had to fall into place. How many sacrifices had to be made."

Torric's heat flares behind me. I feel his rage through the bond — hot and sharp and barely leashed.

"Touch her and I'll burn you where you stand," he growls.

Alekir doesn't even look at him.

"The Berserker speaks." There's something almost fond in his tone. Almost pitying. "Such fire. Such loyalty. Such *predictability*."

The wind dies.

Just like that — one second it's tearing at us, the next it's gone. The air goes still and heavy, pressing against my ears like we've sunk underwater.

Alekir's doing. Has to be.

"Better," he says. "Now we can have a proper conversation."

A flash of light behind him.

Alenya materializes out of thin air, stumbling slightly, her perfect composure cracked around the edges. Callum's unconscious body drops beside her, hitting the snow with a dull thump.

"They teleported exactly as instructed," she says, breathless. Trying to recover her poise. "I ensured it personally."

Alekir doesn't acknowledge her.

"My lord." Alenya steps forward, urgent now. "The Luthar boy — his magic has changed. The corruption is—"

"Enough."

One word. Quiet. Absolute.

Alenya's mouth snaps shut.

"You have served your purpose." Alekir still hasn't looked at her. His attention is fixed on me — I can feel it like a physical weight, even though I can't see his eyes. "Leave."

"But his light magic—"

He lifts a hand.

She flickers — there one moment, gone the next. Not dead. Just... removed. Dismissed like an inconvenience Alekir couldn't be bothered to tolerate. Just — gone. Blinked out of existence like she was never there.

Callum remains, crumpled in the snow like discarded garbage. My shadows reach toward him instinctively — Linda drifting close, Carl hovering uncertainly — but there's nothing they can do. Nothing any of us can do.

He was bait. This whole time, he was bait.

And Kieran's compassion led us straight into the trap.

I feel Kieran's guilt crash through the bond — heavy enough to choke on. He doesn't move, doesn't react outwardly, but inside he's drowning.

Not your fault, I want to tell him. *You couldn't have known.*

But I can't speak. Can't move. Can't do anything except stand here and face the monster who orchestrated all of this.

Movement at the edge of my vision.

One of the robed figures steps forward, pushing back his hood.

Thorne.

My stomach drops.

He looks... wrong. Not proud, not victorious. His face is drawn, shadows under his eyes, something broken in his expression.

He doesn't look at Darian.

Can't look at Darian I realize.

I feel Darian's reaction through the bond — a spike of fear and fury and something that might be betrayal. His light magic flares brighter, defensive, instinctive.

Thorne flinches.

Alekir doesn't acknowledge him. Doesn't need to. The message is clear enough — Thorne is here because Alekir wants him here. And Darian's reaction tells me everything I need to know about what that means.

Thorne's jaw tightens. He still won't meet Darian's eyes.

"The corruption was elegant work," Alekir continues. He's walking now — slow, deliberate steps that bring him closer to our group. The snow parts around his feet. The sickly green light seems to bend toward him. "Centuries of planning. Generations of preparation. And at the center of it all..."

He stops.

Directly in front of me.

"You."

Bob bristles. Mouse's growl deepens. My shadows press closer, defensive, protective — but they feel small suddenly. Insignificant against whatever this creature is.

"You don't even understand what you are," Alekir says. Soft. Almost gentle. "What you represent. What you can *do*."

"I know enough." My voice comes out steadier than I feel. "I know you destroyed the Valkyries. I know you've been trying to break Absentia for centuries. I know—"

"You know *nothing*."

The word hits like a slap.

"You are a child playing with forces older than your bloodline. Older than this realm. Older than the concept of realms themselves." He tilts his head, and I catch the faintest gleam of something beneath that hood — eyes that burn without light. "You think this is about destruction? About conquest?"

He laughs.

It's the worst sound I've ever heard. Cold and hollow and ancient.

"This is about *correction*. About restoring what should never have been sealed. About freeing what your ancestors trapped out of fear and ignorance."

My heart is pounding so hard I can feel it in my teeth.

"The God of Chaos," I whisper.

"The Guardian of the Threshold." Alekir's voice turns reverent. "The Keeper of the Path. The one who was meant to guide souls between worlds — until the Valkyries decided they knew better. Until they sealed him away and claimed his purpose as their own."

I feel the others shifting behind me. Processing. Trying to understand.

But I can't look away from him. Can't break whatever hold his attention has on me.

"You think I care about preserving this realm?" He sounds almost amused. "Absentia was never supposed to exist. The Valkyries built a bridge between life and death and called themselves gods for walking it."

His voice goes cold. Ancient. Bitter.

"I'm going to burn that bridge. Free the God they imprisoned. Let Chaos do what Chaos does — consume everything your ancestors stole from the natural order."

"By killing everyone I love," I snap. "By corrupting the bonds. By breaking—"

"By using the tools available to me." His voice goes sharp. "The corruption was necessary. The bonds had to be... guided. Shaped. Made ready for alignment."

He gestures at the six men behind me.

"Six bloodlines. Light. Shadow. Chaos. Elemental. Berserker. Shifter." His pale hand moves through the air like he's conducting an orchestra. "All connected to you. All bound by magic older than memory. All *perfectly* positioned to open the Gate."

The Gate pulses behind him. Brighter now. Hungrier.

"You think you chose them," Alekir says softly. "You think the bonds were accidents of fate and feeling. You think your love is *real*."

"It is real."

"It is *engineered*." He takes another step closer. "Every connection. Every kiss. Every moment of passion and protection and desperate clinging need — all of it built on a foundation I laid centuries ago."

I feel the others react through the bonds — denial, fury, hurt.

"You're lying," Finn says. His voice is sharp, but I hear the tremor underneath.

Alekir finally looks away from me.

"Am I?" He turns to face them — my men, my bonds, my *family*. "Ask the Dragon how it felt when the bonds first stirred. Ask the Shadow Prince why his magic recognized her before his mind did. Ask the Chaos Boy why he's been drawn to her since before they ever met."

Silence.

Heavy. Horrible.

"The corruption didn't create the bonds," Alekir continues. "It shaped them. Ensured they would form in the correct order. Ensured the alignment would be... compatible."

He turns back to me.

"You are the Key, little Valkyrie. You have always been the Key. And now..."

He gestures at the Gate.

"It is time to fulfill your purpose."

I should be terrified.

I *am* terrified.

But underneath the fear, something else is stirring. Something that feels like defiance. Like fury. Like the same stubborn refusal to break that's gotten me through everything else.

"No."

The word comes out clear. Steady.

Alekir pauses.

"No?" He sounds almost curious. Almost entertained.

"You don't get to tell me what my purpose is." My shadows surge around me, making themselves known. "You don't get to claim my bonds. You don't get to decide what's real."

I feel the others behind me. Feel their support flowing through the connections — imperfect, complicated, *chosen*.

"I don't care what you engineered," I say. "I don't care what you planned. These bonds are *mine*. These people are *mine*. And whatever happens next—"

I meet the darkness beneath his hood.

"—we decide together."

Alekir is silent for a long moment.

Then he laughs again.

"Oh, I do so enjoy the defiant ones." He sounds genuinely pleased. "They always align so much more... completely."

He turns away from me. Faces the Gate.

"Bring them into position," he says to Thorne. "It's time."

Thorne hesitates.

Looks at Darian for the first time.

Something passes between them — guilt, regret, a desperate plea for forgiveness that Darian doesn't acknowledge.

Then Thorne nods.

And Alekir begins to speak in a language I don't understand, his pale hands rising toward the glowing stone.

But I notice something.

Through all of it — the threats, the revelations, the posturing and manipulation — he never once looked at the men behind me as a threat.

He looked at them as tools.

He looked at *me* as the only one who mattered.

Six bloodlines. Seven bonds. One Valkyrie.

He's not afraid of them.

He's only watching me.

Chapter 38
MALRIK

He never looked at us as threats.

I catalog my brothers' positions without turning my head — instinct, maybe, or the strange leadership that's fallen on my shoulders since this nightmare began. Torric is a furnace barely contained, heat rolling off him in waves that make the snow steam at his feet. Aspen stands ice-still beside him, frost creeping up his arms in sharp crystalline patterns. Finn's chaos crackles erratically, sparking and dying like a flame that can't decide whether to catch.

Darian burns.

His light magic — pure now, uncorrupted — blazes around him like a second skin. He's not controlling it. Can't control it. The power is too new, too raw, too tied to the emotions I can feel hemorrhaging through the bond.

And Kieran stands behind Kaia like a wall of ancient stone, every muscle coiled, ready to throw himself between her and whatever comes next.

None of us matter to Alekir.

We're pieces on a board. Tools shaped for a single purpose. The only one he sees as real is her.

That should comfort me. It doesn't.

Thorne approaches.

His movements are careful, deliberate — the gait of a man walking through a minefield he helped plant. He looked at Darian once, at the end of Alekir's speech. That single glance held more guilt than words could carry.

"Into position," Thorne says quietly. His voice cracks on the second word. "Please. Don't make this harder than—"

I step between them.

Thorne stops.

"Don't touch him." My voice comes out low. Controlled. The voice I learned in my father's court, when showing emotion meant showing weakness.

Thorne's expression fractures. "I wasn't going to."

"Then step back."

He does.

I feel Darian's gratitude through the bond — sharp and desperate and threaded with something that might be shame. His light flickers dangerously, unstable, and I reach back without looking. My hand finds his arm. Anchors him.

I've got you.

I don't say it out loud. Don't need to. The bond carries it.

A surge of gold-white light splits the air.

I spin, shadows rising instinctively — but it's not an attack. It's an arrival.

Lady Virath materializes beside the Gate's outer ring.

She's nothing like I remember from the council meetings.

The elegant politician is gone. In her place stands something *wrong*. Her pristine white robes crackle with an aura that doesn't belong in this realm

— too bright, too sharp, like light that's learned to cut. Her golden hair whips around her face despite the stillness Alekir forced on the air. And her eyes—

Her eyes are too deep. Too empty. They devour the light around them, leaving only a hollow chill.

She's not hiding anymore.

And she's not alone.

The sky *tears open* behind her.

Nightwraiths pour through — dozens, then hundreds, filling the air like a plague of shadows given teeth. They circle above us, blocking what little light remains, their shrieks splitting the silence Alekir created.

Torric's fire blazes higher. Aspen's frost spreads across the ground. Finn's chaos crackles wild and desperate.

But there are too many. Far too many.

Lady Virath smiles.

"The preparations are complete," she says, and her voice carries that same hollow wrongness as her eyes. "The ritual circle holds. The bloodlines are assembled."

"And the Academy?"

"Blind. Scrambling. Exactly as planned."

I feel something cold settle in my chest.

She was never following Alenya. She *outranked* her. All those board meetings, all those political machinations, all those demands that Kaia prove herself — it was never fear.

It was positioning.

"You've done well," Alekir says. "The Light Faction's representative, hiding the darkness in plain sight."

"Someone had to ensure the path remained clear." Lady Virath's gaze finally slides to Kaia. Cold. Assessing. "Your Professor Lira was becoming... inconvenient. Asking too many questions. Getting too close to the truth." Her smile sharpens. "She's been handled."

I feel Kaia's reaction through the bond before I see it.

Horror. Grief. Rage so pure it makes my shadows writhe.

Kaia doesn't move. Doesn't speak. But her shadows surge around her — Bob growing larger, Mouse's growl vibrating through the plateau, Patricia's notebook blazing with furious light.

I want to kill Lady Virath for that. Want to let my shadows tear her apart.

But Kaia's darkness wraps around my wrist. Holding me back. *Not yet.*

Alekir is watching us. Watching *me*.

And then he laughs.

It's different from before — not cold and hollow, but bright. Almost giddy. The sound of someone savoring a joke only they understand.

"Oh, but the best part—" He gestures between me and Darian, pale fingers conducting some invisible orchestra. "The Shadow Prince and the Light Faction's fallen star. Standing side by side. Protecting each other."

He claps his hands together.

"Isn't it *delightful*?"

The word hangs in the air like poison.

"Did no one ever tell you, Malrik?" His voice drops, intimate and cruel. "About your father's... indiscretions?"

My blood turns to ice.

"The Shadow King did so love his Light Faction lovers. The political advantages. The secret alliances. The *children* they gave him."

No.

"You share the same blood." Alekir's pale hand moves between us. "The same father. The same legacy."

The world stops.

I feel Darian go rigid beside me. Feel his shock crash through the bond like a wave — denial, horror, something that might be recognition.

"Brothers," Alekir says, savoring every syllable. "How perfectly poetic."

I can't breathe.

Memories flash — fragments I'd buried so deep I'd forgotten they existed. A boy in the palace halls. Younger than me. Dark-haired. Watching me with eyes that felt familiar even then. My father's hand on my shoulder, steering me away. *Don't concern yourself with him.*

That was Darian.

That was my *brother*.

"He was the heir," Alekir continues, gesturing at me. "You were the spare experiment." His attention shifts to Darian. "Placed with my followers because your proximity to Malrik completed the circle. Light and Shadow. Royal blood on both sides. The corruption latched onto you so beautifully because you were *designed* for it."

Darian makes a sound like he's been gutted.

His light magic flares — wild, uncontrolled — and he staggers. I catch him without thinking. My shadows wrap around his shoulders, steadying him, anchoring him the same way I anchored Kaia through her panic attack.

I've got you. I've got you.

"Touching," Lady Virath observes. "The lost princes, united at last."

I want to destroy her. Want to let every shadow in Absentia tear her to pieces.

But Kaia's presence in the bond holds me steady. Her grief. Her fury. Her desperate need for us to survive this.

Not yet. Not yet.

Alekir spreads his arms wide.

"Now. Shall I tell you what happens next?"

He doesn't wait for an answer.

"The Gate requires six bloodlines. Light. Shadow. Chaos. Elemental. Berserker. Shifter." He paces before the glowing stone like a professor delivering a lecture. "All connected to a Valkyrie. All bound by magic older than memory. All *aligned*."

The Gate pulses behind him. Brighter. Hungrier.

"Your ancestors sealed the God of Chaos out of fear," he continues. "They called it protection. Called it duty. Called themselves *heroes* for trapping a force of nature and claiming its purpose as their own."

His voice turns bitter. Ancient.

"The Valkyries were never meant to guide souls. That was Chaos's role. The threshold between life and death — that was *his* domain. But they feared what they couldn't control. So they sealed him away and built Absentia on his bones."

"That's not—" Kaia starts.

"That is *exactly* what happened." Alekir rounds on her. "Your bloodline stole the sacred duty. Fractured the cycle. Trapped souls in a realm that should never have existed. And for centuries — *centuries* — I have worked to correct their arrogance."

Lady Virath steps forward, her voice ringing across the plateau.

"The Valkyries were thieves," she says. "Arrogant children playing with forces they didn't understand. They took what belonged to Chaos and called it righteousness."

Her gaze finds Kaia.

"Your parents were the worst of them. So convinced of their own virtue. So certain they were protecting the realms." Her smile is a knife. "I enjoyed watching the light leave their eyes."

Kaia's shadows *scream*.

Bob lunges — but Kieran catches him, holds him back. Mouse is snarling, growing larger, darkness pooling around his form. Patricia's notebook is a blaze of furious light.

And Kaia—

Kaia is shaking. I feel it through the bond. The grief. The rage. The desperate desire to tear Lady Virath apart with her bare hands.

But she doesn't move.

She's waiting. Calculating.

Good girl.

Alekir and Lady Virath turn toward each other, voices rising in what sounds like a ritualistic argument — timing, energy, the precise moment of alignment. Their words blur into noise, magic crackling between them.

I gather the others closer.

"Now," I breathe. "While they're distracted."

Finn leans in, chaos sparking at his fingertips. "Please tell me we have a plan that isn't 'die heroically.'"

"We align," Kieran says quietly.

Torric's heat flares. "Are you *insane*? That's exactly what he—"

"He doesn't know." Darian's voice is barely audible. Raw. "About the purification. He thinks the corruption is still..."

He trails off. Can't finish.

"It's a gamble," Kieran murmurs. "But it may be the only one we have."

Kaia says nothing. She's watching Alekir, breathing too fast, shadows coiling tight around her.

Calculating.

Alekir turns back toward us.

Lady Virath joins him, standing in perfect alignment beside the Gate. Thorne steps behind them, torn but obedient, unable to meet anyone's eyes.

"Enough delay." Alekir's hands rise. "The moon reaches its apex. The bloodlines will align. And the Gate—"

His pale fingers trace symbols in the air.

"—will finally open."

The Gate pulses like a heartbeat.

The stone beneath our feet begins to glow — six points of light arranged in a perfect circle, waiting for us to take our places.

I look at Darian. My brother. The boy I saw in the palace halls and forgot because my father told me to.

He looks back at me.

Something passes between us — the beginning of something. A recognition that we're bound by more than magic now.

Brothers.

The word sits strange in my chest. Heavy. Impossible.

But real.

I take my position.

And pray to whatever gods might still be listening that we're not about to end the world.

319

Chapter 39

KAIA

The six points of light wait for them. Not me — them.

Because I go last. The Key doesn't turn until the lock is ready.

"Take your positions," Alekir commands, and I hate that we're doing what he wants. Hate that this might be exactly the trap he laid. Hate that I have no idea if the purified bonds will matter at all, or if I'm about to kill everyone I love.

Torric moves first.

He steps onto his point and fire erupts around his feet, contained within the symbol, his rune blazing on his chest. He looks at me — really looks at me — and I feel his fear through the bond. His love. His absolute refusal to let me face this alone.

I try to memorize his face. Just in case.

Aspen takes the position beside his brother. Frost spreads in perfect crystalline patterns, his ice-blue eyes steady despite the terror bleeding through our connection. He nods once. Slow. Deliberate.

I see you, that nod says. *I'm here.*

Finn's chaos crackles as he finds his place. He opens his mouth — probably to make a joke, something to cut through the weight of this moment — but nothing comes out. His green eyes are too bright. His hands won't stop shaking.

He's scared.

We're all scared.

And I might be leading them to their deaths.

Darian moves like a man walking toward his own execution. His light magic blazes around him, pure and golden, no longer fighting what he is. He meets my eyes as he takes his position, and the emotion that crashes through the bond nearly buckles my knees.

Trust. Despite everything. Trust.

What if I'm wrong?

Malrik's shadow magic writhes around him. He stands tall, steady, and when he looks at Darian — his brother, gods, his *brother* — something passes between them. Then his gaze finds me.

Steady. Certain. Even now.

I don't deserve that certainty.

Kieran takes the final position, completing the outer circle. His ancient presence settles into place like a stone dropped into still water. He doesn't look at me. Doesn't need to. The bond carries everything — his fear, his hope, his desperate prayer that this works.

Six bloodlines. Six men. All of them trusting me.

All of them ready to die for a gamble none of us are sure will work.

The center of the circle pulses. Waiting.

For me.

I look at each of them one more time. Torric's fire. Aspen's ice. Finn's chaos. Darian's light. Malrik's shadow. Kieran's dragon I can see in his eyes.

My family. My heart. My home.

If this goes wrong — if the alignment tears us apart, if Alekir was right and I'm just a tool he designed — at least we'll be together.

At least we chose this.

I step into the center.

Seven bonds. Six bloodlines. One Valkyrie.

The alignment is complete.

Alekir spreads his arms wide, and his voice rings across the plateau like a sermon.

"The Key stands in her rightful place." His pale fingers trace symbols in the air, and the Gate responds — pulsing brighter, hungrier. "The cycle returns to its natural beginning. The Valkyrie bloodline fulfills its ancient crime by opening what it sealed."

Lady Virath's hollow voice joins his, her corrupted light magic flaying the air. "Six bloodlines. Seven bonds. The perfect alignment."

Above us, the Nightwraiths tighten their circle. Their shrieks split the silence, hungry and eager.

Every word is wrong.

Every word twists what I am. What we are.

My body is shaking — not in fear, but in *pressure*. Power building inside me like a storm that's been waiting my whole life to break.

And then—

The bonds ignite.

Not Alekir's corruption. Not engineered obedience.

Choice.

I feel it in my chest — six threads of light and darkness and chaos and berserker and elemental and shifter, all pulling toward me at once. Not because they were designed to. Not because someone forced them.

Because they *want* to.

Because *we* want to.

The magic responds.

Shadows rise around me like smoke pulled upward. Bob surges larger, darker, his edges sharp enough to cut reality. Mouse grows until he's the size of a panther, his growl vibrating through the stone beneath our feet. Patricia's notebook blazes. Walter pulses overhead like a captured star.

Light spills from Darian's hands and threads toward me — golden and pure, weaving through my shadows like it belongs there.

Finn's chaos sparks jump across the circle like fireflies, connecting us in patterns that shift and dance.

Torric's flame coils around his wrists, then reaches for me — not burning, just *warm*.

Aspen's frost spreads in symmetrical fractals, beautiful and deadly, meeting my shadows at the edges.

Malrik's darkness stretches toward me like instinct, like coming home.

And Kieran's dragon anchors it all — ancient and patient and *here*.

This is not what Alekir created.

This is what we *built*.

The ground trembles.

The Gate's black stone pulses, light leaking from every seam. The symbols beneath our feet blaze brighter, hotter, responding to the alignment with a hunger that makes my bones ache.

Alekir is laughing. Triumphant. Ecstatic.

Lady Virath's hollow eyes gleam with victory.

And yet—

Something is wrong.

I feel the alignment pulling in a direction Alekir doesn't expect. The magic isn't twisted. Isn't corrupted. It's flowing *clean* — smoother and purer than anything I've ever felt.

Too smooth.

Too clean.

Too *correct*.

Kieran's voice cuts through the noise — soft, horrified.

"Kaia... this isn't corrupted magic."

I know.

I've known since the moment I stepped into the circle.

"This is true alignment," he breathes.

Alekir freezes.

Just slightly. Just enough for me to see the first flicker of doubt cross whatever passes for his expression beneath that hood.

"No." Lady Virath's voice goes sharp. Panicked. "This is wrong. The corruption should be—"

She whirls toward Alekir.

"STOP HER."

Light erupts from her hands — golden and wrong and aimed directly at my chest.

The bonds respond before I can think.

Torric's fire intercepts, a wall of flame that swallows her attack whole.

Aspen's frost seals the ground around my feet, anchoring me.

Finn's chaos jumps and explodes her blast into a shower of harmless sparks.

Darian's light flares like a shield, pure gold meeting corrupted gold.

Malrik's shadows wrap around my waist, steadying me, protecting me.

And Kieran—

Kieran *shifts*.

The sound is thunder and breaking stone. One moment he's a man — the next he's a dragon, massive and ancient, scales gleaming like black gold in the Gate's light. His wings spread wide, blocking out the sky, and he positions himself over all of us.

A living shield.

Lady Virath screams in fury, launching blast after blast — but they break against his scales like waves against a cliff.

The Nightwraiths dive toward us, shrieking — and Kieran's roar shatters them. Just *shatters* them. Dozens of them dissolving into nothing.

He's not protecting me.

He's protecting *us*.

All of us.

We're aligned

"You FOOL—" Alekir rounds on Lady Virath, and for the first time his voice cracks. Loses that ancient patience. "The cycle is correcting itself!"

"Break the circle!" She's desperate now, firing blast after blast that my men intercept without even looking at each other. "Break her concentration!"

I'm not concentrating.

I'm not controlling this.

The alignment is controlling *me*.

Power pours through the bonds — into my body, through my chest, into the circle, then back again. A loop. A cycle. The way it was always meant to work.

My feet lift off the ground.

Just a few inches. Just enough to make my stomach drop.

And then the pain hits.

Searing. Pure. Like breaking through a barrier that was never meant to hold.

My wings burst from my back in a rush of heat and blinding light. Every nerve ending screams as they unfurl — massive and glorious, glowing with that same blend of violet, gold, light and shadow. Their edges ripple with the essence of every Valkyrie who chose to bind their soul to mine.

My sisters.

Light threads through the shadows. Chaos sparks at my fingertips. Fire and frost orbit my body in impossible harmony.

This is larger than me.

Older than all of us.

Alekir screams something I don't understand — words in that ancient language, desperate and furious — but it's too late.

The Gate is opening.

A sound like the world inhaling.

Light erupts vertically from the black stone — not sickly green anymore, but *white*. Pure. Blinding.

Snow lifts off the ground. The Nightwraiths scatter, shrieking in terror. Lady Virath shields her face. Thorne stumbles backward, finally breaking free of whatever held him in place.

Alekir stands perfectly still.

Watching.

Waiting.

And I feel it before anyone sees it.

Something stepping through.

Something ancient.

Something *vast*.

The light dims. The wind dies. The world goes quiet in a way that makes my ears ring.

A figure emerges from the Gate.

Not monstrous. Not what I expected.

He looks… old. Human, almost. A man with weathered features and eyes that hold the weight of millennia. His robes are simple — dark fabric that seems to shift and move like living shadow.

But the *presence*.

The presence is wrong in ways I can't describe. Like standing next to a star. Like drowning in an ocean that's also the sky. Like every ending and beginning compressed into a single point of awareness.

The God of Chaos.

He steps fully through the Gate, and reality *bends* around him. Not breaking — adjusting. Making room.

Alekir falls to his knees.

"My lord." His voice is reverent. Trembling. "At last. After all these centuries—"

The God doesn't look at him.

The God is looking at me.

His ancient eyes — human and not, mortal and endless — fix on my face with an intensity that steals my breath.

"Valkyrie," he says.

His voice is quiet. Almost gentle.

But it echoes through my bones like thunder.

He wasn't looking at Alekir.

He was looking at me.

Chapter 40
FINN

I can't breathe.

I can't think.

I can't fucking *joke.*

The God of Chaos stands twenty feet away, and my magic is screaming inside my skull like it's trying to claw its way out of my body. Every instinct I have — every survival mechanism, every defense I've built — is just... gone.

There's nothing funny about this.

There's nothing funny about *him.*

He's still looking at Kaia. Those ancient eyes fixed on her face like she's the only thing in this entire godforsaken plateau that matters.

He's looking at the one he's about to destroy.

The thought slams through me, and I want to move. Want to throw myself between them. Want to do *something* other than stand here with my chaos magic writhing uselessly around my fingers.

But I can't.

None of us can.

The God's presence is a weight. A pressure. Like standing at the bottom of an ocean that's also the sky. Like being crushed and expanded at the same time.

"My lord." Alekir's voice cracks through the silence — reverent, trembling, *desperate*. "At last. After all these centuries of waiting, of preparing, of holding your purpose sacred—"

The God turns.

Slowly. Deliberately. Like time itself is bending around the motion.

And when those endless eyes fix on Alekir, the soulbinder actually flinches.

"You speak of purpose." The God's voice is quiet. Gentle, almost. But it resonates through my bones like thunder. "Tell me what you believe my purpose to be."

Alekir straightens. Tries to. His form flickers — smoke and malice struggling to hold shape under that gaze.

"Destruction," he says. "The end of what was stolen. The Valkyries sealed you away. Built their precious Absentia on your bones. Fractured the natural cycle and called it *balance*." His voice rises, gaining confidence. "I freed you. I corrupted their bloodlines, broke their seals, twisted their legacy into the key that would—"

"No."

One word. But the weight of it makes the plateau tremble.

"You understand nothing of what I am."

Alekir goes silent.

"I am not destruction." The God takes a step forward, and reality *bends* around him. "I am transition. The threshold between what was and what will be. The guardian of the space between life and death."

Another step.

"The Valkyries did not steal from me. They *partnered* with me. Guided souls through my domain. Maintained the cycle I was created to protect."

Alekir's form wavers. "No. No, the prophecies said—"

"Your prophecies were lies you told yourself." The God's voice doesn't rise. Doesn't need to. "You slaughtered the Valkyries. Corrupted their souls. Trapped them in forms of shadow and hunger. You broke the threshold I was meant to guard and called it *liberation*."

I watch Alekir try to speak. Try to argue. Try to do anything other than stand there while centuries of delusion crumble around him.

"The berserkers who protected them," the God continues. "The bloodlines that maintained balance. The souls that should have passed through my domain — all of them twisted. Trapped. *Suffering*. Because you wanted revenge for a crime that never occurred."

"I was *betrayed*—"

"You were *wrong*."

The God raises one hand.

Just one.

And Alekir — the ancient soulbinder, the monster who destroyed the Valkyries, the nightmare that's haunted Kaia since before she was born —

Alekir *screams*.

It's not dramatic. Not drawn out. Not the theatrical death of a villain who gets to monologue his way into oblivion.

It's just... done.

One moment he's there — smoke and malice and centuries of hatred given form.

The next, he's gone.

Consumed by the very chaos he tried to unleash.

The plateau goes silent.

For one heartbeat, I think it's over. Think we might actually survive this. Think maybe—

"NO!"

Lady Virath's corrupted light blazes as she throws herself forward. Her hollow eyes are wild, desperate, her perfect composure shattered into something feral and afraid.

"You can't— the ritual— the alignment is *complete*—"

She whirls toward Kaia, hands raised, magic building—

"The Valkyrie corrupted the cycle! She's the one who—"

The God doesn't even look at her.

One gesture.

Not violent. Not cruel.

Just... dismissive.

Lady Virath's scream cuts off mid-breath. Her corrupted light flickers once — twice —

And then she's gone.

Same as Alekir.

Same as the Nightwraiths still circling overhead.

I watch them dissolve. Dozens of them. Hundreds. Shrieking as they scatter, as they try to flee, as the God's presence simply... erases them.

Like they never existed.

Like none of this ever happened.

The plateau falls silent.

Really silent.

No Alekir. No Lady Virath. No Nightwraiths. No army of corrupted souls waiting to tear us apart.

Just us.

Kaia — still hovering, wings spread, power radiating from her like heat from a star.

The six of us — frozen in our positions, bonds still blazing, magic still connected.

The God — standing before the open Gate, reality bending around him like water around a stone.

And the wind.

That's it.

That's all that's left.

I should feel relief. Should feel triumph. Should feel *something* other than this crawling dread that won't stop building in my chest.

Because the God is turning again.

Slowly.

Toward Kaia.

Oh fuck.

Oh fuck oh fuck oh fuck—

He's not done.

He destroyed Alekir for corrupting the cycle. Destroyed Lady Virath for serving him. Destroyed the Nightwraiths for existing.

And now he's looking at the Valkyrie who just ripped open the Gate he was sealed behind.

Everyone tenses. I feel it through the bonds — Torric's fury, Aspen's desperate calculation, Malrik's shadow magic coiling like it's ready to strike, Darian's light blazing brighter, Kieran's dragon form shifting to put himself between Kaia and—

The God stops.

Not threatening.

Not attacking.

Just... waiting.

Looking at her with those ancient, endless eyes.

And then—

I hear it.

Behind me.

A sound.

Soft. Wrong. *Familiar*.

Like whispers made of shadow. Like movement without motion. Like a thousand things breathing at once.

Every hair on my body stands up.

I turn.

Slowly.

Terrified of what I'm going to see.

And my heart stops.

They're everywhere.

Shadows.

Just there.

Filling the plateau behind us. Spreading across the snow like spilled ink. Rising from the ground, from the rocks, from the very air itself.

Walter hovers at the front, pulsing with that strange purple light. Mouse stands beside him — panther-sized, violet eyes gleaming. Bob's form is massive, sharp-edged, flanked by shadows I don't recognize.

Shadows that look like Bob.

Shadows that look like *Valkyries*.

And behind them—

Thousands.

Hundreds of thousands.

So many they block out what's left of the daylight. So many I can't see where they end. So many that the weight of their presence makes my chaos magic whimper and go quiet.

They're not looking at the God.

They're looking at *her*.

I move without thinking. Slow. Quiet. Careful, like any sound might shatter whatever fragile balance is holding this moment together.

Kaia is still facing the God. Still hovering. Still radiating power like she's become something more than human.

She doesn't see them.

She doesn't know.

I reach up — her wings are too high, but her hand is close enough — and my fingers close around her wrist.

Gentle.

Trembling.

She looks down at me. Violet eyes blazing with power I don't understand.

I pull her down, she lets me. I lean in.

Right at her ear.

"Kaia."

My voice is barely a whisper.

"*Look.*"

Chapter 41
KAIA

Finn's fingers close around my wrist.

Gentle. Trembling.

I look down at him — his green eyes too bright, his face pale, his chaos magic curled tight against his skin like it's trying to hide.

He tugs, and I let him pull me down. Let my feet touch the ground. Let my wings fold against my back, still humming with power I don't fully understand.

He leans in. Right at my ear.

"Kaia."

His voice is barely a whisper.

"*Look.*"

I turn.

And my heart stops.

They're everywhere.

Shadows.

But not like Bob. Not like Mouse or Walter or Patricia.

These shadows have *faces*.

Faint. Flickering. But there — eyes and mouths and expressions I almost recognize. Women. Warriors. *Sisters*.

The Heart of Eternity burns against my chest, and something ancient stirs in my blood. Something that knows them. Something that's been waiting for this moment longer than I've been alive.

Walter hovers at the front, pulsing violet. Mouse stands sentinel beside him. Bob's massive form anchors the line — but behind him, stretching back across the plateau, filling the snow and the sky and every space between...

Thousands.

More than thousands.

A sea of shadow that swallows the horizon. So vast I can't find the edges. So dense the dying light can't break through.

And I feel them.

Not just see — *feel.*

Their longing. Their grief. Their hope.

Centuries of waiting. Centuries of wandering. Centuries of holding on for something that might never come.

For *someone.*

They're looking at me.

Every single one.

And then — like a wave, like a breath, like the world exhaling —

They bow.

All of them.

A tide of shadow sinking to the snow. Walter dips. Mouse lowers his massive head. Bob's sharp edges soften.

Silence.

No wind. No breath. Nothing but the weight of a thousand souls kneeling before me.

I don't understand.

I don't—

"*You.*"

The God's voice slices through the stillness.

I spin back to face him.

His ancient eyes burn into mine — and for the first time, something like fury twists his weathered features.

"You dared to bring them *here*?"

The words thunder through my bones. Through the bonds. Through everything I am.

Behind me, Torric's fire flares. Aspen's frost crackles. Finn's chaos sparks wild and desperate.

The God takes a step toward me.

Reality bends.

I don't step back.

I plant my feet. Spread my wings. Let the power still coursing through my veins rise to meet him.

I don't know what's coming.

I don't know if I can survive it.

But I'm done running.

I lift my chin.

And I face the God of Chaos.

THANK YOU

To the readers who followed Kaia from that cold open to the edge of everything—thank you for trusting me with the fall.

This book broke me a little. In the best way. Writing the finale of a story you've lived inside for so long is... a lot. But every DM, every keysmash review, every "I'M NOT OKAY" message reminded me why I started.

You made the shadows real. You made Bob's judgment meaningful. You made me ugly-cry over my own characters, which is honestly embarrassing but also the point.

To Kaia, Finn, Malrik, Torric, Aspen, Kieran, and yes, even Darian—thank you for not letting me rest until I got it right.

And to everyone asking "is this really the end?"

Not quite.

Book Four is coming. The shadows aren't done with us yet.

Oh, and one last thing:

Survival Tip #47: When facing a god, bring backup. Preferably the kind that's been silently judging you for three books.

Bob approves this message.

About the Author

Zora Stone writes romantasy with teeth: fierce heroines, protective men who'd burn the world for them, and enough emotional wreckage to keep things interesting. When she's not plotting betrayals or steamy chaos, she's drinking iced coffee, dodging laundry, or daydreaming about enchanted forests.

You can find her online at:

Website: ZoraStone.com

TikTok | Instagram: @ZoraStoneAuthor

And on Amazon and Goodreads.

Want behind-the-scenes chaos and sneak peeks? ZoraStone.com/Influencers

ALSO BY ZORA STONE

The Ether Chronicles

Crown of the Mist
Into the Ether
Ashen Oath
Veil of Echoes
Shattering the Void
To the Final End

Arcanum Academy

Shadows of Change
Shadows Rising
Shadows Found
Shadows Revealed

Author's Note

Shadows Found was the book where everything collided.

Every thread. Every bond. Every secret buried since page one.

Writing it felt like standing at the edge of a cliff and jumping anyway — trusting the story knew where it was going even when I wasn't sure I did.

If you just finished that ending and your heart is pounding and you're screaming "THAT'S WHERE YOU LEFT IT?"

Yeah.

Same.

Book Four is coming. And I promise — *I promise* — it will be worth the wait.

The shadows have been patient for centuries.

They can wait a little longer.

(You, however, are allowed to yell at me in the meantime.)